Dark Hunter

I0664414

AVA K MICHAELS

ISBN: 978-0-9935223-5-2

Book Formatting by Jill's Badass Book Formatting

AVA'S NEWSLETTER

Sign-Up for my Sassy Lassies VIP Clan and get a Bonus Freebie in your welcome email!

Sign-up at WWW.AKMICHAELS.COM

CHAPTER ONE

HIS FINGERS PLAYED with the steel of one of his favorite throwing knives in the pocket of his suit jacket... cold, silent, and deadly; just like him.

The action calmed him as he repeatedly ran the blade under and over his fingers and palm. It was small enough to carry anywhere on his body, and he had a couple more secreted away. One in his boot and another in a sheath at the base of his back... Hell, he rarely went anywhere without some kind of weapon, and blades were his favorite.

"Want another one, boss?" Joel, the barman, asked Lazarus as he sat in *Fortune*, one of the nightclubs he owned, pondering the file he'd received earlier. One that held a woman's life in his hands. Literally.

The information contained within had already determined her fate; she'd die. And he'd take great pleasure taking her last breath. He'd watch closely as her eyes dimmed, growing glassy and grey as the life left them. They all did. Every last pair he'd gazed into as he'd taken their lives had followed the same route as their last breath left their body and their heart stopped beating... eyes glazing over and dimming until he was certain there was no longer anything left behind but a shell.

He'd put that on hold for the night, however, because if he dealt with the case now, his fury would take over and things would get ugly fast; a bloodbath would ensue, and that's not how he carried out his *assignments*.

He was certain he wouldn't be able to contain the darkness inside, absolutely positive it would break free and wreak bloody havoc. No doubt about it. It was hard enough keeping it

1

harnessed on a good day. It had taken him a lifetime to learn how to do so. Fuck, it had taken many lifetimes to learn how to keep it in check. But on a day like today, after reading that shit? It would be impossible. So here he was, doing his damnedest to relax while trying to get the images out of his head from reading the file had brought.

He wasn't sure that was achievable, not until he carried out his sentence anyway.

Even the loud music as it thudded around him while the club started to fill up didn't help like it usually did, and he had yet to decide whether he'd stay and *play*. Or not.

He was riled up and maybe it was too dangerous for him to risk. He hadn't made his mind up, but a few drinks would certainly help to relax him.

"Aye, sure." He nodded over the bar and another whisky appeared, sliding across the sleek black bar top, his hand catching it before it dropped over the edge.

"You in for the night, boss?" Joel swiped a cloth over the already pristine bar, ensuring it was kept clean... as always. His dark brown hair combed to perfection to match his immaculate white shirt.

"I've not decided yet." He raised his drink while Joel tipped his head and smiled; the guy always had a smile on his face. It earned him a ton of tips and he was a great worker, but sometimes his unending cheerfulness irritated the hell out of him.

Once, just once, Lazarus wanted him to moan about something... anything. Hell, there was enough in the damn world to gripe about, but no. Joel was always happy, no matter what was happening around him, or if the world was going to shit.

"I'll keep 'em coming then." Joel gave him another of his damn smiles as he ran the cloth over the bar... again.

"Aye, you do that." Lazarus' fingers sped up, flicking his blade through them and attempting to calm the anger flaring to life inside him. "Looks like you're going to be busy tonight, rushed off your feet, Joel."

Joel set up a round of drinks for a lanky young man who looked like he needed a good dinner, or ten; he was so damn thin. But he certainly had money to burn as he ordered enough shots to sink the *Titanic,* which Joel poured out, two-handed and at breakneck speed, laughing and joking as he did.

"There you go, and remember to watch the clock; there's two for one at midnight." Joel pushed the tray over, grinning.

"Really? Thanks. Here." The guy threw a bundle of cash over, a *big* bundle. "Keep the change and thanks for the tip. I'll be back."

He rang up the drinks and counted the money out, a large amount of cash going into his jar before answering, "Yeah, it's going to be busy but that's good. It means the time goes fast and usually ends up with a lot of extra in this jar, so I'm happy."

"I bet," Lazarus snarked back but he bet that Joel didn't notice. He was right.

"Another?" He held up the bottle of his whisky, waggling it around, and that smile was still pasted onto his face.

"Aye, fill her up." Lazarus pushed his glass over and Joel topped it up.

"So, have you decided?" Joel asked, at the same time putting together an order for one of the waitresses, his hands grabbing drinks and glasses while she read them off her pad and quickly placed them onto her tray before returning his attention to Lazarus, who knew he should be happy at having such a good worker under his employment instead of annoyed.

"I'm staying for now."

"Okay, I'll make sure to tend to you." Joel gave him a nod

before he sped off to deal with other customers, still fucking smiling.

Lazarus watched as Joel and Alma, the other bartender on duty, took care of business. The two of them working quickly to get orders out, both for the customers standing at the bar and for the waitresses who were shouting orders at them. He couldn't help but be impressed, they were good at their jobs, but that's why they worked for him; he only employed the best. His bar manager, Matteo, was at the opposite end, helping out as they started to get busy. Lazarus checked his watch, noting the other bartenders would be arriving shortly.

After that, Matteo would disappear to his office to do his paperwork and whatever else he had to do to run the place, only coming back if he was needed. He liked that he could leave Matteo in charge; hell, he had so many businesses that he'd be run ragged if he had to deal with the day to day running of them all.

It didn't stop him from dropping in without notice though. That always kept them on their toes, and if he found anything amiss, they soon saw a side of him that kept them on the straight and narrow from then on. In fact, he relished that part, especially when it was a new staff member and they were unaware of who, or more importantly, *what* he was.

That first time, that first look, when he unleashed his power, his darkness... *that* was glorious.

Lazarus couldn't help but take pleasure from the fear that washed over them... No, not fear... downright terror as they saw the beast inside him. Saw what he was capable of.

Hell, he couldn't help himself from relishing in the emotions that rolled off them; he lapped them up like a baby at its mother's breast. He couldn't help who he was, what he was, or what gave him pleasure.

Swirling the amber liquid around in his glass, he inhaled the tangy, almost citrus-fruit aromas wafting up together with a slight honeysuckle scent... nice. One of his favorite whisky blends he'd had shipped over from Scotland, but not one of the most expensive. Those he kept for special occasions, but, before he could take another drink, a disturbance at the entrance caught his attention. His sensitive ears picked up everything as his doormen yelled at someone who was obviously attempting to get past them.

"Good luck with that", Lazarus thought briefly before a body rushed inside, quickly followed by the burly men who manned the door.

He didn't think twice, slamming his glass down and hopping off his stool, Lazarus sped forward to intercede the body completely dressed in black. He took in the disheveled state of the person, dirt on their clothes and one important detail hit him as he closed in: a long dark braid swung down their back. All the way to curvy hips encased in denim and knee high black boots.

"What the fuck?" he cursed under his breath as he sped forward.

His feet moved with lightning speed as he covered the distance in a blur of movement, passing people whose heads spun around wondering what the rush of air was that had caused their clothes to flap around them, and seeing nothing because he was already gone. Their dazed and confused faces as they looked all around were comical but nothing new to him.

His eyes were glued to the intruder, that long braid swinging around, and Lazarus couldn't believe a female had managed to get past his men and into his club. How the hell had that happened?

And what was going on with her? She was obviously hurt and running from someone. He could scent blood, the smell intoxicating and growing stronger the nearer he drew to her. She was looking back over her shoulder, keeping an eye on his men, who were pursuing her, and she didn't see him until the last moment. Her eyes dark and cold as they locked with his blue ones. Lazarus was surprised to see not a hint of fear staring back at him. Not even when he tackled her; deftly stepping to the side, his arms grabbed her roughly around the waist, sweeping her off her feet and spinning her around with the speed she'd been careening toward him.

She'd tried to veer away, her eyes darting all around, but there was nowhere to go. Bodies were everywhere and her legs knocked a couple who shouted in annoyance before they saw his men and quickly moved away. A circle emptied around them, people worrying they'd get caught up in whatever was going down as his guys came stampeding toward them...nobody messed with them.

"Hey, what do you think you're doing?" He held her back to his front, his mouth at the shell of her ear as his keen sight took in the wounds on her face.

She'd been in a fight, that much was clear, and she'd taken quite a beating. The left side of her face was puffy and bruising already, a cut at the side of her eye was bleeding profusely, and she had a split lip to boot.

"Let me go," she replied coldly, struggling in his arms violently and with a strength that defied her size.

She continued to struggle until he tightened his hold. His steely grip a clear warning that she was going nowhere unless he allowed it, and that wasn't happening anytime soon. Not until he found out what the hell was going on.

Raised voices behind him had him turning to look over his shoulder...two men had turned up and were now arguing with his staff. And they didn't look happy. One had a bloody nose and the other appeared to have a knife wound to his upper arm.

"Did you do that?" he whispered, his lips so close to her that he felt her skin as he spoke, her body shuddering. Then she kicked his shin and moved her head back fast to try and bash him right in the middle of his face.

Hell, if he hadn't seen it coming and didn't have reflexes as fast as he did, he'd be sporting a broken nose, and a lesser man would probably have loosened his grip and allowed her to escape. Then again, that was probably her plan.

Damn it, she was a firecracker, but he merely tightened his grip again. She inhaled sharply as he did; her body tight against him, her scent invading him, and he could feel her tensing her muscles as she readied to make another bid for freedom. Aye, as if that was going to happen. Was she deluded?

"I said: let me go," she repeated, her voice just as cold, but Lazarus felt the change in her body. She wanted to run, that much was obvious, but it was more than that. She was desperate to escape. He could sense it in every cell of her being as she wriggled in his arms.

Why? What the fuck was going on?

He put her down onto her feet, holding onto her arm with a vice-like grip, and turned around, keeping her behind him as he faced the men.

"Who the fuck are you and why are you chasing this woman into my club?" he snarled, anger rising up. Why? He wasn't sure. Yet.

The one with the wound on his arm pushed forward, trying to look around him to see the woman.

"Give her to me, now, and we'll get out of your hair. We can forget all about this."

Lazarus looked him up and down, his senses going into overdrive. Scum was the first word that sprang to mind. Lowlife was the second, and bully was the next. He knew this kind of man. Seen their type over and over again...and he loathed them.

Despised was more accurate, and he wasn't about to hand this woman over to him. Not a fucking chance.

He was tall, almost as tall as Lazarus, and he was wide, but there was no muscle mass there; it was pure blubber. Lazarus would bet his last dollar that this thug would use his size to intimidate, especially women, and he wouldn't put it past this ass to do more than that. He could scent it on him, see it in him, and he *knew* his kind.

"What's your name? As I said, this is *my* club. I own this place, so give me the damn courtesy of answering my fucking question before I lose my patience. Trust me, you don't want me to do that."

Lazarus glared over at the man, allowing some of his supernatural powers free, including permitting his eyes to turn fiery red and his fangs to spring free. He never hid the fact of what he was, but he also didn't advertise it either, unless it was to his advantage. And at this moment, he wanted this fucker to know exactly who and *what* he was dealing with; a powerful and deadly Vampire.

It worked, in spades. His face losing all color as he stumbled back. His blood dripping slowly down his arm, falling through the air with a soft whisper before landing on the floor... *plop*. A dull noise as the crimson globules made contact, his ears heard them loud and clear and his nostrils flared to take in the essence of the man before him.

"Sorry, I didn't mean to offend you." His wheedling tone drew his attention back to his face. "My name's Evan Smythson, and this bitch here broke into my loft where me and my buddy had just returned after a few drinks. She attacked me with a fucking knife and broke his nose before escaping out the damn window. We chased her and she came in here so we followed."

He waved his arm back to his friend, as if attempting to get him to back him up, but he didn't. The other man remained in place and silent. Interesting.

"And you've never seen her before?"

Lazarus kept his eyes pinned on Smythson as he shook his head before blustering out, his uninjured arm raising to stab a finger toward the woman behind Lazarus, "Never. I don't know this crazy ass whore. Maybe she was gonna rob my place and didn't expect us to come back. I've no fucking idea. All I know is she attacked *us*."

Lazarus tipped his head, retracting his fangs and looking back at the female he still held. Her eyes were full of hatred as she glared over at Smythson. Pure, unadulterated hatred. Not the look of someone who had broken in with plans to rob a place, and certainly not a look of someone who didn't know him. She did. You didn't look at another person with such loathing for no reason.

"But you two managed to get the weapon from her, didn't you?" Lazarus pressed, raising his eyebrow and spearing this piece of shit in place.

Smythson's feet shuffled, looking back at his buddy who hadn't said a word and who had moved away by several yards. In fact, if it weren't for Lazarus' men, he was certain the second man would've fled by now.

"Well, yeah, but it took both of us to do it. She fought like a madwoman." He held his injured arm out, looking for sympathy. Yeah, that wasn't working. "Like some kind of crazy ninja chick. I've never seen anything like it."

"So..." Lazarus inhaled slowly, looking Smythson up and down and leaning over to look at his friend and then back to him again. "...two big, strong men against one woman. You get roughed up and you manage to get her weapon away, and then you decide to get your own back. Right? You rough her up a bit, as I can see from her bruises, cut eye, burst lip, instead of just calling the police. And I can guess what happened next."

Smythson's face turned white, anger rising as he shook his head vehemently and took a step back. He looked like he wanted to turn tail and run, but he didn't, or rather he couldn't. Not with his men at his back and his cold dark eyes keeping him pinned in place.

"No, no, that's not what happened." Sweat started to pour down his face, fear showing as he realized Lazarus knew what he'd had in mind for the woman Lazarus now held behind him.

"Yes, it is," Lazarus spat out, pointing a finger straight at him. "I know your type. You're a bully and you didn't like a woman coming into your home, you liked it far less that she got some hits in on you. So you had to teach her a lesson. What was next? Were you going to *really* teach her a lesson? Huh?"

That's when he felt it. The woman's entire body stiffened behind him briefly before the scents assaulted his nostrils: anger, disgust, and topping it all was fear. Hell yeah, that's what was going to happen in this fucker's loft. Only, it didn't because she fought back even more and somehow managed to get out.

How she did that was a mystery, one he'd like to figure out. One that was taking root inside him and slithering around like a snake seeking its prey; just like *he* normally did. This woman wasn't all she appeared to be, and with every passing second, Lazarus wanted to know more.

"But she got away, didn't she?" he pressed again, his voice low and filled with venom. "Did she hurt your ego, Smythson? Is that why you ran her down? Or is it because you wanted to continue the game?"

She began to wriggle, tugging her arm in a vain attempt to break free, but he held fast as he motioned to his men.

"Get them out of here, and if I *ever* see either of you again, then I promise you that you'll regret it. And by that, I mean in any of my clubs, on the street outside, or…oh shit, I just mean in general. Stay away, got it? And another thing, if I hear that you've hurt a woman, any woman, in any way whatsoever, I promise I'll come for you. Believe me, you don't want that to happen."

He waited as they were manhandled out, enjoying the way they were treated; especially when Smythson complained and he was rewarded with a swift punch to the kidneys. Yeah, that would hurt for a while and probably have him peeing blood for a week. His friend was wiser, keeping his mouth shut, as he had done the entire time he'd been there. Although, that had Lazarus's *spidey senses* tingling. Sometimes the quiet ones were the worst. Maybe he'd check him out when he had the time. He had Smythson's name now so it would be easy enough for him to track his friend down; he was good at that.

"You can let me go now."

Her voice settled over him like a dark whisper, causing a reaction inside that he couldn't quite put his finger on. Without a doubt, this woman intrigued him. How she'd managed to get the better of those two men was something he'd like to know. Never mind the fact she'd broke past his men and inside the club. The phrase *some kind of crazy ninja chick* stuck in his head. What had Smythson meant by that?

But more importantly, what was she doing in his home in the first place? Lazarus didn't get the feeling that she was there to rob the guy. So what? In fact, he was one hundred percent certain that wasn't the case.

And why was he still holding onto her instead of releasing her and allowing her to disappear into the night?

Dark Hunter

CHAPTER TWO

SHE TUGGED HARD, trying to free herself again. Her strength amazed him as she pulled with all her might, but he held firm, his fingers digging into her skin as he turned to look down at her. The bruising on her pale, porcelain skin looked worse by the second, marring the beauty of it. Her dark eyes glared up at him angrily while she continued to fight against his hold on her, his stomach clenched tightly in reaction to her look. Why? What was different about this woman?

"Come with me." He hauled her toward his office behind the bar.

He wasn't gentle. If he relented in his vice-like grip on her, she'd break free, and he'd have to chase her down. She wouldn't escape him, of course she wouldn't, but he didn't relish having to race after her either.

"What? Where are you taking me?" She fought against him, rather valiantly in Lazarus' opinion, but it was no use.

Surely she'd know that? She seemed to be intelligent, and she sure as hell knew by now that he wasn't human; so why was she still struggling?

Her feet dragged across the floor as he pushed through the throng of people that now crowded the place. Not one batted an eyelid. They were too busy enjoying themselves or, more likely, they were drunk or high. Didn't matter, Lazarus wanted to get her away from the noise so he could see her better and talk. Maybe then he'd get to the bottom of what had happened earlier. Why he felt the need to do that was a bit of mystery to him.

Maybe he was bored. Or maybe he wanted to think of

something other than the file he'd received earlier...anything would be better than what he'd read inside *that*. Whatever it was, he wanted to know more about this slip of a girl who'd taken on two hulking men and made it out in one piece. Battered and bruised, aye, but still in one piece and still ready to put up a struggle, going by the way he was having to drag her ass behind him.

As they neared the bar, Joel leaned over and, for once, he didn't have a damn smile on his face. "Do you need my help, boss?"

His help? He honestly thought he needed his help? Lazarus had to stop himself from laughing in his face before he answered. "I've got it, Joel."

"Okay, but if you need anything just let me know." Joel's eyes raked over the woman and then back to him. "I'll keep an eye out, just in case."

"Fine," Lazarus shot back, wondering what Joel thought he could do to help. He was a great barman, but he weighed next to nothing and he doubted he'd be able to stand up against the woman he was dragging behind him. Not when she'd managed to deal with Smythson and his friend.

She'd probably lay Joel out in ten seconds flat.

He carried on around the side of the bar to his office, his lips tugged up at the thought of Joel coming to his rescue. That would be the day.

"In here." He pushed her in front of him, followed her inside, closed the door, and went to his desk to pull out a first-aid kit. "Sit down so I can clean you up. That cut above your eye might need a stitch or two."

"No." She crossed her arms over her chest, her face closed down with no emotion whatsoever showing. Good trick for a human female who'd just gone through what she had.

In his experience, most of them would be a gibbering mess

right about now.

But he was a Vampire, an extremely old one at that, and just because she attempted to show nothing to him didn't mean he couldn't read what was going on inside. Her heartbeat thudded wildly in her chest, her blood rushed through her veins so fast he was certain it was taking everything in her power to keep her breathing slow and even and portray that look she was giving him right now. That took a lot of training; it wasn't something just anyone could do.

Lazarus realized this was no ordinary woman. Not by a long shot.

Not if she could depict such a calm exterior while inside was in utter turmoil. Her dark brown eyes met his with pure defiance, although he was certain there was more behind them. What? He wasn't certain but, again, he couldn't figure out why he wanted to know. Why he was wasting his time with her. But he did and he was.

Lazarus tipped his chin up, sitting on the edge of his desk as he kept his eyes locked with hers. She didn't look away either, and again he was fascinated by her. Most people would balk at his direct look, and the way she was conducting herself was impressive.

"You do realize I'm a Vampire, right? I can hear your heart beating so fucking fast inside you that you must surely feel like you're going to pass out. It must be taking a hell of a lot of concentration for you to slow your breathing so you can come across as if you're all nice and calm, when in truth you are anything but. So, let's start with something simple like introductions. My name is Lazarus Báis, and I own this place, it's one of my clubs. You are?"

Remaining exactly where she was, not moving one inch, she didn't say a word, her eyes flitting to the door several times. Lazarus saw her brain working out if she could make it without him intercepting, and if he were human she might have taken the chance. He saw it clearly when she made the decision. Her shoulder's slumped down slightly and her jaw ticked...anger. She was angry she couldn't make a dash for the door.

But he wasn't human and she knew that. She wasn't stupid. Another point he found remarkable, especially in the circumstances. Most people would be making bad decisions and choices right about now, as fear took over.

So she stood where she was with blood seeping from the cut at her eye, the left one, and it had slowly slid down the side of her face, a thin river of crimson marring her fair complexion. His eyes left hers to watch it, transfixed as it reached her chin and finally dripped to the floor.

To anyone else's ears it would not have been heard, but to him it made a soft splat as it landed on the oak wood; his nostrils flared and his mouth opened, inhaling the scent and savoring it.

Fuck. She was A Negative. One of the rarest of blood groups and his most favorite of all.

It was a delicacy among his kind and cost a pretty penny, not that money was an issue for him, but for others...it could cause them to *take* rather than buy. Lazarus couldn't allow her to just walk away with open wounds, not in a club that was accessible to others of his kind. She'd be in danger...and again, he wondered why he was making it his business.

"Because you don't want to clean up after the mess." He told himself as he slid off his desk.

"I'm trying to be polite and you are making it difficult, so I'll dispense with the niceties." Lazarus stalked toward her, not even trying to hide his menace or the underlying power he held within. She didn't move, not a fucking muscle.

Jeez, she had balls.

He stopped toe to toe with her, his dark blue eyes boring down into hers. Dark chocolate with hints of amber and a few

16

specks that reminded him of an expensive whisky he liked to drink. Fuck it, her eyes were gorgeous, full of fire and an enthralling...he shook his head, forcing himself to focus back on what he'd been about to say.

His voice harsh and cold as he reached up to catch a stray drop of blood, staring at it briefly before forcing his eyes back to hers. "For your own good, you have to clean this up. I'm not the only Vampire out there and you have open wounds and a rare blood type that they'd kill, literally, to get their hands on. Some of them don't have the same self-control that I have; although, I admit I'm beginning to lose mine." He ran his tongue over his lips for effect. "So, unless you want to become an evening snack for a less than stellar and hungry Vampire, I suggest you do as I say. Get *that* cleaned up and cover it with a bandage or something. And I won't ask again, what is your name?"

Lazarus released more of his power, his strength, and his darkness; the beast that hid just beneath the surface, which he always fought to keep a tight leash on.

It washed over her like a sea of night, filled with everything that scared children in their nightmares; from monsters under the bed to the boogeyman in the closet and everything in between. That inherent terror that was hidden deep within every human and which was so easy to use against them. He watched as it hit her. Saw goosebumps rise on her skin, her arms tightened around herself as she shivered involuntarily before him, before his power...before the blackness inside him. Before the monster that he truly was.

"Ariana," her voice trembled, "Ariana Harmon."

She spoke the truth. There was no doubt about that. Lazarus would've known if she'd lied, and the way her hand shot to her mouth a second later, as if she couldn't quite believe she'd uttered the words, told him far more than those two words; she'd wanted to hide her true identity from him.

Why? Everything about this woman brought more questions than answers. And with every second that passed, he found himself wanting those damn answers.

Lazarus stepped away, his lip tugged up on one side. "Pleased to meet you, Ariana."

"Fuck you," she bit back, turning her back on him and stomping over to the medical kit.

She definitely had guts. Telling him to fuck off was one thing, but turning her back on him was another. He was a threat to her. One he'd just shown, and she'd turned away from him, giving him her back. That was an insult, plain and simple.

"Ariana, do you want to explain what happened earlier? Why you went after Smythson?"

She'd opened the kit and pulled out some swabs and betadine, wiping over her open wounds gingerly before she shrugged. "I've no idea what you're talking about."

"Really? Let's go over the facts, shall we?" He went to his wet bar in the corner, pouring himself a large drink. He didn't offer her one. After all, she wasn't his damn guest.

He strolled toward her then sat down behind his desk, where he had a good view of this woman who was an enigma. She was beautiful with soft features and soft skin...but his trained eyes saw her toned muscles and a body that didn't come from Pilates or yoga. No. She trained and trained hard. She could also fight and had used a knife on Smythson, so she had knowledge of weapons. Just who the hell was she?

His keen eyes and senses focused on her as he settled into his chair, taking in everything as he started to talk, but she refused to look his way, concentrating on the swab in her hand as she cleaned her burst lip and wincing as the betadine made contact before she steeled herself once more. She carried on with a steely resolve.

"You were obviously after him, it was his loft you went into, and it was *him* alone that you used the weapon on. The other guy? You only defended yourself against him. No weapon used. So it doesn't take *Sherlock fucking Holmes* to figure out that it was Smythson that was your intended target. You didn't go there to rob him, you were there to hurt him, or kill him. I've not decided on that yet. So, Ariana Harmon, why would a young woman, who weighs next to nothing, go up against someone like him? That's what I'd like to know. Indulge my curiosity; after all, I kicked him and his friend out of here and helped you out of a rather sticky situation."

"I would've lost them." She didn't look over at him, continuing to clean herself up. The scent of her blood diminished as the tart scent of the antiseptic took over, but it still clung to the inside of his nostrils. Damn, it smelled divine.

"You sound certain of that, in fact, you sound convinced." Lazarus leaned forward, right into her line of sight so she could no longer ignore him.

She was infuriating. Never before had he had to work to gain the attention of anyone, far less a female. Yet, here he was, doing just that. For what? And for whom? A young woman he'd only just met and who he'd never meet again. What the hell was he doing? It would be so easy for him to use his power, to compel her, but he didn't do that... Why?

That was another question he'd yet to find the answer to.

"They are both unfit, slow, and none too bright. Well, Smythson is, the other guy I've no idea about. Regarding his intelligence that is. He wasn't exactly fit though. I found that out quickly enough." She finally lifted her eyes to look into his, holding a piece of blood soaked gauze. "I would've made it to the restrooms, cleaned myself up, loosened my hair, took off my jacket to reveal a skimpy top, and swooned out like I owned the damn place, using my hair to cover the side of my face that was injured. It's all in the way you act. If you act like you belong and

19

there's nothing wrong, then people don't take a second look at you. *They* would've looked right on over me, and I could've walked out of here. Or... I could've just ran straight on and to the back and out the fire escape and into the alley. Did you *see* them? They would've been winded by the time they crossed to the other side of the club. They were already slowing down when they arrived here. Another few minutes and they would've given up, especially when they saw all the nice young and scantily clad young girls. They would've grabbed a beer and started to figure out how to nab one of them. Why do you think I came in?"

Lazarus sat back, digesting her words. Most made sense, and he was impressed with her plan because she was right in her assessment of Smythson and his associate. They were out of shape and would've been out of breath soon; in fact, they already were when they'd arrived, and they probably would have given up shortly afterward.

She was also right about what she said of looking as if you belonged in a situation and people not seeing you. That was a technique he'd used many times himself, and it worked like a charm.

But when he came to the end of what she said, his synapses fired up, as well as his anger.

He played her words over and over in his head...

No. He hadn't misheard her. She'd said exactly what he'd thought.

His fury boiled inside him. He couldn't hide it as he sprang forward, his voice laced with it as he spat out.

"What did you say? What do you mean by that last bit? About the young girls and them figuring out a way to *nab* one? What the fuck are you talking about?"

CHAPTER THREE

LAZARUS SHOT TO HIS FEET, sending his chair shooting back to crash against the wall. He slammed his hands onto his desk as he leaned over toward Ariana. His lip curled back while he snarled at her, holding nothing back. "Tell me what you mean by that? Now. I'm not messing around, Ariana. I want you to explain what you said."

She stepped back, her eyes popping open wide like a damn doll's. For the first time since they'd arrived in his office, he saw a flicker of fear in them, but she recovered quickly. Her face closing down again. She dropped the gauze she'd been holding, and her hands disappeared into her jeans' pockets to portray a look of nonchalance.

He wasn't fooled; he'd seen them shake just before she'd shoved them inside the dark denim. His outburst and his quick as lightning movements had rattled her, and he suspected she hadn't meant to say what she had.

She'd slipped up, and she knew it.

"What?" she asked.

One word. That's all he got, and he knew damn well why. She was rattled, and if she said anything more before she controlled herself, he'd hear it in her voice.

Damn it, she was fucking good at this; well trained. Where the hell had she had this type of training?

Fighting, he understood. Martial arts, aye, that he got too... but this? This was something else entirely. She'd been trained in far more than mere combat, and now he was even *more* interested in the woman standing before him, and her secrets. Ones that she was doing her damn best to hide from him.

"Don't play games with me, Ariana Harmon." Lazarus stood back, coming around the desk to crowd her. "You know what I mean and I want to know what you're referring to. If it's what I think, then you tell me now because I'll go and deal with those fuckers in my own way; for what they did to you and possibly to others."

Ariana's eyes bored into his, her back straightening. She'd gotten herself under control and she was facing him with fire in her belly, heating those chocolate orbs as they blazed up at him now with a look as if she wanted nothing more than to punch his lights out. Yeah, good luck with that, he thought.

"You don't touch them because of me. You hear me? That's not your business, Lazarus Báis. I don't need you to do anything for me, understand? And I just meant they looked the type, sleazy, that's all. Nothing more. He's never laid a finger on me... he wouldn't be breathing if he had. You can trust me on *that*. And what kind of name is Lazarus Báis anyway? Bit over the top, isn't it? I mean, come on? Lazarus? Really? And what about Báis? Where's that from and what does it mean?"

He knew she was deflecting, and he also knew she meant what she'd said. About Smythson not hurting *her*, but there was an underlying meaning there... Was she suggesting he'd hurt others? Was that why she'd gone after him?

Then she did something that put him on alert. Her eyes flitted to his side. Or rather, the pocket where he had the knife he'd been playing with earlier.

It was just a glance. A second. But it was enough to tell him that she must've felt the weapon when he'd held her in his arms earlier in the club. She knew he was carrying and she was wondering whether she could get to it and use it. Damn. She was good, but she had no chance in hell of getting it from him. The fact that she had realized it was there in the first place was another matter. It was another fact that seemed to point to her having had professional combat training. Had she been in the army? No. She definitely didn't come across as that... So what?

"Well?" she prodded. "Is it a joke or what?"

Lazarus smirked malevolently down at her, deciding to play her little game. For now anyway.

"I've changed my name numerous times over my life, but Lazarus seems a good fit, don't you think?"

Ariana snorted derisively. Although he was certain she was covering her true intentions: deflecting from Smythson, he allowed her to. For now. If she thought he was finished then she was very much mistaken.

"I guess. What about Báis?"

Leaning down toward her, his lips brushed against her ear as he whispered. "It's Gaelic, I *am* Scottish after all, and it means: Death-spawn."

He stayed where he was for a second or two, hearing her heart speed up and jackhammering in her chest. A gasp escaped her as she fought to control her reaction to his words. A flush of red started on her neck and worked its way up to cover her cheeks as he stepped back to watch while she lost some of her aloofness and the cool exterior she'd fought so hard to portray. Ariana's eyes flew to his, then lowered, unable to withstand his scrutiny as he unashamedly took in the ethereal radiance that shone from her blushing skin. He was mesmerized by her strength and vulnerability at that precise moment; the way she was shocked by his revelation, the vein in her neck throbbing violently out of control while she battled to recover herself.

She was magnificent in that moment, and he wanted nothing more than to sink his fangs into her neck and taste her sweet blood while he drove his cock into her.

"Suits you." She spat out, her head high and eyes cold as ice.

"I thought so." He returned with a shrug. "Now, back to Smythson, and don't think I missed your play on words, Ariana.

You said he didn't hurt you, but the way you said it suggested he might have…"

He was about to question her more when there was a knock at the door. He was ready to roar at whoever it was to leave them alone, but he never got the opportunity. The door swung open and one of his security men, Edvin, stuck his head in. He was huge, blond, and Slavic, his accent still heavy.

"Boss, we have a problem with one of the Vampires, he is refusing to leave one of our dancers alone." Edvin ran a hand over his buzz cut. "He says he wants to feed from her but she is not wanting this. I cannot get him to leave. Can you help? She is crying and he has her in his grip saying her blood is… Fuck, I can't understand his babbling."

Edvin looked between them nervously, then back out into the club. It took a lot to get the guy on edge the way he was. He was half-Wolf after all, and strong as fuck. If he wasn't able to deal with a situation, then it was serious.

"Shit." Lazarus turned to Ariana. "Don't go anywhere."

"Sure." She went back to the med kit. "I need to fix this cut or it's going to scar."

Lazarus frowned, not sensing a lie as she carried on tending to her injuries. Striding to the door, he asked, "Where is this fucker?"

"In the far corner." Edvin pointed. "He's crazy, boss. I've not seen anyone act like this before; I mean, Vamps. It's like he's lost control or something. I didn't want to do anything to put the girl in further danger. He kept calling me a *dirty fucking dog* and every time I tried to get near, it seemed to make him angrier. So I thought it best to get you."

"Fine. I'll deal with it. I'll be back in five; don't let her leave." He jabbed a finger toward Ariana. "Understand? Do not let her leave."

"Sure, boss." Edvin nodded, closing the door behind him.

It took him almost ten minutes to deal with the issue. The Vampire was a new customer, and one who definitely wouldn't be returning. He'd found him with one of the dancers curled on his lap, white as a sheet and deep in shock. The sight was one that he couldn't allow. Not in one of his clubs, where anyone could snap it on their damn phone.

Luckily, he was in a dark corner and his men had secured the area. If they hadn't, then they'd all be looking for new jobs in the morning.

"It's okay," he addressed the girl, whose name he didn't know. She was one of the new batch that had started the previous week, and he'd not been in since then. "I'm Lazarus and I own this club."

Her body shook but her eyes locked with his. He wasn't sure if she knew who he was, or *what*, but if not, then he'd probably end up scaring the shit out of her even more.

"I'm a Vampire too, so I'll deal with this fucker for you, okay? I won't harm you. I promise, but I have to take care of *him*."

Her head moved. Not exactly a nod, but it gave a jerky shake.

The rogue Vamp who held her snarled. "Wait! I need to feed and she tastes so good."

Lazarus' attention moved to the shadowy figure of the Vamp behind the slip of a girl. A young man's face barely visible, with fangs descended and blood dripping down the side of his mouth. He could sense that he was not an old Vamp, but he wasn't a newly turned one either. He should know better than to act like this, especially in public.

"You have one decision to make here, and one only." Lazarus released his own fangs, curling his top lip back at the same time as he released some of his power and allowing it to flow forward. "You either release her, or I'll end you; right here and now."

"No, the only thing I have to do is feed. I need her blood; it's exquisite. I want more."

Her scent wafted toward him as the fucker's tongue lapped at the open wound on her neck. Fucking hell. He couldn't believe it. Two in one night. Another scarce type, O Negative. She had to go. After tonight, this dancer would be getting a payoff and was out of here. She couldn't be let loose in any of his clubs with that rarity flowing through her veins, and she had to be warned not to work *anywhere* Vampires frequented. Not if she wanted to stay alive.

He'd also make sure to find out her name and pass it around to everyone who owned establishments like his, which allowed his kind to patronize their places. They wouldn't want this kind of trouble at their door either.

He turned his attention back to the bloodlust lost Vamp. Now that he knew what the damn problem was, he knew time was of the essence. If he didn't act quickly, he was certain the guy was going to rip her throat out and drain her dry, and going by how pale she was... He'd drank a fair bit already.

Her head lolled to the side. A flash of white fangs and he knew the Vamp was going in for the kill. Fuck. Using his supernatural speed, he sped forward, one hand snatching for a hold of the girl and one pinning the guy in place with his hand around his throat.

"No! She's mine!"

The guy's shout was filled with anger but also sheer terror at the thought of his prize being taken from him as they fought over the young woman, who now looked to be on the verge of unconsciousness. Her eyes were closed and her body lay limply while Lazarus attempted to free her from the steely grip of the stranger, who refused to give up on his precious meal.

Lazarus released more of his power just before sharp fangs sank into his wrist, tearing a long, deep wound right through his suit and down to the bone. He hissed in protest but didn't release his hold, tightening it further to stop him from retaliating. His grip on the girl loosened, but only after he lowered his face and speared him with a deathly stare, allowing his darkness within to seep out and flow over the weaker being beneath him.

When that happened, when he saw what he truly was, what he held in check, he released his hold on the girl and shrank back from him in terror.

"Take her and get her some help," he pushed her already falling body back toward his men, who darted forward to pick her up and spirit her away, before turning his attention back to the man who'd ruined one of his suits and caused him to leave Ariana Harmon. He wasn't sure which upset him the most.

He dealt with him harshly and advised him that if he ever showed his face in any of his establishments again that he'd end him, with no further warnings given. The man balked beneath his power, shaking his head and apologizing for his *indiscretion*, but Lazarus barely heard a word while he hauled him to the back door and tossed him into the alley behind the club before returning to the office. When he entered, his wound had already healed, but he found no sign of Edvin at the door and the room was empty. His anger rose as he looked around the office before he stormed back to the door, slamming it shut.

Shit. Where were they?

Returning to the bar, he shouted over the music to the nearest barman asking if he'd seen where Edvin had gone and he pointed toward the restrooms. Hell no. Surely he'd not fallen for that?

Lazarus took off running, using his speed and agility to dart around the packed dance floor and arriving at the ladies' room a second or so later. Sure enough, there was Edvin. He stood with his arms crossed and a large line of angry females who were desperate to get inside.

"What the fuck? I told you not to let her leave the office." Lazarus cursed as he shoved the mammoth guard aside.

"She needed to use the facilities, boss, for," Edvin stopped, his face burning scarlet, "women's stuff. You know? She needed to change her... Shit. I'm not good at all that, but she held it in her hand and told me she had to change her... tampon. I emptied the room so she couldn't use someone's phone, and I've not allowed anyone else inside."

Lazarus's heart sank. He knew as they entered that she'd be gone...long gone. "When? When did you bring her here?"

Edvin looked at his watch as Lazarus kicked open every stall door, finding each one exactly as he expected: empty.

"Eight minutes."

The windows in the room were tiny, at the back of the stalls and approximately ten feet from the floor. The last stall Lazarus slammed his foot against, the window was open. Well, not open exactly; it had been completely removed from its frame and lay on the floor. Lazarus pointed to the offending item. Edvin stared at it and then at the window in disbelief.

"What? How? No, she couldn't have gotten through such a small space, boss. How could she?"

"Irrelevant, because she did." Lazarus looked up at the window, the night sky his only view. No, a drop of crimson marred the side of the frame.

Her blood.

He inhaled deeply. Her scent was intoxicating, but that wasn't why he did it. No. He was imprinting it in his brain so he could use it in the future. If he ever wanted to. If he decided to track her down. If he fancied to spend a few hours to figure out the puzzle that was Ariana Harmon... And that might be something he'd do. She had secrets, that one. She was hiding something, and he could easily have gotten them from her with compulsion, but he hadn't.

Why the fuck not?

Hmm, maybe he wanted to *play* with her, maybe his beast wanted to toy with her, maybe he'd have some fun... maybe.

So many maybes and so many possibilities that Ariana Harmon had brought to mind, had raised in his psyche, causing his insides to clench with excitement and his heart to beat just a little bit faster, and that wasn't all. That wasn't the end of what was going on inside him. No, not at all. His beast was prowling around hungrily, impatiently. Just as it did when he was about to dole out some well-deserved justice. His very own dark hunter retribution.

He felt exactly like that as he gazed at Ariana's escape route. Yes, he'd made his decision.

He'd be looking into Miss Harmon and finding out everything about her. Why she was so secretive. Why she could fight like a *crazy ninja chick*. Why she'd gone after Evan Smythson and where she'd trained so she could project a cool-as-a-cucumber façade in the face of true danger: a deadly Vampire.

Ariana Harmon's entire life would be an open book to him soon enough, and she had no clue he was about to uncover every last detail about her. And, once he did, he'd decide what to do with her.

Forget, kill, or play?

The tantalizing aroma of her A Negative tugged up his lips. *Play* sounded good.

His inner demons visualized how he could acquire her seductive crimson by fair means... or foul. It would make no difference to him in the end, or her. If he wanted her blood, then he'd have it.

Ariana just didn't know it.

Yet.

Dark Hunter

CHAPTER FOUR

Ariana sped through the backstreets at breakneck speed, her braid coming undone and her hair flying out behind her. Her head ached, and her heart felt like it would burst as she pushed her body far past its limits.

She'd been sprinting at full speed for over an hour, and after her encounter with that bastard Smythson and his friend, she was running on empty. What was worse were the feelings that lapped inside her guts. Ones she couldn't get rid of and that reminded her so much of ones she'd long thought gone for good.

Fear.

The emotions just wouldn't leave her and seemed to be growing with every slap of her feet on the tarmac as she raced on.

She didn't like to admit that. Hell, she refused to. Not even to herself. Even when her eyes started to blur, her legs began to tremble, and her chest felt as if it would explode. Only one thought in her head: get to safety. And that place was home. Her bolt hole, the only place she truly felt safe, and where she could get her hands on her weapons, curl up in a corner, and fend off anyone who dared to come anywhere near her.

She would kill any stupid ass guy who touched her. Ever. She refused to be a victim again. She was no longer that teenager. That person dead and buried long ago.

She was strong, capable, and a skilled fighter. Hell, if that fat bastard hadn't surprised her by bringing a friend home with him, then everything would've gone to plan. *Her* plan. She always plotted things out meticulously, and tonight was no different. It was organized down to the last damn detail. *Every little thing.* She'd worked on Evan fucking Smythson for weeks, and he should be lying in a pool of his own blood right now. Choking on his own dick.

Instead, he'd be out trolling for another victim while she was running away with her tail between her legs and terror lapping in her belly. Not of him. Not a fucking chance was she scared of him; the fat slug. She'd regroup and re-schedule him to get his punishment because he sure as hell wouldn't escape for his crimes.

"Not a fucking chance." She gasped, the effort of talking caused her to falter and cough before she picked up her pace again.

The thought of her target getting away earlier had her angry as hell and ready to spit fire, but her body was already giving out. Her chest heaved, and she almost puked right there in the street before she managed to get a hold of herself. Once again her thoughts wound back to the bastard who'd slipped through her fingers tonight: Smythson.

He'd pay for what he'd done to the many women and young girls he'd mistreated. She'd make sure of it. Her training kicked in; *improvise, adapt, survive.* The rules of Krav Maga, and the many other martial arts she'd trained in, rolled around in her brain along with the mantra she now lived by, and she'd do just that to take down Smythson. His day of reckoning was coming and he would not escape.

She'd taken a long time collecting evidence, following him and almost getting caught when she saw him assaulting a girl in the alley behind his apartment building. Fucking bastard. That night had stayed with her for weeks afterward, especially in her nightmares. She'd wake in cold sweats, her hand reaching for one of the many weapons secreted in, and around, her bed. The only thing that could calm her wildly beating heart and allow her eyes to close again.

Ariana would have to go to class tomorrow after she'd finished a project she was working on for a customer. At least she worked from home and for herself. The wonders of working in IT; it allowed her to earn enough money to support herself, and she didn't have to actually *talk* to people face to face, well, not often anyway. She outsourced a lot of the work when it came to that side of things and had several people she relied on who she paid handsomely to do the work for her.

The only time she spent in other peoples' company was when she went to her martial arts classes, and there wasn't much talking there, other than when she went to Krav Maga and Ron, her teacher would draw her aside to check up on her. And she tried to get out of *those* exchanges every chance she got.

Tomorrow would be one of those times, and she knew she couldn't escape him, not with the state of her face, but she couldn't not go. Not with the way she was feeling. Not when her insides were shaking and roiling with... No. She refused to allow that back in. Fear was not a word she would ever use again. She was not afraid. She wasn't.

"Yes you are," her brain screamed at her as she slid the key into her lock and collapsed inside her house, resetting the alarms before sliding down the wall to land on the floor.

"What the fuck happened?" She rewound the evening's events, going over everything from the moment she'd run into that club, *Fortune*, and put eyes on the Vampire. "Lazarus, shit, what a stupid name."

She talked aloud as she pulled herself up, thinking of the way he'd casually told her what his surname meant: *Death-spawn*. A shiver ran up her spine when she remembered the touch of his breath against her skin and his body crowding hers. Her belly clenched and her heart started to race again, only this time it wasn't because she was running hell-for-leather through the streets.

A vision of his azure eyes flashed into her head. Intense, broody, hard, and... No. She was definitely not going to go there. She didn't find him attractive. Not even in a cold, detached kind of way. Not even his killer instinct side either. Yes, she'd seen that in him. Clearly. And yes, she'd been pulled toward that darkness because she had it too, but she wasn't going there. It was too dangerous. *He* was too dangerous. It was too dangerous all around.

He could find out her secrets, reveal her to the authorities, and she'd end up behind bars for the rest of her life... or worse. She had to keep her distance from him. She had to keep him away from her and ensure he never found out anything about her, because if he did... Panic started to overcome her as she thought of what could happen.

"He can't find me," she gasped out, her throat dry, her heart pounding as she realized the enormity of her close escape.

Ariana had to ensure Lazarus Báis never found her and that they never spoke again, because if they did, he could blow her life apart in five seconds flat.

All he had to do was look inside her damn head, but why hadn't he done that already? She thought back to their conversations and the way he'd *asked* her everything. Not once did he do that compelling shit she'd heard about. Why? Was he toying with her for some reason? Or did he have another motive?

Her heart sped up to an alarming rate. What if he already knew? What if he'd read her mind already and she'd not even known? Was that possible? Fuck, she had no idea how that shit worked. Maybe he knew everything about her, including her address and the fact that she carried out her own form of *sentence* to those she fucking knew needed it. No. That was unlikely. He didn't seem the kind of man not to bring that up; in fact, she was certain he would have. *Certain*.

Yes.

"You're safe, he doesn't know, and you're safe," she repeated over and over as she went through every room, checking everything was as it should be before double checking her security cameras were operating.

They were, but she still sat down at her desk to go over the feed and see if there was anything on them from the last few hours. She was parched, her tongue sticking to the roof of her mouth, but she refused to move as she used the fast-forward button to check the cameras. When she was sure nobody had been on, or sneaking around, the property, she rose and only then did she go to the kitchen to grab a bottle of water before heading to the shower, still whispering to herself.

"He doesn't know, he doesn't know... he *doesn't* know."

The water washed over her, soothing her muscles and her mind, slowly. She couldn't get rid of everything though. The feelings of unease lapping at her belly remained, so she tried to concentrate on what she'd do in the morning... Fight. She was good at that.

She wasn't sure she'd feel completely at peace ever again, not after what she'd gone through when she'd been younger, but she did her best to get as near to it as possible. And getting fit, strong, and deadly, helped. Ariana didn't allow those ghosts in... never allowed them in. If she did, then she'd sink down into a dark hole, which she doubted she'd ever climb out of again.

It had taken too much out of her the last time and had left her with scars; both physical and mental, which made her who she was today.

The police detective who'd dealt with her case when she was sixteen, lost, broken, and on the verge of suicide, saved her by taking her to meet Ron Shepherd and introducing her to Krav

Maga; it was what took her from the edge of the abyss. Plain and simple.

Ron brought her back from the brink, and she'd trained with him every day for weeks; no, for months after that first introduction. And now she had gained the level that she could train others, she was a Master, but she wasn't interested in training anyone else. All she cared about was learning more, training harder, and gaining new skills so she could carry out her *missions*.

Even that wasn't enough though. She'd sought out other martial arts, more extreme forms to supplement her Krav and make her more lethal, and she took to them like a duck to water. Bloody noses, black eyes, broken fingers, sprained ankles, she'd had all of them and more, but she relished them as she learned her new fighting techniques. Jiu Jitsu was a favorite, as was Thai boxing, both of them demanding physically, but she'd thrown herself into them with fervor and sucked up every lesson, earning herself a reputation in both. She didn't do it for that; she didn't enjoy that part of it. Her only reason was, and always would be, to protect herself and to take down the bastards who hurt others.

Whether that was because the law allowed it, or because they'd never been caught in the first place. Ariana made sure they paid. Yes. She had a secret. A fucking great big one and she couldn't allow that damn Vampire close to her again. Not when he and his kind had those superpowers and could compel her to tell the truth, or worse, get right inside her mind.

"He can't find me," she gasped out again, shaking her head and sending water flying around the shower stall. Her hands shook as she turned off the water, knowing that if Lazarus Báis uncovered what she was up to, he could destroy her.

She refused to allow herself to even think of the man himself, or rather the Vampire.

The cold charm and icy allure that kept her heart thudding far too fast in her chest, and those eyes... When he'd stood towering over her and stared down at her, she'd gotten a real close look at them. His dark splendor washing over her while she attempted to ignore those amazing blue orbs that had her belly clenching.

No, she wasn't thinking of him at all. Absolutely not.

And when she went to bed, a dagger clasped tight in her hand, drifting off into a slumber that was fraught with dreams. Dreams filled with a tall, dark Vampire, whose eyes caught hers like a deer in headlights. His face beautifully ominous, darkly alarming, completely and utterly intimidating.

No matter what she did, how hard she fought, she couldn't tear her gaze away from his dark, dangerous, and deadly stare.

DarkHunter

CHAPTER FIVE

LAZARUS SPENT the next few hours researching two very different women. One would live, and one would die by his hands very soon.

The one who would die was the one whose file he'd received earlier, and the one who would live was the enigmatic Ariana Harmon who'd piqued his interest. So far he'd managed to find out her address, the fact she lived alone, and how she had a successful IT business, but not a hell of a lot more. And that just made him all the more curious about her; she was becoming more interesting by the second, if that was possible.

Ariana Harmon didn't appear to have any kind of social life, or the usual presence online associated with the craziness that most everyone else had nowadays. None whatsoever that he could find... yet. That he hadn't found anything so far didn't mean there wasn't something. It just meant it wasn't in her own name and she was damn good at hiding her trail.

That was no surprise, not when she made her living in IT.

Lazarus sat back from his desk, sipped his drink, and smiled. "Just who the fuck are you, Ariana Harmon?"

Lazarus decided it was time to call in some help. It would cost him, but when someone went to such lengths to conceal themselves, that told him all he needed to know: they had something to hide. And he planned on finding out exactly what that was. If she thought for a moment that she could keep it hidden from him, then she was sorely mistaken.

Opening a secure browser, one he used for getting in touch with certain *contacts*, he fired off an email to one such person. One who was more than a match for Miss Harmon's skills. She might work in IT, but he doubted very much she could deal with the person he was about to employ.

A very skilled hacker he used when he needed information that he couldn't get on his own. He was expensive, but worth every last cent, and he went by the name of Hoax. He'd been responsible for some *big* international hacking jobs that had him on the shit-list of several countries and Law Enforcement Agencies, as well as Interpol. He'd get him the information he wanted. In fact, he'd soon find out everything about her, right down to what she ate for dinner every damn night.

Anything she did online from paying bills to concealed social media accounts, Lazarus would know about it, and as soon as he'd dealt with his *other business,* he'd also be on her case. Ariana wouldn't even know he was there, watching her every movement, but until then, he'd place someone else he trusted to keep watch on her. Her entire life would be known to him. Everything.

She had secrets and he wanted to know them. Every last one.

"Why?" he mumbled to himself, frowning at the screen as he continued to type.

His beast prowled around impatiently inside. It had been over three months since he'd last allowed it out to *play,* when he'd received the last file and he'd carried out his own form of retribution for the crimes contained within. Lazarus felt restless, agitated, and on edge, as he always did when his darkness hadn't been allowed out, hadn't been set free, had been forced to remain hidden inside him, shackled and contained. When he hadn't been out *hunting.*

Shaking his head to clear it, he finished his request, immediately sending the payment. Hoax wouldn't even look at his request unless the money was in his account, and he wanted him on the job as soon as possible.

A knock on the office door drew a snarl out of him. He didn't want any intrusions right now. "Enter." He growled before the door opened, and Edvin stuck his head in, looking sheepish and unsettled.

"Can I speak with you? Just for a moment?"

"Don't tell me there's another problem? If there is, then I'll be less than happy, Edvin."

"No, no." Edvin's face paled as he came in, closing the door. "I wanted to apologize for my actions earlier, boss. I can't believe I was so stupid with that girl. Allowing her to do that, using her woman's *stuff* against me and me being embarrassed about it. Shit, that was dumb. I wanted to offer my help in finding her. I'm good at tracking, you know that. My shift just finished and I can start now. I have her scent from the blood on the window. I could go and track her for you and see how far I get. It's the least I can do after my failure."

Lazarus knew the man was good. He was part Wolf Shifter after all, but he already knew where Ariana lived. That wasn't the information he wanted or, more importantly, what he needed. He wanted every little detail of her life, every minute and secretive thing that she hid from everyone else. What he was after was what he could use against her if it came down to it.

"I'm grateful for the offer, but it's unnecessary. It's already taken care of. You don't need to worry about it." Lazarus raised a brow. "But don't ever fall for that trick again, Edvin, women are crafty creatures and will use whatever they can against us. Whoever said they were the weaker sex must've said so as a fuckin' joke."

Edvin's head fell back, a rumble of laughter erupting before he agreed. "Yes, boss, they are as cunning as a fox and as slippery as an eel. I'll remember, don't worry, but I am sorry and I won't let you down again."

"I believe you." Lazarus knew the Wolf wouldn't. He could sense his utter despair at his failure.

He was a good worker. Always had been... up until now. He was certain Edvin wouldn't make the same mistake twice. Sometimes you had to fail to learn a lesson in life. He wasn't usually so forgiving, but Edvin was a good man and a good employee, who was in charge of the other men who worked in the club. He'd be a fool to lose him over this; it was Ariana's conniving that had been at fault here.

That was something he admired her for, and, at the same time, he was angered by her actions. Both emotions vying for supremacy every time he thought of how she'd ran from him.

"Thank you. I'll be on my way then. Good night." Edvin backed up, looking far better than he had when he'd arrived.

"Good night." He turned away and promptly forgot about him, getting back to what he'd been about to do and sending another email to the person he wanted to follow Ariana's movements for the next forty-eight hours.

That would give him enough time to do what he had to, and then he'd take over in dealing with the wayward Miss Harmon.

This one was easier, and he knew she'd never know she was being tailed. It was who he always used, because he was also a Supernatural; a Witch by the name of Acelin Keeling, and he used a nifty cloaking spell whenever he was following anyone. That always came in handy. His targets never knew he was there, in the literal sense. Acelin was the perfect solution to his Ariana problem, until he could deal with her himself.

She'd be followed while he took care of his own business and while Hoax was getting him her information. When he was done with his *hunting*, he'd have everything he needed to know about her, and then she'd be his. He was looking forward to it. In fact, he was excited about it. The thought of following her, watching her when she wasn't aware of his presence, it caused a frisson of... something to flutter inside him. What? He wasn't completely sure, but there was definitely something there and he was ready to explore it.

He received a reply from Hoax within moments, his request granted and stating he'd start immediately. He'd have a report within thirty-six hours. Wonderful, even faster than he'd anticipated, but he guessed this was child's play to the master hacker and computer expert. Didn't matter, all that did was that he got what he wanted.

Acelin took longer to respond, minutes dragging out. Lazarus stared at the screen until he was ready to throw it through the room. His hand slid inside his suit pocket, wrapping around his blade to play with the cold steel, his fingers feeling the sharp edge and the slight curve that helped it to sail through the air to its target if thrown, but if used in close combat, that bow in the blade slid nicely around a throat. These were hand-made to his own specifications, and he had them crafted by a master who weighted them just for him so they were flawless and lethal.

They were a work of art. A deadly work of art.

As the minutes ticked by, he brought the knife out and stared at it as it laid in the palm of his hand, loving the feel of the cool metal against his skin. As he focused on the lethal beauty, a vision of his father swept unbidden before him, when he'd given him his first weapon as a young boy.

He'd just won his first bout in the fighting pits and he'd been the youngest to ever enter. His father had banned him from doing so, but he'd disobeyed him. The anger inside him was out of control and the darkness had already taken root, slithering around.... NO! He couldn't go there. Not now. Not when he had a mission the next night. If he allowed himself to think of that time, that horror, he'd slip into a rage he wouldn't be able to control.

He had business to take care of.

He slammed closed his memories, locking them up tight before they were released to wreak havoc on his life and his plans.

"Come on, Acelin." He smashed his hand on the desk before reaching for his phone, on the verge of calling Acelin, which he knew the Witch hated. He was a freak about phone calls, saying they could be tracked, and preferred to use his dark-web email for contact. Finally, Lazarus saw a reply pop up on his screen and he clicked on it quickly... and her fate was sealed. Acelin had agreed to take the job.

When he'd finished with his own business, she would then be his... so to speak.

He was fortunate in that he was thousands of years old, and with age as ancient as his came a great reward. One that he rarely allowed others to know of, another one of his *secrets*, and one he guarded well: he could go out into the sun.

Lazarus knew of only one other Vampire who had his particular talent and he lived in Paris. He'd run across him on a trip there, over twenty years ago, and he wasn't quite sure who had been more surprised when they'd met while Lazarus had been admiring the Mona Lisa in the Louvre. That was a meeting he thought of from time to time, and the resulting afternoon they'd spent together once they both got over their shock and initial distrust of each other.

But Lazarus kept that fact close to his chest and didn't announce it to anyone. When he went outside during the day, he tended to dress down, and he certainly didn't do business with anyone. No, definitely not. Well, not anyone he planned on staying alive anyway.

Ariana Harmon would be different. She would never know he was there, and she definitely wouldn't expect a Vampire to be following her during daylight hours. Plus, he was an expert in covert operations; shit, he'd had centuries in training. She didn't know what was coming her way, but when he was finished with her, he'd know every last dirty secret she was hiding.

First, he had to finish his other errand, the one that had been rolling around inside his brain all day and night, turning his stomach at the same time as calling to the darkness inside him... So eager to be set free and dole out the justice that humanity had failed to do. So many times humans betrayed their own kind, but he was there to do what their broken society could not.

No matter. His beast would gladly carry out the sentence, but not tonight. Not when it was so near the surface and his control over it so slight.

No. He had to feed and rest before he went anywhere near the woman in the file for fear of losing control of the beast inside, of the darkness that hadn't been released for too long.

Tomorrow. Yes, tomorrow night he'd release his dark hunter and wreak his retribution. She'd never see the light of day again; he'd send her soul to the dark depths of Hades where it belonged.

Then he'd turn his hunting skills to the beautiful, enigmatic but devious, Ariana Harmon, who had her own secrets. Secrets he was going to uncover as he unraveled her piece by piece.

CHAPTER SIX

ARIANA'S NIGHT was consumed with nightmares; some from her past, that dark time she tried so hard to forget, and others where a dark figure with no face chased her. She felt exhausted when she dragged herself from bed a few short hours after falling into it. Attempting some meditation after her shower was fruitless and she gave up after half an hour; instead going for a run, exercise always her fallback to just about every stressful situation.

This time, however, proved not to be the case. It was, in fact, the opposite. From the moment she left the sanctity of her home, Ariana couldn't shake the feeling that eyes were on her. Following her wherever she went. Including when she ran across the park, which she normally loved to jog through, taking in the nature that abounded around her. Her special training she'd done in Israel was going into overdrive, alerting her that there was someone trailing her, but whoever it was, they were damn good because no matter what she did, she couldn't catch even a glimpse of them.

So much for paying all that money for elite training. Hell, she couldn't see a damn thing, but she could *feel* someone was there. What the hell was going on?

Darting through the trees, swerving around them, and increasing her speed to try and lose her tail, Ariana still felt as if she were being watched. She no longer saw the beauty around her, the wildflowers that she would normally slow down to take in their glorious colors and untamed splendor. Now she was trampling over them in her haste to lose the person she was certain was right behind her, destroying them with no care whatsoever. The pretty flowers she loved so much disappearing beneath her feet. All rational thought gone as she used every trick in the book, including backtracking, to no avail.

She had to stop, head against a large oak tree to catch her breath when she'd ran much farther than normal in her attempt to lose the tail she was certain was there.

When a hand landed on the base of her back, followed by a faltering and soft voice, she almost jumped out of her skin. She spun around ready to knock out whoever it was to find a little old lady, who looked to be about a hundred. Okay, that was a bit of an exaggeration, but she was ancient as she stumbled back, almost falling on her ass.

"Are you all right? You look as if you're scared, dearie. Can we help?"

Her husband, Ariana presumed it was her husband, grabbed her before she fell, while Ariana rushed to help, apologizing.

"I'm sorry; you surprised me." She helped the woman to steady herself before looking all around once again and coming up with absolutely nothing. Again.

"We saw you running toward us and you looked like you were running *from* someone." The man looked back the way she'd come. "Are you sure you're all right? We can call someone for you if you like? We've got a phone."

"No, that's very kind, but I'm fine." Ariana felt herself flush at their offer. They were old and fragile, but they'd still offered her assistance. Not everyone in the world was bad it seemed. "I was supposed to meet a friend for our run but she didn't show up. I was hoping she was late and would catch up; that's all."

The lie slipped out easily while she continued to scan the area.

"I see. Okay. Well, be careful, a young woman like you should take care running through the park on her own." The man waggled his finger to make his point as his wife nodded her agreement.

Ariana didn't argue, didn't tell them she could snap both their necks in ten seconds flat if she wanted to... that would be unkind. She gave them a smile instead and thanked them for their offer before turning away and resuming her run.

She carried on for another mile or so, her neck aching at the twisting and turning while she checked time and again for the invisible person she felt certain followed her, and she ended back at her house thinking she'd gone crazy. Stone cold nuts.

But no, she knew better. She went abroad for several intense advance courses, and she fucking *knew* someone was shadowing her. She wasn't imagining it... was she?

Another shower and a light snack later and she was on her way to class, hoping that would help. Today was an advance Krav session, set aside for those who were at the higher levels, not quite as high as her Master certification but close enough that she'd be put through her paces and be able to let herself go and not hold herself in check like she usually had to. Ron ran them a couple of times a month and they proved so popular that people came from all over to take part. It wasn't often that you could truly test yourself against others at such levels. She was one of a few females in the area at a level that allowed her entrance to today's class, but she was the only one who took part in these particular *events*. Whenever a new person arrived, they always raised an eyebrow toward her and tried to take her on, which ended with them getting their asses handed to them.

She sought out other martial arts and took part in various classes that took her to the edge of her physical and mental ability, but she always returned to her first mentor. The man who she looked on as the one who'd saved her from oblivion. She incorporated them into her fighting whenever needed because the fact was... if she needed it, she'd use it.

First rule of Krav in a dangerous situation is if you can, then you get away as fast as you can. In truth, this was a rule Ariana no longer lived by. She used her skills for her own means now, and running wasn't one of them. Second rule, if you can't run then you deal with the threat with full, and deadly, force. You do not ever hold back until the threat is down and out with absolutely no chance of getting back up to hurt you. In other words, don't stop until they drop. And your aim in a fight situation? Inflict damage, not pain. The reason for that was simple; different people have different pain thresholds. Pain is subjective; damage is not.

There were others, many, and she'd learned so much, but the main ones she focused on was how to protect herself while inflicting damage on her opponent, lethal damage. She'd done everything in her power to be as strong as possible, as powerful as possible, and in control of her own fate. Nobody ever again would be able to walk up to her and just do what they wanted. She had the skills to take that person down, and out. With the training she'd had from the different martial arts over the last few years, she was pretty damn deadly. She took what she needed from each, which was pretty much Krav, but she'd just taken it a step further and incorporated all the others into her fighting too. Her Thai Boxing, her Jiu Jitsu, and several others; she used them all, loved them all, *relished* them all.

One saying ran through her mind every single day. A small, quiet man in Israel had said it to her many times. Usually when she was picking herself up from the ground when she'd been knocked down for the hundredth time: Courage strengthens. Fear weakens.

It had taken her a long time to realize that he hadn't meant anything about her fighting capabilities, it was much deeper than that. He'd seen something inside her. His inscrutable stare unnerved her to the point where she'd look away, and that's when he'd say the words in his broken English before reaching to grab her shoulder and forcing her to face him. He'd give her a nod before turning to leave. Every damn time. It took dozens, if not more, of these occasions before the words finally made sense to her, and she lived by them from that second on.

She parked in front of the grey building that Ron held his class in, picked up her large water bottle and towel, then got out, noticing the car park was already filling up. Her adrenaline started from the second she walked in, noticing several new faces, who Ron was talking to. His face inscrutable as usual, but she knew he'd be checking them out, every detail of who they were and their credentials. He wouldn't allow them to take part if they didn't pass his strict inspection, and it wasn't just what level they held in the craft. Hell, no. It was what Ron *felt* about their whole aura as he talked to them and looked right into their eyes. Ariana always wondered what he saw when he looked into hers.

Did he still see the terrified and broken girl who had turned up that first day? Or did he see the woman she'd become? The one with secrets? So dark, so sinister, so fucking *right*.

It didn't matter because he'd never said anything. Not once had he asked her. Ron had only ever asked, "How're you doing, Ariana? Is there anything I can do for you?"

Always wanting to help. Always offering his assistance, but he couldn't do anything for her. Not anymore.

He'd done what she'd needed. Ron had taught her how to be strong, how to defend herself, how to fight back, and how to teach those fuckers a lesson. That was all she had needed from him.

"Okay, let's get started." Ron broke away into the middle of the room. "You all know the rules. This is an open fight session, *but* we are not here to kill each other, people. We are here to test our skills. Understand? I *will* step in if things get nasty and, trust me, you don't want that happening. Who wants to go first?"

Ariana rushed forward, Ron looked down at her and shook his head, seeing the bruises and cuts on her face. She knew he was going to say something so she beat him to it.

"I'm fine."

"You don't look fine." He leaned down, checking her out. "I'd go so far as to say you look as if you've been in a street brawl, Ariana. Should you be here?"

"I said I'm fine, Ron. Let's get started, shall we?"

She knew her tone was sharp, and his raised brow and curl of his lip wasn't what she wanted to see as he stepped away. He was upset with her and she hated that.

"As usual, Ariana, is first up. Who wants to take her on?" Ron walked around, arms out to the side as he spoke to the crowd, but he didn't look at her again, which she was grateful for. She didn't want to see the worry in his eyes or the reproach for the way she'd talked to him.

She'd already kicked off her sneakers, and the only other items she had on to prepare for the match was some strapping around her hands, her hair already tied up into a bun. It could be used against her otherwise. Nothing else. She started to do some warm up moves in the middle of the mats, which covered most of the floor, as the group fanned out. The ones who'd sparred with her before backed off; they knew better. She didn't hold back and not one of them had won against her. They hated to lose, especially to a petite woman.

One of the men who had been chatting to Ron cracked his neck and stepped forward, eying her suspiciously. He was large, over six feet, broad and muscular, with dark hair cropped almost to his skull. He had dark brown eyes and a nose that looked as if it had been broken a few times. He was obviously of a Krav rating to be here, so she'd have to take care in the first few minutes to get a measure of him. That was prudent when taking on someone new, but once she'd done that, once she'd figured out his style and his weaknesses, *that* was when she'd up the game and go in for the kill.

Ron joined them in the middle. "All right, you know the rules; I won't bore you by repeating them, but I will say that if I have to step in because you're taking things too far, then you'll be banned from taking part again. Understand?"

Ariana tipped her chin. Her opponent looked around the room with a wide grin, playing to the audience. "Sure, no problem."

That act spoke volumes to her. Told her more about him than those three words that fell from his lips, and she knew deep inside that he'd do whatever it took to win. Including breaking the rules.

Ron looked at him, eyes squinting. "Don't test me; you won't like the results if you do."

Ariana stepped up, whispering, "It's okay, Ron. I've got this."

His eyes swept to hers and she gave him a quick nod before stepping back. Ron looked at the new guy once again, giving him a death glare, then turned on his heel and stomped away.

Ariana's heart leapt with delight, both at his faith in her, especially after seeing her injuries, and at the chance to test herself against the asshole who now smirked at her. As Ron walked away, she heard a few sighs of relief from those watching, excitement and anticipation now filling the air around them.

Ariana shut everything out, focusing on nothing but the hulking figure before her; his stance, his muscles, which ones were, at this very moment, tightening and giving her advance warning of his movements. Every little nuance of his body that would give her a split second's notice of what he was about to do, what attack he was about to release upon her, and more importantly, what she'd do to avoid it, striking him as she did in all her bouts; fast, furious, and with one aim in mind: put them down so they don't get up.

This hulking beast before her was already giving away signs, his left leg moving slightly, thigh muscles tensing. He was about to spring forward using that to propel him. That meant he was going to lead with his right side, and she was right. A second later, he dashed forward exactly as she suspected, a roundhouse punch coming her way.

So that's what he was going with? Pure strength? Hell, no. That wasn't going to work with her. Not with her agility.

Ariana deftly dropped down, side sweeping her leg and bringing him crashing down to the mat before she leapt up and danced away. Of course she could've landed a few kicks to him while he recovered and climbed to his feet, but she allowed him to rise, his face red and angry.

Anger.

He was the type who would let anger take over when bested by a woman, especially one as small as she. It was already showing as he grunted, fists up in front of him, eyes glaring down as she pranced around him, using her smaller frame and speed to her advantage as she moved deftly about the floor.

Ariana added fuel to the fire by winking at him, speeding up and going in to land a punch to his kidneys before ducking out of his way as he tried to grab hold of her. Hell, he was supposed to be good? Ariana wondered how he'd got in, just as agony exploded through her when he landed a swift kick to her hips. She didn't see it coming, his leg moving so fast it was a blur, but she fucking felt it as it landed. She flew up and through the air to land hard on her back. She didn't have time to think of the pain, knowing he'd be on her in seconds if she didn't move now. So she inhaled sharply, focused, rolled over twice, and flipped to her feet.

Shit, maybe she'd underestimated this fuck-head, but she wouldn't do that again. Now the game was *on*!

They fought hard and dirty; punches, kicks, and everything in between, until she saw her opening when he'd lost his cool again. Fury fueling his movements and thoughts, he'd lost it completely, and for a brief moment, she'd wondered whether she'd have to put him down completely to end the fight, and then it came.

He barreled toward her, leaving himself completely open, and she side-stepped, spun around, and put every last ounce of strength inside her to roundhouse kick him in the gut. He flew back and went down like a ton of bricks, spluttering, coughing, gasping, until finally he turned over and puked everywhere.

That was it. Game over.

One of the rules was: if you puked, you were out. And he was doing it in glorious fashion in front of everyone. Ariana was sure he'd never live it down, but she didn't care. All she bothered about was the fact she was the one left standing and her stomach contents weren't cascading over the floor in such a spectacular fashion for all to see.

The room erupted into a cacophony of whistles, whoops, and stomping feet. Ron rushed forward to grab hold of her. "Are you okay? I was about to call a halt to this, but I knew you'd hate me if I did. But fuck, Ariana, that guy's an asshole, he's *barred*. Fucking barred, for life."

She fought to breathe, her body aching from head to toe, but damn she felt so *alive*. "I'm all right," she gasped. "I just need water and a shower."

"Ariana! Ariana! Ariana!" chants started up around them as people surged forward.

"Looks like you've made a few new fans." Ron gave her another hard look. "Are you sure you're fine?"

"I'm sure." She blushed as complete strangers started to tell her how well she'd fought, and what a douche the other guy had been, mainly because it was obvious what his intentions had been from the get go. It took her a while to extricate herself and find her water, and by then Ron had managed to regain control and had set up the next bout as well as grab the mop and bucket to clear up the mess her opponent had made. She was too tired to stay and watch though, her body sore and in need of a nice warm shower, so she slipped away.

Ariana never noticed the man who'd seen it all, captured it all on his cell, and who followed her all the way home. Nobody did. How could she? How could anyone? He was hidden from view by strong magic, and Ariana had nothing in her arsenal to fight against that; she was powerless in the face of such things.

She was exhausted by the time she got home, her mind and her body, bruises popping up all over, but she had salves for those. Ariana was used to them, and after some food, a very long shower, and catching up on work, she headed to bed where she slept like a baby.

The video of her fight already sent to the deadly Vampire who'd set his sights on her, together with all the other information gathered. It was now in his grasp. Soon he'd have his eye on everything: on her home, on her security, on her *life*.

CHAPTER SEVEN

LAZARUS LOOKED into the horrified eyes of the woman whose throat he held. He had no compassion for her whatsoever. None.

And he knew she knew it. She would be able to see it in his eyes as he slowly lifted the dagger, the moonlight glinting off the blade through the window behind her as he released his fangs to further terrify her. He wanted her last moments to be filled with as much fear as possible, and it was working, the scent of urine wafting up as she lost control of herself.

Perfect.

He brought the sharp blade down, inflicting a wound across her collarbone, not deep enough to cause her death, but certainly one that was painful. Her blood dripping down her skin as she writhed and fought against him to no avail. Stupid woman, he was far stronger and he was going to end her this night. No doubt about that.

She knew it too; her entire body was filled with terror now, but it was more than that. He could see it. Sense it. *Feel* it in her as she realized her fate was sealed.

Filled with a dark fury that ran through him like hot lava, he'd thought of spending the rest of the night torturing her for hours but decided against it. It would end up with too many questions being asked when she was found, and that wasn't how he wanted this to look. Wasn't how he usually worked. No. He'd stick to his plan and make it appear like a break in gone wrong, even though he wished nothing more than to spend more time with her. He knew he had to finish this now, before he lost control.

He'd already stolen a few items from several of her neighbors so this would look like she'd woken to find an intruder in her home and he'd taken her life in a panic. He didn't like the thought of leaving her so early, so quickly, the darkness inside of him craving to be let loose to wreak bloody vengeance, but he fought to rein it in. Barely containing the beast as she continued to kick and scratch in a futile attempt to break free.

"No. Please, don't."

Her frail whimper did nothing to him. Not a damn thing. Her eyes sought his in a vain attempt to change his mind. Aye, as if that was going to happen. Was she deluded? Or had she just lost her mind?

Lazarus leaned down, fangs almost at her neck as he whispered, "A warrior of darkness has come calling and you can't escape my dark hunter." He plunged the dagger into her chest, deep, hard, and right into her heart.

He felt it go in, heard her heart pop like a balloon, heard her blood slowing as it failed to pump the crimson liquid, and saw the moment her life left her eyes, far too quickly. She deserved to suffer further for her misdeeds. So much more.

Another job done. Another piece of shit who had managed to get away with despicable crimes, but he wouldn't allow it. Not a damn chance would he allow her crimes to go unpunished.

No. He'd been given her file, knew her guilt, and he'd carried out the sentence.

She didn't deserve to live. Not after what she'd done. Murder was bad enough. When it was that of a child it was worse, but to have done that multiple times as a care-giver and to get away with it on a technicality? No. That was something he'd never allow to happen.

She'd changed names and changed cities because of the

many times people had hounded her out of her homes due to what she'd done. And no wonder.

Thirteen babies she'd murdered in her care. Murdered newborn babies. She hadn't even shown any remorse, but due to a balls-up and a loss of evidence she'd been released. His contact, and friend for over twenty-five years, had been one hundred percent sure, as had every other agency, that she was guilty. And when asked by a reporter what she had to say, she'd just smirked at the camera.

How could anyone do that? He couldn't understand and nobody else could either. That's why Clive Parnell, his inside man at the FBI, had sent him her details, and her current address.

He allowed her corpse to drop to the floor and lie in the pool of blood that spread out around it, staring down with not one ounce of compassion for the woman who'd caused so much heartache to so many.

Maybe, just maybe, they'd have a second's peace when her death came to light.

He hoped so anyway as he leaned down, wiping clean his blade on her nightdress before storing it away in a hidden sheath at his waist. Then he looked around to check that he'd removed enough items to ensure the authorities would have no doubt that a robbery had taken place. Some jewelry, cash, and drawers left open with the contents strewn around would hopefully do the trick, and her purse, which he'd leave emptied and lying on the roadside outside.

His job done, he silently slipped out, moving with his Vampire speed, a blur to any eyes that happened to be awake in the middle of the night and looking this way. He threw her purse away and carried on. His motorbike parked a few streets over, far enough away not to be linked to the crime, but close enough that he didn't have to run for miles. It would take him several hours to get back to the city, but that would give him time to think of what club he'd frequent when he arrived. He owned quite a few and always ended up visiting one after he carried out one of his jobs.

After all, he needed to *unwind* and there was no better place to do so than one of his own establishments. There was always plenty of willing *companions* to choose from, and if he picked carefully, he might get one who was amenable to his particular tastes. And that was definitely on his agenda tonight. After spilling that much crimson, his inner demon was demanding his due and, he had to admit, he didn't feel like bagged blood. No, tonight his tastes were definitely leaning toward straight from the vein of a willing partner, and that was exactly what he'd have. Hell, if need be, he'd use his supernatural abilities, whatever it took, but by the end of this night, he'd be feasting on warm blood.

Speeding over a manicured lawn and around a corner, he spied his prized bike parked where he'd left it, in a dark corner behind a large SUV.

"Hey, you; what're you doing?"

A gruff voice followed by a hulking figure stopped him in his tracks.

Who the hell was that and what were they doing out in the middle of the night?

"I asked you a question. You're not from around here, so what the fuck are you doing here, biker boy?" The figure drew closer and, damn it, a growl accompanied him, a deep one. There was the culprit, a big black Rottweiler at his thigh.

Lazarus couldn't allow him to remember seeing him in the area. Not once the body was found. This was the last thing he needed, especially when the dog leaned forward, sniffed, and promptly started to shake and whine, trying to pull its owner back the way they had come.

"What the fuck? What's wrong, boy? What's going on?"

His dog's unusual behavior, its fear at being in Lazarus' presence, had put the man on guard. So Lazarus darted forward, grabbed him by the neck, and brought forth his Vampire abilities in full force. Fangs extended, eyes red. The dog broke free, howling and hightailing it back down the street.

The man was large and muscular, his hands tearing at him to break free, but he held fast and drew him forward, forcing compulsion inside him. In less than a second, the guy's eyes were blank while Lazarus went to work.

"You never saw anyone on your walk with your dog, no humans, not me, not anyone, but you and the dog caught sight of a coyote and the dog decided to go after it. It tore free and raced after it. You're going to turn around and go in search of your dog now and forget you ever saw me. All you'll remember is seeing a brief sighting of what you thought was a coyote and your dog running after it. You got that?"

"A coyote. Yes, dumb dog chased the coyote. I've got to find him. I've got to go find him or the wife will be mad. Got to go find Bobo."

"Bobo? Jeez what a dumb name for a Rottie." Lazarus shoved the man away, spinning him around and watching as he rushed away while yelling for his dog at the top of his lungs.

He waited until the man was no longer in sight, then reached into his jeans' pocket, lightly touching the hi-tech remote. The purr of the engine remotely igniting to life was one of his *must have's* when he was planning to build the bike and, with his deep pockets, it was easy enough to incorporate. He required such technology at times, for fast getaways when the police were just around the corner.

Well, what was a Vampire to do? He couldn't just kill them all.

Of course he *could*, he was more than capable of doing so. But he wouldn't. That was the whole fucking *point*.

He was taking the trash out that they couldn't because their hands were tied by stupid laws. And he was not. He didn't care what their courts said. He wasn't bothered that a piece of evidence had been lost and a scumbag had walked free. It wasn't their fault that someone had fucked up and yet another lowlife got off. So he'd give them a helping hand and take out their garbage for free.

That he enjoyed it was just a bonus.

He loved seeing the look of horror on their faces as they realized what was coming. Who he was, *what* he was, was just a little extra for him. But he refused to take out any errant police that might appear before he was free and clear. No, he wouldn't do that.

So he had his little gadget to ensure he could get his beloved bike away before any prying eyes saw it and started asking questions. And, if that wasn't possible, he had his *failsafe* button, but he sure as hell hoped he never had to use that. Lazarus *loved* that damn bike, he didn't want to have to blow it up.

So far he'd been lucky. He'd never been anywhere near caught and none of his *jobs* had ever caused any kind of suspicion from the authorities. All because he was careful, and possibly because the police didn't give a shit about the fuckers he killed either. Maybe they didn't look too hard, and he also paid attention to details. Like tonight. All in all, it worked out just fine.

Before he set off, he had to make a call. He didn't always, but this time he felt it right to do so. With his bike purring nicely, ready and waiting, he stopped, sighed, and just did it; the phone being answered on the third ring, even though it was the middle of the night.

"Laz? Everything all right?"

Clive Parnell sounded wide awake, and he was one of a very few people who Lazarus would call a friend. He was also an FBI Agent and had been for almost thirty years.

"Aye, everything's fine, Clive."

"You had time to read through the file I sent?" Clive whispered, as if someone was listening in, even though they always used secure lines to communicate.

Lazarus wondered if his friend was worried about his home being wired.

"I did." He paused, and Clive jumped right in.

"I couldn't hold that one back. I tried, Laz, for a long time I held onto it, but I finally caved when the last appeal by the parents for a retrial was thrown out. This case has haunted me for a long time. A long time."

Clive sounded just that: haunted. Even through the phone he sounded like ghosts from hell were in the room with him as he spoke, and Lazarus knew how that felt.

"It's all right, Clive. I read it and her fate was sealed as soon as I did. You don't have to worry about her any longer."

"Really? You'll take the case on?"

Clive's voice rose in relief. Or was it excitement? Lazarus wasn't quite sure.

"I've already done so. The case is closed," Lazarus replied coldly.

"It is? Did you..."

"I did," Lazarus butted in, "I used compulsion and got a full confession. She admitted her crimes, fully. You know I do that every single time, Clive. I never carry out any sentence before I do that. I have to know. I need to be certain. Me, myself, not just a file of evidence, no matter how compelling. Even if you tell me your gut says someone is guilty, and I believe you, you know that. I still need them to say it. I have to hear it from their own lips. I need their confession before I do anything."

"I know that too, my friend," Clive's voice hitched. "I do. I understand it, you know I do. I'm just so... fucking relieved about this one. I can't tell you how much, Laz. This is one that I'll be happy to see the end of. Finally. Thank you."

"No thanks, Clive. Never thanks for this. You know the rules."

Clive let out a bitter laugh. "Yeah, I do. Okay, I'll just say goodnight then. I might pop in and see you soon. Grab a drink or two and catch up."

"Aye, do that. Bye for now."

Lazarus hung up.

So the only decision he had to make now was: which club?

As he rode back, pushing the bike as fast as he could and winding in and out of the few vehicles he came across on the road, Lazarus decided where he'd stop. *Monarch*. It suited his mood and, more importantly, he wouldn't stand out too much with the way he was dressed. Being the boss, he could get into any of the clubs he owned, some of them did have dress codes, but *Monarch* was a little lax in that department. Although, still one of his most profitable businesses; maybe *because* of that fact.

It drew in high-end customers who preferred the more casual approach, some well-known musicians used it as their regular haunt, as well as those desperate to meet them. Which ended up with the club being packed out most nights, with weekends having long queues to get in, unless your name was on the VIP list.

That was another moneymaker; VIP party rooms rented out for birthdays and special occasions. They made a bomb and were booked out up to a year in advance. Although, they always kept one available for emergency bookings for big names, or friends and family occasions for staff.

Or... if the price was right.

Lazarus, or his management, never turned down the opportunity to make big bucks. *Monarch*, like every other establishment he owned, was only a cog in the wheel of his many businesses, and the main aim was always the bottom line.

Lazarus had money, lots of it, but he never missed the chance to add to his coffers, especially when he had such a dangerous *hobby*. If that came to light, he would have to move on, fast, and the money he transferred around the world to off-shore accounts would come in handy if he ever had to jump ship and leave everything behind at a moment's notice. He hadn't worked his ass off for centuries to live like a pauper now.

He'd lived that life when he was a boy, such a fucking long time ago, and he refused to ever do it again.

A snarl escaped unbidden as images from his past flooded his mind; dark, horrendous, and deplorable scenes played around inside him. Ones that he rarely allowed to break free, ones that were usually locked up tight in a box wrapped with chains as thick as his arms and sealed with a stout iron padlock. Somehow they'd broken free and were performing on a loop, over and over, the same scene that had shaped the man he'd become from the terrified boy witnessing... no!

He couldn't allow those images back in; he couldn't let himself fall down into that insanity again. Thoughts of his life back then when he had a different name, one people wouldn't even be able to pronounce now, Cinioch. The verbiage was so different on the tongue back then and sounded alien even to his own ears now as he whispered it aloud. But he remembered his family, his mother especially because he saw it all from where she'd hidden him.

Every last detail.

But he couldn't go there. He had to force the horror away. That time when his mind and soul had *shattered* and he'd been forged into the beast he now was.

Everyone thought it was being a Vampire that Lazarus had to control. They were wrong. It had happened long before that. It had happened that day. A day when he was a mere boy and he was never the same again afterward, the darkness had taken root inside him, deep inside him, growing, flourishing, until it was part of him and his soul was irrevocably tainted.

CHAPTER EIGHT

LAZARUS SKIDDED to a halt on the side of a bend, his heart banging in his chest like the whole damn drum section of the Vienna Philharmonic. His skin felt like it was on fire and he fought to regain control of himself, of his thoughts, of his mind, forcing every last image back into the ornately carved wooden box. He concentrated on the patterns, forcing himself to hone in on the details his imagination had created for this most important part of his psyche. His brain thrusting each horrendous picture inside that precious prison in his brain before slamming the lid closed.

Then he began the slow process of manhandling the reams of thick and heavy chains over and under the container, looping them through each other to contain his memories once more before finally retrieving the massive padlock to seal the restraints in place. Only when he mentally secured the final piece in his armor did he breathe easy once again, wondering what the hell had happened.

He hadn't had a relapse like that in decades, falling down that rabbit hole was not something he needed right now. The last time had taken him down a slippery slope, floundering in memories that drove him to spend too many nights partaking in activities that he'd rather not dwell on. Luckily, he'd managed to keep from taking any lives that mattered, seeking out low-life bastards and others of his kind who wouldn't be missed while he'd struggled to claw his way back up from the hell he'd sunk to, battling to regain control of the darkness inside him. It had taken him several weeks to fully get back to normal, so he knew what to expect if he ever lost control again, but that wasn't going to happen. Not now.

Lazarus had too much to do, too many games to play, especially with one particular female, which he couldn't get out of his head. It was rare that someone caught his attention like she did, and after living as long as he had, Lazarus was excited at the thought of the game ahead.

He was waiting for updates from Hoax, the hacker who was doing his deep search on Miss Harmon, and he'd have a concise report waiting for him in the morning from Acelin, the Witch who'd been following her every movement since the morning after he'd last seen her. It would be interesting to see what both of them produced, and what secrets they'd uncovered before he started his own reconnaissance.

He pushed all thoughts of her aside, for now anyway.

For the next few hours, he planned on burning off some energy and he was certain of finding a playmate in *Monarch*. Someone he could spend an hour or two with and feed from. Aye, that was definitely on the menu tonight, again. He'd get back to bagged blood tomorrow, if he felt like it. It wasn't as if he fed from live donors every damn night, not like some Vampires he knew, and he fed on bagged blood more nights than not, so he could allow himself the freedom of some fun tonight.

Getting on his way again, a feeling he wasn't familiar with flooded through him; excitement. With so many things to look forward to, especially the puzzle that was Ariana Harmon, he felt a buzz inside him that he hadn't for a very long time. Together with his night of enjoyment, the information from Hoax, and the reports from Acelin... Yes, he had a lot of things to look forward to and he was going to enjoy every last one of them. Starting with a few hours of pleasure tonight.

Pushing the bike to its limits once again, the miles fell away and he was now on the home stretch, weaving in and out of the little traffic still on the roads of a city that never seemed to sleep... a little like Lazarus. He tended to rest for a few hours during the day but rarely for much longer, and he sometimes went for days without any at all. However, he was almost always up and out during the night, feeling at home in the grey and charcoal shadows brought on by the evening. He could easily hide, slip, and slide from one place to another without a sound. Their eyes inferior to his in so many ways that they could barely see their own hand before their faces...far less the predator stalking them, who was sometimes barely inches away.

Yes, Lazarus welcomed the night like a lovers embrace because it's where he belonged. Like the blackness that lived inside him; it wasn't a friend, definitely not, but it'd been there for so long that he welcomed its dark caress, its evil kiss, its malevolent strength, and he used it whenever the situation required it.

He didn't lose control now, only rarely did his beast break free, and seldom did it wreak bloody havoc... unless Lazarus allowed it. And when that happened, it was gloriously sinful and immoral but usually directed toward someone who deserved such punishment, albeit he *did* occasionally use his inner demon for his own ends. Not often, but he couldn't deny the fact that he had.

His shoulders shook as he barked out a sarcastic laugh, thinking of the few times he'd allowed his beast free rein in his business dealings... and the aftermath. He'd soon earned a reputation of being a man never to fuck with.

Now he was ready to relax and let loose, *Monarch's* sign flashing up ahead caused his lips to tug up and anticipation to grow at the thought of what was ahead as he slowed, the engine purring like a big cat as he glided down the alley to the back door. Hell, he'd probably get thrown out of the line up front if he was an ordinary guy standing waiting to get in. Although

Monarch's dress code was less strict than some of his other establishments, he wasn't sure he'd pass, not the way he looked right now, dressed like a badass biker looking for trouble.

Yeah, his doormen would probably send him on his way for sure if he'd been standing in line on his own. But he wasn't going out front because he owned the damn place and he was going in to find a nice warm body to work off the pent-up energy buzzing around inside him, and, hopefully, she'd be willing to offer him something else too. Something he'd been craving the entire ride over. Something that he wanted more than a warm pussy. His fangs ached against his gums, desperate to break free and to sink into soft skin and drink down some sweet, sweet blood.

Lazarus strode to the door, inputting the entry code on the keypad, and almost ripped the door off its hinges in his eagerness to get inside and find a willing partner to share the next few hours with. The sounds hit him as soon as he stepped through into the dimly lit hallway, even though he was right at the back of the building, the thud of the music still made it through to his sensitive ears, as well as the muffled voices of a packed club; he estimated close to capacity going by the amount of noise he could hear.

A cacophony of voices fighting to be heard above the music assaulted him as he strode nearer to the main floor, stopping to check himself before he joined the masses. His eyes scanned down his body and then, more importantly, his hands and arms; no signs of what he'd done were visible. As expected. Lazarus was always careful whenever he carried out any of his *extracurricular activities,* and he never left behind any evidence, or departed a scene with anything that could tie him to it afterwards.

Shoving the sleeves of his leather jacket up to his elbows, displaying his tattoos, some of which had to be redone several times over the years to keep them from fading since he'd first had them done in his boyhood. His first ones he'd never get rid of, but others he'd covered up with newer ones in recent years when the mood took him. The one place he'd refused to have them when he was a youth, and which had caused him many a fight with his father, was his face.

The sight of his brother with blood pouring down over his new tattoo had scarred him, and he refused point-blank to have one. His father had beat him more than once until Lazarus had proved himself in the fighting pits against youths much older than him, beating them to bloody pulps when the darkness inside him had taken over and he'd fought like a demon, something that had earned him status among the men. Including his father.

He was the only member of their Clan who had no tattoos on their face. Something unheard of and for which he was glad of now. It would've been difficult for him to have lived his life through the centuries marked with the tribal ink covering half of his features.

"Oh my goodness! You nearly gave me a heart attack!"

A shriek came from Dina, one of his waitresses, as he slid through the door and into the club, appearing as if from nowhere beside her. Lazarus' quick reactions saved her tray of drinks before they tumbled to the floor, as he caught it deftly in one hand.

"It's just me, Dina. No need to freak out."

"Mister Báis, I'm sorry." Dina's face blushed, her hand shooting out to take the drinks back. "I didn't see you there."

"That's okay, I came in the back." He looked around, noting he'd been right, the place was packed. "Busy night, huh?"

"Yeah, it's been non-stop for hours." Dina sidled away, checking the tables off to the left. "I've got to get these orders out."

"Of course, don't let me hold you up." He watched as she expertly wound her way in and out of the mass of people hanging around before he turned his attention to making his way to the bar.

He needed a drink or two himself. Hell, he'd probably just take the full bottle and still not have a buzz on, but at least he'd enjoy it and it would get him off to a good start. The scents of the humans assaulted him as he made his way and fired up his synapses so his senses were heightened further, searching for that heady aroma that would sate him and his beast. At least for a few short hours.

CHAPTER NINE

"Hey, boss." Ria, one of the bartenders, smiled over at him as he arrived at the end of the bar. Her tattooed left arm a blaze of color as she waved at him, leaning over the bar to hand her customer a tray laden with drinks before she turned back to him. "What can I get you?"

"Busy night, Ria?" Lazarus shouted so her human ears could hear him over the thudding music and the hundreds of voices reverberating around them.

"Sure is; just the way we like it." She laughed, canting her head to the overflowing tip jar.

Lazarus raised an eyebrow at the jar. It was jam-packed full with notes. "Definitely a good night. Now, can you give me a bottle of something good and strong; I don't much care what it is just so long as it's not cheap or shit."

Ria tipped her head to the side, her hand rising and a finger tapping her chin briefly before her eyes grew wide and a wicked smirk appeared on her dark brown painted lips. "I've got just the thing for you. We got a new order in yesterday and this has been going down a storm. It's expensive and strong as hell; although, we usually sell it in tiny shot glasses for ten bucks a pop. I'm sure you'll be fine though."

She dipped beneath the bar briefly before reappearing with a black bottle, which had gold and white lettering on the front. "What is it?"

"It's a premium reserve Absinthe that's strong as fuck. Oops, sorry, boss; but it is. It's like, shoot, over eighty-nine percent proof, and most people can only stand one or two shots of it but, as I said, you'll be fine, won't ya?"

She looked at the bottle and then up at him, frowning. The look of concern on her face was comical as Lazarus reached over, snatching the bottle quickly. "Sure, I'll be fine." He motioned to the horde of people crowding the bar. "You should get back to work."

"What?" She stared at the unopened bottle in his hand, then at the people who were already shouting orders at her; some of them none too happy at being kept waiting, waving hands around with money while their voices rose indignantly. "Oh yeah, right."

And with that, she rushed away to deal with the horde waiting to be served, and he cracked open the bottle and took a swig straight out of it without bothering to use a glass, and boy was Ria right. The liquid slipped down his throat, stinging as it went. Just what he needed. He took several more gulps before he focused his attention on the crowd. His eyes scanned back and forth at the multitude of people who were crammed into the club enjoying themselves.

Some were obviously extremely drunk, swaying back and forth to the music. Those, he completely ignored. He wasn't interested in dealing with a drunk-ass. He preferred his liaisons to be with someone compos mentis. His senses were firing on high alert, sight, hearing, and most importantly... scent. Inhaling again and again, left, right, back and forth, head held high as he sought his... Shit, why lie to himself?

Prey. Plain and simple.

His beast wanted to play and he wanted to taste sweet, warm crimson as it slipped over his lips, dripped along his tongue, and finally slid down his throat. Yes. That's exactly what he sought and that's why he was now seeking someone to sate his needs. Not a fuckbuddy, but someone to fuck and feed, hence prey. Not a weakling. Not some damsel who would faint at the first sign of his power... or fangs.

Lazarus needed someone with some fire in their soul who would get his juices flowing and satisfy his beast too... always that too.

At first he was overwhelmed with the horde of odors assaulting his sensitive senses. So many different aromas coming at him from all directions, and a lot of them were not agreeable; sweat soaked bodies abounded together with various whiffs of sex, obviously there were couples who'd already been lucky among the throngs of people. That's not all though, there were many bouquets that filled the club, dozens of different perfumes worn by the women, a handful of aftershaves worn by the men, and various drugs partaken by the more adventurous, or just plain stupid.

Lazarus could smell it all and it took him several moments to filter them out and hone in on what he was looking for; something fresh, alive, exciting, and willing.

There!

Her eyes caught him looking. Dark pools of emerald in an oval face so pale he wondered if she ever saw daylight. Then he saw her dark red hair and wondered if it was merely her heritage instead. A spark of interest flamed to life within, her chin lifting haughtily as her jean clad hip jutted out. His eyes dropped to take all of her in; she was shorter than he'd like, but she wasn't stick thin like so many of the others around her. Shit, he hated those; nothing to hold onto.

Her ass, round and plump, filled the denim as it stretched over it. The top she had on was sheer silk... and blood red. Perfect. He could see a matching lace bra beneath it, which was barely containing her large breasts sitting high due, no doubt, to the push-up she wore. Fuck. He was already imagining his fangs sinking into the pure white skin of those mounds as his cock pounded inside her... Yes. She'd do nicely for tonight.

Lazarus raised his eyes to hers, tilting his head and raising a finger in a come hither gesture, then waited to see what she would do. Would she come willingly? Or would he have to work to get her to his bed?

After all, he was dressed like a goddamn biker, with his tattoos showing and a bottle of booze in his hand with no glass. Would she run? Or would she come?

She looked around, at him, then away... and back again. He could *see* her mind working as she tried to decide whether to come to the *bad boy* ... or not. Then she looked over her shoulder at a group of girls who were dancing wildly to the music blaring all around, and then back at him. Then she did something that had his cock twitching inside his jeans. She sucked in her bottom lip and started to nibble on it with her teeth, obviously a nervous reaction as she attempted to make her decision.

Damn. It looked so erotic as he stared hard at her, but she was unaware of the reaction she was having on him, until he gave her a smirk and a nod, urging her to come to him. "Come here." He mouthed, knowing she wouldn't hear him, but she would know exactly what he'd said.

He'd been on the verge of saying, "I won't bite." But that would've been an out and out lie, so he restrained himself.

Then he saw it. The second she made the decision. Her back straightening, her chest expanding as she took in a great gulp of air, and then her legs followed as she started to move in his direction, without even a glance back at her friends.

She faltered half way, her eyes darted back to her friends briefly before she looked to him again. Her eyes falling on his body to take in his muscular form, the tatts on his arm, and finally landing on his face, one he knew was handsome but also cold and dangerous. He saw it every damn time he looked in the mirror. Was that what was drawing her in? Did she want a taste of danger?

He hoped so, because he sure as hell was ready to give it to her.

Her feet started moving again. Quicker this time, faster and faster until they almost danced across the floor and she ended up right in front of him. Her head barely reached his chest as she tipped it back to look up at him. Instead of the shy smile he expected, she wore a confident look in her eyes as she reached a hand forward to touch his tattooed skin.

"Nice ink."

"I know," he replied, holding the absinthe bottle out. "Want a drink?"

"I'm not much of a drinker." She shook her head. "I prefer to have a clear head."

"Good." He leaned down, his lips at her ear as he whispered. "I don't want you drunk when I make you come so hard you can't breathe, or when I sink my fangs into those amazing breasts and drink your sweet blood. Then I'll have you screaming over and over as you fall apart with ecstasy."

He heard her gasp, her heart galloping in her chest like a fucking racehorse, and he waited for one of two things to happen; she'd either turn tail and run, or she'd stay and take him up on his offer.

He hoped it was the latter.

That would save him from using his powers on her. Because he'd decided as soon as she'd touched his skin, there was no way she was getting away from him. No fucking way. There was only one way this night was ending, and it was her beneath him as he sank inside her pussy and drank her blood.

"What?" she stuttered while he licked up her neck, moving back to stare into her emerald eyes.

And *there* it was. Dilated pupils.

Yes. She was going to say yes even though she was scared. He could see it inside her, *feel* it as he saw her thigh muscles clenching at the mere thought of him taking her while he fed. Oh yes, this one wanted what he was offering.

"I won't kill you." He stated firmly. "I'll give you the best night of your life. Plain and simple fact. I own this place. I'm not about to kill anyone. What's your name?"

She looked flustered, a hand shot up to her throat as if she expected him to launch himself at her, but she answered, "Kimmy, my name's Kimmy."

"Well, Kimmy, as I said: I'm the owner of *Monarch*, so I can assure you that I won't be carting you off just to drain you dry. What do you say? Are you coming with me?"

"How do I know you're telling me the truth? Anyone can just say that? You're the owner?" She looked him up and down with disbelief.

Lazarus took her hand and backed up to the bar, raising his voice. "Ria! Hey, Ria, tell Kimmy here who I am, will you?"

Ria was handing over drinks to a guy but, when she was done, she darted over, frowning. "What?"

"I said: Tell Kimmy, here, who I am."

Ria looked at Kimmy and grinned. "He's my boss, that's who. He owns this place, and other clubs in the city. Hell, he owns a lot more than clubs, girl, but not sure what that's got to do with anything. Why? Oh, do you mean his name? It's Lazarus, if that's what you want to know. Sorry, I'm not sure what you want me to say, boss?"

"That'll do, Ria, thanks." Lazarus turned back to Kimmy. "Told you. Now, are we on or what?"

Her cheeks pinked up to a nice rosy glow, her breathing quickened also, and her eyes were locked on his as she answered. "Yes."

"You need to get anything? A purse perhaps?"

She shook her head. "Nope, I'm good."

"Let's go." He grabbed her hand and led her back the way

he'd entered, and as soon as they got outside, he smirked when she saw the bike.

"Hope you like them, 'cause that's how we're getting to my place."

"Holy shit." She clapped her hands. "I've never been on one, but yeah, I've always wanted to. Just don't kill us. Okay?"

"I promise."

His cock was already rock hard, his beast itching to get out and play, and he now had someone he could amuse himself with. A *someone* his inner beast had deemed it wanted; perfect.

DarkHunter

CHAPTER TEN

LAZARUS NEVER WORRIED about taking anyone back to his homes. Plural. He had several in every city he had businesses, but again, he never had concerns with having liaisons in his homes simply because he wiped the memory of the addresses from their minds before they left.

The last thing he wanted was any of them turning up on his doorstep. Particularly if he felt they were 'fang-bangers,' or if they had any sort of actual *feelings* for him. He didn't do emotions. He didn't *have* emotions. Unless he counted anger, hatred, and rage; he had those in spades. Anything else? No.

He had no time for any others.

Right now, all he wanted was to expend the energy buzzing inside him because if he didn't... he felt as if he'd explode, and if that happened, god help everyone and anything that got in his way.

"So, this is where you live?" Kimmy breathed as she handed over her helmet.

"One of the places." He shrugged. "I have several, but this was the closest." He placed their helmets on the nearest table. "Enjoy the ride over?"

Kimmy nodded up at him, her chest heaving as she tried to catch her breath and her eyes scanning the apartment.

"It was exhilarating, but terrifying too. You drove very fast."

"I did." He moved in, his arm wrapping around her waist to pull her in against him. "I was eager to get you alone so I could do this."

Lazarus pressed her tight against him, his hard length evident as he leaned down to cover her mouth with his. She opened willingly, his tongue entered with a harsh push to claim hers roughly, demanding entrance with no sense of gentlemanly manners. No playing around as he devoured her lips with a kiss that set his senses on fire and stole her breath away, swallowing it down while she gasped and her fingers clawed at his chest to tug him closer.

Her intoxicating female aroma wafted up between them, overpowering him and expressing her growing arousal... all from one kiss.

Lazarus pulled on the sheer material of her blouse, loosening it from her jeans until his hand could slip beneath and feel her warm skin. Kimmy's resulting moan was like a prize won when his fingers trailed across her back, rising to hold her firmly against him. Deepening the kiss further, he could sense her arousal growing, feel it rising higher while her tongue lashed against his in a tango of desire. And when he grabbed her hair in his other hand, seizing her locks tightly at the base of her neck, her legs weakened and her body crashed against him while a mewl of pure yearning poured down his throat from hers.

Tearing his lips away, he shook his head once. "Not here, Kimmy. I want you spread wide and naked on my bed."

She didn't talk. He doubted she could, but she gave him a brief nod before he scooped her up and strode along the hall toward the bedroom. As soon as he entered, he clicked the lights on with his elbow then zeroed in on the massive bed in the center of the room. Her heart was thundering in her chest, forcing her blood through her veins at an alarming rate that had his fangs pushing against his gums and aching to be free, but he held them in check... for now.

If he revealed them at this moment, she'd probably have a coronary and that would put an end to his *fun* far too quickly.

"Undress." He ordered a moment before releasing her onto her feet, stepping back and crossing his arms to watch.

Kimmy paused, looking at him as if she were a deer caught in headlights and only just realizing where she was and who she was with; alone in a room with a deadly Vampire. Her face paled, her breathing hitched, and her scent was now a mix of arousal and fear... *fucking beautiful.*

Lazarus raised an eyebrow, canted his head, and opened his arms to the side. "You want to leave? Are you scared?"

Her eyes flitted to the door, betraying her as he stepped forward. "You've come all this way and I've not harmed you, have I?"

He was on the verge of using his powers to compel her to remain, but he much preferred his companions to be willing to enable him to truly *feel* their emotions. However, if she wanted to flee, if she tried to escape, then he wouldn't allow it to happen. He wasn't a good guy. He never purported to be.

He didn't lie to himself; he was a beast and, tonight, she was his prey.

Lazarus slipped off his jacket, slowly, and made his movement seem casual and not the calculated act it was... one to make her feel more at ease. Tossing it on the chair nearby, he turned back to her before reaching to tug the ends of his t-shirt up slowly, revealing his sculpted abs. Her eyes immediately drawn to them as he continued upward to expose his bare chest, tearing his top over his head to drop it onto the floor.

His keen eyes saw her stomach muscles contract, and he could sense a rush of heat flooding her body while she gazed upon him. His jeans hung low and her eyes dropped to the V that ran down inside the denim, her tongue darted out to run along her bottom lip. Yeah, he had her now.

"Are you staying?"

Kimmy's head popped up, her cheeks flushing at being caught, but she surprised him by giving a cocky smile; albeit, her heart rate didn't slow and her scent couldn't mask the fear that still permeated the air around her as she whispered, "I'm staying."

Her words floated toward him like gossamer, he could feel them landing on his naked skin and his muscles rippled in anticipation. Lips tugging up at the sides, he allowed a fraction of his power to seep out. His eyes began to burn and his fingers played with the button on his pants.

"Undress." He repeated, forcefully, demanding, insistent, with his hungry eyes locked on hers.

She took a quick glance at the bulge in his pants before complying, her fingers clumsily undoing the buttons on her blouse until finally it fell free to expose her pale skin and lacy bra, which was barely managing to contain her full, luscious breasts. And he saw why she had no purse with her, a lanyard hung from her neck with a bank card tucked inside and a key. It sat right between her plump mounds, the ones he couldn't wait to feed from, his fangs desperate to break that flawless skin. A low growl rumbled in his throat at the thought, startling her.

Dropping his jeans quickly, kicking his boots off, and discarding them and his pants, he stepped toward her in all his dark magnificence. He knew he had to distract her, his growl had scared her, her face was whiter than before, and her eyes were anxious with her teeth nibbling her lips while her fingers tangled in the silk of her crimson blouse. Moving fast, he was in front of her, running a finger down the side of her face before following it up with his lips; soft kisses to calm and distract.

He was a master at distraction. A master at seduction. A master illusionist. All he wanted was to calm her down, get her naked and into his bed. He'd fuck her, of course he would, and she'd love it, of course she would, but his end game was, and always had been, to taste her glorious blood and feed from those tits of hers, which had been calling to him from the moment he'd seen her.

Wrapping an arm around her waist, he pulled her tight against him, his cock thick and hard between them. His hips grinding against her while his mouth found hers in a searing hot kiss full of raw passion. His tongue filled her mouth, lashing with hers in a frenzy of desire while he swallowed down her gasps and moans, her arms around his neck and her fingers tangling in his hair to hold him tightly in place, as if she feared he'd abandon her.

Stupid human. She was going nowhere. Not until he got what he needed.

Not until his beast got what *it* craved. Until it was satisfied and once again wasn't tearing at his skin to break free and wreak havoc. He had to give it its due or suffer the consequences of battling against it in the coming days, and he had better things to do with his time...

Ariana Harmon.

The name settled over him like a whisper. A frisson of excitement fluttered in his belly as a vision of her face filled his mind. The thought of hunting her caused his cock to harden further, twitching painfully. Yes, he was looking forward to seeing her again. Why? He wasn't sure. All he knew was there was something about her that drew him to her, and that had never happened to him before... ever.

But that was for later. Tonight was for satiating his hunger and enjoying his time with little Kimmy, who now trembled with equal measures of desire and fear in his arms.

DarkHunter

CHAPTER ELEVEN

KIMMY TREMBLED when he sat on the edge of the bed, releasing her on unsteady legs. "You still haven't undressed for me, beautiful."

She blushed a gorgeous shade of rose red, reminding him of the wild flowers that used to bloom in the summer on the hills of his homeland; a bittersweet memory that brought him both sadness and pleasure in equal measures. Shrugging off her blouse, it floated to the floor softly; to human ears, it wouldn't be heard, but to his it sounded like butterfly wings, a whisper on the wind as it fell to pool at her feet.

Then she pulled off the lanyard, dropping it with a dull thud onto his thick carpet, his eyes zeroing in on her breasts as she reached behind her to unclasp her bra. The red lace loosened to free those magnificent mounds that he'd been dreaming about since *Monarch*. He wasn't disappointed when she revealed them; they were astoundingly beautiful, and real too. Not fake like so many were nowadays. Full, round, and ripe for the taking... his taking. He could almost taste them as he gazed upon their beauty, his mouth filling with water, and his fangs pressing painfully against his gums.

Should he allow them free yet?

He took a deep breath in, inhaling her scent. Arousal was all around her. So much so that he could barely detect fear at this point. So he allowed his fangs out to play ...not their full length...not yet.

Kimmy's eyes widened, her chest heaved, and he felt fear exploding inside her when she saw them, especially when he ran his tongue over them for dramatic effect.

"It's all right, Kimmy. Don't panic," he said aloud. To himself, he thought, *not yet.*

She didn't say anything; words seemed to have escaped her, but her hands continued down to her jeans, unbuttoning them.

"You're gorgeous, absolutely beautiful." He gave her some encouragement, not wanting to lose her at this late stage of the *game.*

Sliding the denim down her thighs, she kept her eyes on him, whether it was because she liked what she saw or due to her fear of losing sight of him, he wasn't entirely sure. No matter.

"I'm gonna make you come so hard, Kimmy; so fucking hard that you'll not know what way is up."

Her breathing hitched, her heart rate skyrocketed, and finally she was naked before him, shyly standing there quivering with her hands moving to cover her body.

"No, no, no. Don't do that. I want to see all of you, Kimmy, because you *are* beautiful, baby. Now, come here."

She stepped toward him, her steps tiny and filled with doubt, and she was doing that lip nibbling thing again as she closed the distance between them. His hand shot out, snatching her wrist like a snake going in for the kill, pulling her quickly the last few inches until she was trapped between his thighs. Her breath whooshed out of her in surprise, her mouth a perfect little pout as she stared down at him, her hands landing on his shoulders to steady herself while his legs wound behind hers to keep her exactly where she was.

He kept his eyes on hers as he leaned forward, his lips opening to release his tongue to sample her skin, dragging it along her belly slowly. "Hmm, you taste divine," he mumbled, one hand reaching up to tweak a nipple while the other dipped between her thighs to search within her folds. What he found was exactly what he expected, she was beyond aroused, even if she was scared.

Dipping a finger inside, Kimmy inhaled sharply, her legs wobbling and her blood thundering through her body like a damn freight train. It was calling to him like a siren to sailors, but he held himself in check. It was too soon to allow himself free rein yet.

His steely control was hanging on, barely. His need to feel her warm blood dripping down his throat was growing with each passing second. Like a tropical storm brewing inside him, growing and growing until he knew it would blast out of him like a fucking hurricane unless he timed things *just right*.

But he was a master at these scenes. He'd done them a hundred times before, a thousand... *more*! So many that he'd lost count, but he played the game well and enjoyed them immensely; as did the women. They had an encounter with a deadly Vampire, toyed with death and lived to tell the tale and, at the same time, had great sex. Tall tales to tell their friends afterwards, many of them embroidered he'd bet.

His thumb circled her clit and a moan escaped her. His lips kissed her skin and his hand cupped her breast, which was just waiting on his fangs to pierce it. Her legs grew weaker, trembling more and more as he worked her harder with his thumb while his fingers probed inside her hot core. His cock was hard and needy, desperate to be inside her.

Now was the time to take the next step, so he used his Vampire abilities to move so fast she was on her feet one second and, in the next, she was flat on her back in the middle of the bed with him between her thighs and caging her body.

"Oh!" she yelped, her eyes wide and alarmed, her breath caught in her throat as the carotid artery throbbed frantically.

Lazarus didn't give her time to think, dropping his head to cover her mouth with his. Together with his fangs, the venom ready and waiting to do its magic, he nicked her lip and his toxin went to work. His kiss was short and sweet, pulling back to watch as she relaxed beneath him, wanton and desire heightened beyond mere human capabilities.

Her skin was delicate with not a mark on it, so much so that he wondered if she ever went out in the sun. It held no signs of the usual damage that humans bore from the ultra-violet rays that so many of their kind sought. It was porcelain pale, pure, and perfect. The only marks were her areolas and nipples that stood out in stark contrast, a dark coffee color, and were outstandingly adorable. Ripe for the picking, and he was just the person to take advantage.

She reached for him, her hand running down the side of his face as if in awe at his magnificence and power, which he was no longer shielding. His fangs growing and lengthening in his mouth to their true size, showing her what they were truly like, what *he* was really like. What he was capable of. One swipe of his mouth, of his fangs, and he could tear her throat clean apart, kill her stone dead.

He refrained from allowing his claws to appear. That would be overkill and would hamper any kind of lovemaking. Hell, he'd rip the bed to shreds and most definitely would end up injuring her, or indeed, killing her. No, fangs were all that was required for this encounter.

Nudging her thighs further apart, he positioned himself at her willing entrance. "Are you ready?"

"Yes." She urged her hips up toward him, her chest heaved, and her eyes already glazed over.

Hell, did he release too much venom?

"I'm going to feed from you, Kimmy. I'm going to fuck you, but I'm also going to drink your blood."

He thrust inside her, his cock filling her fully. A soft whimper escaped her, but he didn't stop, he started to thrust, one hand beneath her ass to angle her hips so he hit just the right spot. "There, knees up and keep them there."

"Yes! Yes! That's amazing!"

She squealed, so high pitched it hurt his sensitive ears. That had to stop.

Releasing more of his power, he allowed his eyes to burn brightly. Knowing they'd be a demon red. The result was instantaneous; Kimmy's enthusiastic noise ceased. Her fear skyrocketed but her desire continued as he pounded inside her due to the type of venom he'd injected into her system. He'd promised to give her the best sex of her life and he would deliver that. He had left out the details of how that would transpire.

He knew she'd calm down shortly, they always did when they realised he wasn't going to slaughter them beneath him. But this moment, these few seconds when their terror spiked was magnificent, and he soaked it in like a sponge. The heady aroma leaking from her pores was intoxicating in its dark splendor. *This* was what he craved. *This* was what his beast sought, and it was now that he had to feed. Right this very moment, he had to taste her sweet blood when the endorphins had flooded her system. It would be so fucking magical.

His mouth opened wide, fangs showing in all their tainted majesty as he shot forward and sank them into her celestially perfect breast. His razor sharp teeth broke her skin with no resistance, piercing through with a barely perceptible pop and finally... *finally* her essence flooded inside his mouth. It was delectable, wondrous, and downright decadent as he took his first drink, holding it for a few seconds before allowing it to dribble down his throat, slowly, to savor the blissful and revitalizing liquid.

It was a heady mix of spicy with sweet undertones that slid down like soft velvet, energized with the endorphins of her fear, which gave it a succulent piquant that set his senses on fire and his orgasm speeding to the fore with every swallow he drank. He knew the chemicals would change quickly, in just a few short heartbeats, once Kimmy realized he wasn't going to rip her throat out, so he drank quickly, pulling on her breast over and over as if he hadn't fed in weeks and garnering as much of the heavenly ambrosia as he could before it changed.

But through it all, even though she'd been absolutely terrified, she'd continued to meet his thrusts with her willing hips in silence. Her core clamping around his cock as she neared a cataclysmic orgasm that she would never again experience, unless she sought out another Vampire.

He opened up his mind, reaching out to Kimmy's, searching for her feelings, her sensual consciousness as she rode the wave of passion that was thrumming through her body, rising and rising with each crash of their bodies and each pull of her blood into his mouth until he got a hint of the bittersweet change in the liquid. The sweet ambrosia had altered as all fear of him dissipated. He disengaged his fangs, drawing his tongue over the holes to seal them over and ensure they healed without leaving a mark on her flawless skin, then he retracted them back into his gums and pounded into her without abandon.

She clawed at his back, her fingers digging in and nails scraping down in long trails as her legs hooked around his ass while her head rolled from side to side, mouth wide, mumbling over and over incoherently. Her body was slick with sweat, she reeked of the pungent scent and it permeated the air around them, but still their bodies slapped together.

A low moan flew out of her throat, her head flying forward so she could look into his face and her emerald green eyes glassy and lust-filled as they locked onto his. Her movements beneath him growing more frantic, like a woman possessed, and she was. She was possessed with one thing and one thing only, to reach that zenith that would tip her over into pure unadulterated ecstasy. She was on the edge, her body quivering beneath him, her walls already starting to shudder and tremble around him as he thrust inside her and, finally, she fell over with a loud wail.

Her eyes rolled back into her head so all he could see were the whites—weird—while her entire body went into a full body orgasm. His own was imminent, but he took a brief second to marvel at what lay beneath him, the sensory overload that was happening to Kimmy's body and her senses. She was completely at the mercy of the bliss overwhelming her system, and she was absolutely out of it.

Her body shuddered, shook, and shivered beneath him as wave after wave of rapture ran through her from the top of her head to the tip of her toes, with her sheath clenching his cock so tightly he could barely move. It felt so good that he reached the brink in seconds. His own climax exploded out of him with a thunderous roar tearing free to echo around the room, so loud that the lamp on the bedside table trembled, shook, and finally exploded into a thousand pieces.

Lazarus fell forward instantly, shielding Kimmy's body with his, and just in time before the shards landed all around them. She was still in a stupor, shaking beneath him and mewling softly while the sharp pieces from the disintegrated porcelain gored into his naked skin in dozens of places.

He saved her from harm, his body taking the brunt of the fall-out of the destroyed lamp while she recovered beneath him. His enhanced healing already kicking in and forcing the shards out as he withdrew from her warmth.

"That was... amazing." She gasped, unaware of how close she'd come to being speared by the exploding lamp.

Hell, he doubted she was even aware of it.

Lazarus rolled to the side and off the bed, retrieving her clothes. "Here, get dressed and I'll take you home."

"What?" Kimmy looked aghast. "I thought..."

Lazarus sighed, knowing what was coming and cutting her

off. "No, Kimmy, don't think. This isn't the start of anything so don't go there. I told you what was going to happen and it did, didn't it? I didn't let you down, did I? So let's act like grown-ups and get dressed."

Her eyes flashed with anger as she floundered off the bed, snatching her clothes. "You're a bastard. You know that, don't you?"

"Yes, I do." He grabbed his jeans and tugged them on, knowing he'd have to use his compulsion on her before they left to remove his address from her memory, but if she continued this, he might have to remove more. It looked like she was possibly going to be a problem; hell, he hoped she wasn't a fucking fang-banger. Had he read her wrong?

"I don't want to see you ever again, and if I do, that'll be too damn soon." She flounced to the other end of the room where she started to dress.

It looked like she wasn't going to be a problem after all.

Good, because he had business to take care of, and he didn't have time for a fang-banger hanging around.

CHAPTER TWELVE

LAZARUS OPENED his emails eager to see what Acelin had to report, his heart speeding up as he thought of the information he'd find on the mysterious Miss Harmon. After his night with Kimmy, he felt invigorated, even if she'd ended up pissed at him. Most did.

He didn't end the night with flowers and a promise to take them to dinner. Never did. That upset a lot of women. But he wasn't interested in a damn *relationship*; he wanted to feed and to appease his beast.

He'd got that and now he was feeling much better, settled and ready to get to work on his next project. But he needed information before he could do that, and that's where Acelin came in, or rather, his report.

His stomach lurched when he logged into the dark web email, seeing a new one from the Witch waiting on him, as well as one from Hoax.

"Which one to open first?" he murmured aloud, moving the arrow of the mouse to hover between them.

"Acelin," he decided, knowing Hoax's would be longer and have far more details.

When he got in, he was surprised to find a video attached, but he left that until he'd read through the written report, which held a few surprises, including the fact that Ariana had gone to a local martial arts class and taken part in a fight 'meet.' According to Acelin, she'd been, in his words, 'outmatched' but won the bout and had been well-known to those present.

"I fucking knew it." Lazarus shook his head at the screen, clicking on the video footage and watching.

There she was, tiny in comparison to a colossal figure of a guy facing off against her. Jeez, she looked like she was going to get her ass handed to her. But he watched avidly as the fight progressed, with Ariana and the man getting down and dirty, to her being hit hard more than once but getting up lightning fast and out of her opponents way before he could follow up. Lazarus leaned forward, keenly taking in her technique as she fought. Hell, she was good, tough as nails and fast. The fucker fighting her was losing and he knew it, his anger taking over time and again, and she used it against him, like a damn pro.

"Where did you learn all that?" he spoke to the screen, tapping it when she landed several vicious blows to her ailing rival. "That's not the usual shit you learn, Ariana, that's serious stuff right there."

And finally, he saw it. She was going in for the kill, and his eyes bored into her as she ended it. She was tired, exhausted, and hurt. But she covered it well as another large muscled guy rushed forward and leaned down, whispering into her ear.

"And who are you? You know her... well. She doesn't let anyone close, but you... you're right up in her space and she's not bothered. That means she knows you and you look worried for her too. Aye, you two know each other. Who are you?"

The crowd of people had surged forward, obviously to congratulate her, but he didn't need to see anything else. He'd seen what was important; how she'd managed to deal with Evan fucking Smythson and his friend and managed to walk away in one piece. Ariana Harmon just got a whole hell of a lot more interesting.

Lazarus carried on reading Acelin's report, latching onto the name of the person who ran the martial arts club; a Krav Maga Master by the name of Ron Shepherd. That was someone he'd be looking up if Hoax hadn't already.

There was further information on her home, including the

fact she had not one but two alarm systems in place, and a large enclosed back garden, which had a ten foot wall topped with glass.

"Overkill," he muttered, frowning as he read.

"What the hell is going on with you? What are you scared of, or are you running from someone?"

He continued to the end of the report, noting she hadn't gone out other than to the martial arts studio and for a run. It had only been a couple of days though, so he hadn't expected a lot of information on that front. The other stuff, the other shit, that was definitely not what he'd expected, but it just made her all the more interesting and had his juices flowing even more for her.

He couldn't wait to see what Hoax had uncovered. Closing down Acelin's email, he quickly moved to open the hacker's when there was a knock on his door. Damn it.

Lazarus was in the offices of one of his property businesses. He'd had a meeting earlier, which had gone well, adding a huge amount to his portfolio, and he'd stayed to go through his emails in private.

"What?" he barked out. "I gave instructions not to be disturbed."

"My apologies." The door opened and a security guard popped his head in. "Everyone has left for the night and I'm doing my rounds and saw the light on."

"I'm still working." Lazarus returned his attention to his screen. "I'll lock up when I leave."

"Sorry to have bothered you." The guard paused, hesitating.

Lazarus looked up, taking a measure of the man. Wait. He wasn't just a man. He was, in fact, a Wolf, and he was large, broad, and looked like he knew how to take care of himself, even if he looked nervous right at this moment.

"What is it?" Lazarus looked him up and down. "You obviously want to talk to me about something, so out with it."

"I do." He stepped in and straightened up to his full height, which was impressive. "I took this job because I knew who owned this company; that was over three months ago. I hoped I could talk to you at some point."

"I see." Lazarus canted his head, taking note of the man and trying to figure out if he was a threat. It didn't look as if he was, he wasn't portraying that in his body language in any way. "And why is that? What is it you want to talk to me about?"

"Two things, sir." He walked closer, still showing no signs of being a threat, so Lazarus remained where he was but still on alert. "The most important one is my daughter, she's gone missing and I'd like your help to find her, or rather... I think she's dead."

Lazarus sat forward, that piece of information, as well as the pain he heard in the guy's voice, gaining his attention.

"I'm sure she is because if she wasn't then she'd come back to me. There's just the two of us and she wouldn't not contact me. I know you're going to say that young girls go off on their own all the time, but not her, not my girl; she wouldn't. We're..."

"Wolves," Lazarus interrupted. "I know what you are and I'm aware that she wouldn't just up and leave, your kind stick together. I know how it works. I'm also aware that you have some kind of link with family. Isn't that right?"

Lazarus watched as a look of pure despair crossed the man's face, quickly followed by pain before he closed it down, a huge paw of a hand coming up to run over his face as he took a moment to collect himself before he said another word.

"Yes, that's correct. That's why I know she's gone, and I need to find who's responsible. I have to, sir. You must understand that. You have to understand the need to find those responsible for killing my girl. Don't you?"

A fleeting image flashed before him, of his home, blood and gore, screams and shouts.

"Mister Lazarus, sir."

"What?" He forced himself back to the present, knowing exactly how the Wolf felt. "Yes, I know, but how do you think I can help you?"

"Because the last place she was going the night she went out was Monarch."

Lazarus' blood ran cold in his veins. Surely he'd heard wrong. "What did you say?"

"Monarch; that's one of your clubs, isn't it?" The guard stepped closer. "I'm not blaming you, please don't think that's why I'm here. It's not. But I'm hoping that you might be able to help me figure out what happened to her. She went into your club that night with some friends, and they got separated. That's the last anyone saw of her. If you can do anything, anything at all to help me, I'd be very grateful."

"What's the police doing?" Lazarus asked, playing for time as his mind went into overdrive at the thought of someone coming to harm in one of his establishments.

"Nothing." He shrugged, but the man's body was wound tight as a drum, and he couldn't blame him. "She's one of hundreds of girls who went out and didn't come home, and she's an adult. Add to that the fact that she's not human and, well, they're not interested."

"I see." Lazarus did see, all too well. Supernaturals weren't high up on the chain when it came to the authorities expending manpower. "What's the other thing? You said there were two things."

Again he played for time, running through how he could try to help, his decision already made up. If this girl had come to harm in his club, then he'd get to the bottom of it. One way or the other. He just didn't know how... yet.

"I'd like a job, another job; not this shitty one, sorry. I'm not trying to be disrespectful, but I'm a Wolf, and being a night security guard here is... pretty damn boring. I'd prefer something better, and I was hoping you could help me out there. Truth is, since this happened, I tried everywhere I knew you owned, including Monarch, so I could possibly meet you, but this was the only place I could get in. I need something more."

"I'd need your details, and a name..."

"Ralf," he interrupted. "Ralf Sawyer, and my daughter is... was Keena. Here."

He rushed forward, handing over a small picture of him and a young woman with long auburn hair. His arm was around her and she was laughing up at him with a look of pure happiness in her eyes as she held an ice cream in her hand. The vision was one of a father and daughter who loved one another and a soft sound escaped Ralf as he stepped back.

The sound was barely there but Lazarus heard it and it cemented his decision.

"All right, Ralf. I'll see what I can do." He kept hold of the image. "I'll need to keep this for now and I'd like to see you at Monarch tomorrow night, say nine, if that suits you?"

"What about my job here?"

"I'll take care of it, don't worry."

"So... you'll help me?" Ralf prodded, his eyes boring down into Lazarus'.

"I can't promise you anything." Lazarus didn't want to give him false hopes. "But I'll do my best to find out whatever I can and, from now on, you work for me. A Wolf shouldn't be working this kind of job. You can do something at my Clubs... security there maybe? We can discuss it tomorrow. The pay is certainly a hell of a lot better."

"Thank you, thank you so much, Mister Lazarus." Ralf's chest puffed out as he took a huge breath in, exhaling it in a great puff. "I can't tell you what this means to me. Not knowing is the worst part. I know she's gone. In my heart, I do, but not really and truly *knowing*... that's killing me a little more each and every day."

"I'll see you tomorrow but, for now, I do have work I have to finish, Ralf."

"Of course, sorry to have kept you so long. I'll see you tomorrow." Ralf backed up to the door. And with that, the massive Shifter disappeared, leaving Lazarus angry and unsettled.

Who had dared to use one of his clubs as a hunting ground? That privilege was for him only, and he didn't kill his prey. He returned them unharmed after a night of glorious sex. No fucking way was he allowing this to go unpunished. Nobody, absolutely nobody, was allowed to hunt on his turf and kill one of their own. Okay, Keena wasn't strictly one of his. She was a Wolf, but she was still a Supernatural and, in his books, that made her off limits. Fuck, everyone was off limits in his establishments.

He'd hunt this bastard down and make him pay for what he'd done, and then he'd make it public in their circle; that way no other hotshot would ever think of doing the same. The fact that it was another Super wasn't in doubt, it had to be to take out Keena. She was a Shifter and would be able to fend off a human with no trouble whatsoever. No, it was one of their own who'd done this.

Not for long. Not once he found out who it was... and he would. He fucking would.

But that was for tomorrow, tonight he still had other business to attend to and he planned on getting back to that right now. Focusing back on the screen, he clicked on Hoax's mail and found his report, as detailed as expected and so long that he downloaded the document and opened it, starting to read every little detail the hacker had uncovered about Miss Ariana Harmon.

It took him a long time, stopping and re-reading at times when he was certain what he'd read was wrong. Some parts of the document were blacked out with notes from Hoax saying he'd been unable to retrieve the originals as someone else had already been in before him and deleted them. He suspected it was Ariana herself. These were documents relating to an incident in her teenage years when she'd gone missing for several weeks, and it looked like she didn't want anyone to know what had happened.

Everything related to that period had been 'cleaned' as Hoax put it. Completely and utterly, apart from some paper copies which he'd managed to get, but that had large black marker over them in parts. This would mean she'd broken in and physically done that too. No mean feat.

Lazarus wondered what the hell had gone on but couldn't figure it out from the information he had on hand.

Hoax had done searches for her but came up empty for that time period, so he was none the wiser of what it was all about. The hacker appeared to be annoyed, his email laced with cuss words, and he was doing what he called a 'deep dive' to see if he could find out more. What he did say was that she'd covered her tracks well, far better than he'd anticipated, but he'd continue his search and get back to him if he uncovered anything further.

He had a ton of information on her life from that point on though, including when she'd been introduced to Ron Shepherd, and that was interesting. It was right after the time when she'd been missing, or not long after anyway.

Hoax had her life laid out before him... almost. There were a few patches where she seemed to fall off the face of the earth, and he wasn't able to track her. He was certain she'd gone abroad, but where or why, he couldn't ascertain. He surmised she'd used false paperwork to do so, and with her own IT skills… that wasn't too far a leap to make.

Her parents called her every week, but she didn't see them, didn't visit. They lived on the other side of the country and Ariana didn't go there, and it looked like they didn't come here to see here either. Her mother, in particular, was always worried about her, always asking if she was okay, but it looked like Ariana tried to keep contact to a minimum. Strange.

She was OCD to the 'max,' as Hoax put it. Her online orders for everything she required being delivered to her home, including an inordinate amount of cleaning supplies and hand sanitizer. Somehow that didn't surprise him.

She also had a very successful business, which she ran by herself, and when he saw what it was, her being able to erase records suddenly made sense. Ariana owned her own IT company and it did very well according to Hoax. She had multiple bank accounts in her own name, and the business had healthy balances, but he saw money being filtered from them to offshore accounts too, and he'd chased them around until he lost them in the dark web. Exactly the place where Hoax conducted his own business.

"She's smart, Lazarus. Fucking ace at this, and I'd bet she has other aliases too. I've got a feeling she's on the dark web looking for people; who or why, I'm not sure. But I know she's there, she's fucking there all right."

Hoax admired her. Lazarus could see it, feel it in the way he'd written that, and so did he, but he had one up on the hacker. He had an idea what, or, rather, the who she was looking for.

Ariana was no normal young woman, no normal IT businesswoman. She was on there with one thing in mind… *hunting.*

What he needed to know was why?

CHAPTER THIRTEEN

Lazarus waited outside Ariana's house, wondering—no—hoping she'd make an appearance for a run. Dressed casually in sweats, he was at the edge of the cul-de-sac sitting in a pick-up with gardening equipment in the back and a ball cap on his head with the front pulled down low. His eyes glued to her front door, itching for it to open to see her emerge.

Hell, he was just desperate to get a whiff of her scent again. That unique blend of aromas that was *her*... Ariana. It was ingrained deep inside him and he'd know it anywhere now. If she was amongst a crowd of a thousand, he'd still be able to find her. No doubt in his mind. None.

He'd find her in a damn stadium packed to the rafters; that blend of fragrances, hints and bouquets of smells when blended were just one persons, and Ariana's was magnificent. So damn alluring with her exclusive blood-type adding its irreplaceable undertone to the mix. Aye, he'd know hers anywhere and be able to track her easily from far enough behind so she couldn't see him. But where the hell would be the fun in that?

No, he wanted to *see* her, *hear* her gasps as she realized she was being followed. See her as she attempted to evade him. How would she do it?

Would she speed up? Duck and dive through bushes, trees, and buildings? Or would she use some of those fighting skills he'd witnessed? Would Ariana attempt to take on the lone man following her? That was a possibility. Hmm... that could prove tricky if she did. She could unmask him and that wasn't on the agenda.

Not for today anyway.

That was a moot point. She had to come out of her damn house first.

He'd been waiting for over two hours. Well past the time that she'd gone for her run when Acelin had followed her; it looked like she might not be going out today. "Fuck," Lazarus snarled, opening his laptop. "More than one way to see you again."

He opened up her company website and checked that she did at least one of the things he was after and then clicked on the *contact us* button. "Liar," he whispered, knowing it should've read 'me' instead of 'us,' and fired off an email marked urgent in capital letters then sat back. His attention flitting between his screen and her door.

A large white van entered the street, slowing as it neared Ariana's home. Hell, yes; looked like she was getting a delivery. With the vehicle in his line of sight, he would see absolutely nothing, so he slid out and grabbed a few tools from the back, crossed the road, and started to walk down slowly.

The delivery guy was already at her door, a number of boxes piled at his feet. Yes. She'd need to sign for them and take them inside because he was certain she wouldn't allow a stranger into her home. No. Ariana wouldn't do that. Or would she? Had he sized her up wrong?

He slowed, pulled a hankie from his pocket, and wiped imaginary sweat from his face as he leaned over, catching an imaginary breather. All the while his eyes were glued to her doorway as it opened and Ariana made an appearance.

Finally, he saw her again in the flesh.

This time was like chalk and cheese to when she'd been in his club as she ran from Evan Smythson and his buddy. This time she was fresh and clean with her long hair hanging loose, and when she stepped forward, the sun glinted off auburn highlights causing it to shine. She wore a plain white t-shirt and what looked to be black yoga pants, which clung to her body and had his imagination going into overdrive as to what lay beneath... taut muscles were a given.

He knew she worked out, so there was absolutely no doubt she was fit, in more ways than one.

There were some faded bruises still visible, to him anyway, but they were almost gone. She must be a fast healer. After her run-in with Smythson and the fight she had at the martial arts club, she should've had a few more on her face, but either she was wearing cosmetics or, as he thought, she'd healed up quickly. She didn't look to be wearing any kind of make-up, her skin was clear and pale. Aye, there were no enhancements worn, so she must have used something to aid in her recovery. Maybe he'd ask her when he got the chance.

He was close enough to inhale her scent, the heady aroma that was *her*... Ariana Harmon. His synapses flared to life as it hit him. Every. Single. One. The hairs on his body stood up on end, the back of his neck tingled, and his beast fired to life inside him, roaming back and forth restlessly.

Why?

Then he saw it. Saw the delivery driver lean forward with a smile playing on his lips and his eyes checking her out; his beast didn't like that. Not one fucking bit. And neither did he. A snarl rose inside him, his lips curled back, and he had to force himself not to spring forward and tear the fucker's heart from his chest right where he stood.

What the fuck? What the goddamn fuck?

Lazarus lowered his head, taking a deep breath to stop himself, and gathered his thoughts at the same time as his eyes squinted upward to keep a watch on Ariana. He couldn't tear them from her as she ignored the guy's obvious interest in her, signing his clipboard and returning it to him with a shake of her head when he seemed to offer to take her delivery inside. Her eyes glinted up at the delivery man, a no-nonsense look that told him to back the fuck up... and he did.

"Good choice," Lazarus whispered, his jaw clenched tight as he watched the scene play out.

Then Ariana paused to look around the street, her keen eyes roamed around as if she were looking for a threat.

Did she know he was there? Or was this just Ariana being... Ariana?

Probably the latter. Her eyes skimmed over him and returned to the boxes before she hefted them inside her home. His keen ears picked up the sound of her locks being put back in place and her alarm being re-set. All before the delivery guy had even walked back to his truck.

And she was gone. Her aroma dissipated around him as he stared at the closed door, knowing she wouldn't step back outside for the rest of the day. The thought wasn't one that had him jumping for joy. Instead, it elicited a snarl and feeling inside him that he couldn't put a name to. All he knew was he hoped nobody crossed his path at that moment because he wasn't sure what he'd do.

He took a deep breath, eyes locked on the house for a few more seconds before he pulled them away as the truck's engine revved. The noise pulling another snarl from him when he remembered the way the guy had looked at Ariana, his head spinning to lock onto the vehicle. Lucky for the guy, he was already on the move, and Lazarus shook his head to get a hold of himself.

"Not a good idea." He squinted at the truck, eying the young man as he passed by and wondering how long it would take to drain him dry but deciding he wasn't worth it.

Lazarus waited until he'd driven away then backtracked to his own vehicle, knowing she wasn't going for her run. He'd seen all of Ariana he was going to for the day, unless he sat around waiting in the off chance she had another delivery. So... what to do? Leave? Or stay? If he stayed, he was certain she'd make him. She was paranoid about security and she'd seen him on the street now. She'd be sure to check and see what he was up to, so he couldn't just sit here and do nothing all day long, and she wasn't going anywhere.

Email. Had she replied to his email? He checked to see and excitement lanced through him when he saw she had.

Bingo!

Opening it up, he saw a brief message from her, one that had his lips tug up as he read through it. She'd agreed to meet with him, or rather, the owner of *Monarch*, to go over his requirements and to help with an urgent security task. One that he'd said was of the utmost importance and needed to be dealt with as soon as possible, and that he'd pay a handsome bonus if it could be done today. She'd said she could fit him in and would be there at seven this evening, if that suited.

Hell, yes; it suited him just fine. There would be nobody else there that early. Well, he hoped not. The rest of the staff didn't start to arrive for at least an hour or so after that, so it would be just the two of them, and he couldn't wait to see her face when she walked in and saw him.

He hit reply and told her that was perfect, and that he'd leave the front door open and to come straight in. He'd meet her at the bar area. His eyes were glued to the screen as he waited, the minutes seemed to drag by before she responded—eight minutes to be exact—and she merely said that was fine and she'd see him promptly at seven.

Aye. She'd see him then and he'd bet she'd be right on time too. Ariana wouldn't be late, and he sure as hell wouldn't be either.

Starting the engine, he took one long last look at her house before backing away. "See you soon, Ariana."

He had his meeting with the Wolf, Ralf Sawyer, at nine; plenty of time for him to have his *reunion* with Ariana. Then he'd talk with the father whose girl had disappeared from his club and fill him in on what he was doing. He couldn't allow that to go unpunished.

Nobody came into his clubs and did that shit. Not if they expected to live. And he couldn't permit it. If word got out that stuff was going down and he'd done nothing... Fuck, no. That wasn't happening. He might be a monster, he *was* a monster, but he didn't go around killing innocents for no reason. He didn't get involved in any of that, not any longer.

That's what made them as profitable as they were. That's what brought the big bucks in, and he wasn't going to allow that to dry up. No way. So he'd sort this out. One way or the other. Ralf Sawyer deserved to know what happened to his daughter, and Lazarus would do whatever it took to get him answers. He'd talk to him, get him set up with a job, and hopefully the Shifter would work out okay.

He'd then get back to Ariana.

She wasn't getting away from him that easily, and he suspected she went out at night more often than day. Ariana was more at home hiding in the dark where she couldn't be seen, in the shadows just like him.

Only difference was she was human, and he was not. She could be so easily killed. He could not.

She appeared to put herself in danger, and he would not allow just anyone to take her life. If anyone were to do that, it would be him. So he had to follow her to ensure she was safe... for now.

ARIANA PACED BACK AND FORTH, going to her window and staring out for the hundredth time... the truck was gone. She knew it was. It was gone the last fifty times she'd checked, but it didn't stop her looking because she was certain that the *gardener* had been off.

Absolutely certain.

There was something about him that was familiar. The way he held his body maybe? His clothes? Hell, she couldn't put her finger on it, but there was something. She could *feel* it. She wasn't losing her mind. Not again. She wasn't.

It had been years since she'd been in that dark place, and she was strong now. No longer that weak girl who jumped at the smallest noise, or whenever a man came near her. No. She wasn't that person any longer; but that man, there was something about him that caused her skin to itch, and her attack alarm was going off like a damn siren inside her.

She'd seen him before. There was no doubt about it. She just couldn't place where or when, but he was a threat, and she wasn't about to let her guard down. If he came anywhere near her, he'd soon find out she was no easy target. He'd get a taste of the true Ariana; the one who would take him down and out before he had a chance to lay a hand on her, before he could open his mouth and utter a threat.

Yeah, they liked to do that. Talk. Say what they were going to do before they did it. Well, that didn't work on her. Before he got a sentence out, she'd have him fucked over and he'd never utter another threat to anyone again.

But he wasn't there. Hadn't been for some time, but doubts slithered inside her brain. Slipping, sliding, and creeping around while she stood still as a statue with her eyes glued to the street, watching for any sign of the figure she knew didn't belong. That she knew was a threat. That she knew she'd seen before. That she knew had been watching her.

DarkHunter

CHAPTER FOURTEEN

LAZARUS COULDN'T SETTLE HIMSELF, couldn't get Ariana out of his damn head. Not for a second. All day long she'd been in there and he hadn't been able to concentrate on his work. Hadn't been able to do one iota of anything that even resembled a constructive piece of labor. Nada, zip, zilch.

The way she'd looked earlier when she'd come outside, alert but also something else too... she'd looked vulnerable, upset even. As if something was troubling her. What? He wondered about that for a long time and couldn't get the sight of her out of his damn head.

He'd attempted to go over some contracts he'd been sent, his eyes glazed over and images of Ariana replaced the words on his screen. He'd then tried to check the profits for his clubs over the past month to ensure everything was running as they should, the numbers ran together and the video of Ariana's fight sprang into his head.

The sight of the man she'd fought caused him to snarl and slam his hand on the desk, sending things flying in all directions with one thought... he wanted to tear him limb from limb.

"What the hell?" he ground out to the ceiling, running a hand through his hair as he tried to figure out what was wrong with him. It wasn't as if he wasn't going to see her again. Hell, he would see her soon, in a few hours, and he had other businesses to run. He had no time for this daydreaming shit, and it was beginning to annoy the hell out of him.

His phone ringing and vibrating across the desk caused another flare of anger to rise up inside him, for no good reason, while he snatched it up. A name he didn't expect to see flashed on the screen.

"Clive? What's up?"

"Lazarus, did I wake you? I know it's early for you."

"It's okay, Clive. I'm awake." Lazarus heard the tension in his friend's tone and knew it wasn't a call just for a chat. He was right.

"I don't like doing this. I really don't, Laz." Clive stopped and he could almost see him running a hand over his face like he always did when he was upset.

"Just tell me," Lazarus pressed him. His mood was already up shit creek so he couldn't be bothered hanging around and waiting for Clive to spit out why he'd called.

"All right. I've got another file for you." Clive paused again and Lazarus jumped right in, the thought of expending some of his pent-up energy sounded good right about now.

"What is it? Or rather... who?"

"He's a gang leader, one who's gotten away with a ton of shit for over ten years, but he's worse lately. He's branched out into underage girls, Laz. He's selling them on the dark web and we all know it. Every damn one of us knows, but we can't pin him down. Some of them are barely into double figures, ten years old for fuck sake!" Clive stopped and he could hear him take a drink, probably bourbon or something just as strong, before he carried on.

"We've been trying to stop him but he keeps slithering out from under us. You know what it's like; nobody will say a word against him, and if they do they end up dead in an alley soon afterwards. Shit, I can't allow it to go on. I just can't. It's killing me more each day, and last night we found one of the girls. She was dead. Barely twelve years old and dead. I won't tell you what had been done to her, but she had his brand on her arm so we know where she came from. Right here in this city, even though she was found all the way across the country."

Lazarus' beast woke with a fury, rampaging inside him at the thought of the fucker who would sell kids to animals who would use and abuse them; he felt the same. He couldn't allow that. Not a chance in hell would this animal be living and breathing for much longer.

"Send me the details, Clive."

Clive exhaled loudly, as if he'd been expecting him to refuse. Why? Didn't he know him by now?

"Thank you, my friend. You know I can never repay you for what you do... for what I can't."

"No payment necessary," Lazarus returned, and it was true. He relished in this, savored the times when he could release his dark hunter and allow his beast to wreak vengeance on these lowlifes.

"Still, thank you, Laz. I've gotta go. I'll send the file now."

"Fine." Lazarus was ready to hang up, already wishing he had the file in his hands. "Wait, Clive, send me his details over the dark web, to the email we use at times. I don't want to wait on the courier."

"Are you sure?" Clive sounded surprised at the break from their normal protocol, but Lazarus needed something to stop him from obsessing about a certain female. One who he was growing more and more preoccupied with.

This fucker would take his mind off Miss Ariana Harmon, even if only for a few hours. It was something... anything to stop him visualizing her dark eyes, which held secrets he wanted to uncover. Her silky hair that caught the sun when she'd stepped out of her house to retrieve her parcels earlier, and fuck, don't even think about those lips that were plump and... No.

Don't fucking go there.

"Aye, send it over. I've other matters to attend to, but I'd like to have a look at it now," Lazarus ground out, pushing the visions of Ariana from his mind.

"Okay. I'll do it."

Clive didn't sound happy about the change in their usual way of doing business, but he didn't care.

"Clive, I don't need the entire file. All I need are the bare bones; his name, description, and where the fuck I'll find him. I can get anything else myself. You know that, so there's no need to worry."

"Sure, Laz, of course. Just be careful. This guy's never on his own. He's always got his right-hand man with him and at least one or two other bodyguards. They'll be armed to the teeth too. I don't want—"

"I'll be fine," Lazarus butted in. "I told you not to worry... about anything. Leave it to me."

The thought of a fight, a true fight, one with more than one and with people who wouldn't just lie down in terror before him... Shit, that had his juices flowing.

"Be sure to call me and let me know you're okay," Clive added while Lazarus was already thinking of which weapons to take with him.

"Aye, no problem," he replied absentmindedly, hanging up and tapping his chin, his mind already on the new issue at hand; taking out a gangbanger with a horde of armed men guarding him.

"Hmm, now can I get this over and done quickly or not?" he talked to himself as he flicked over to the dark web with a few fast and practiced keystrokes, opening up a browser and logging into one of several email accounts.

As soon as he was in, he saw it, the mail from his friend and FBI Agent, sitting there waiting on him. Adrenaline flooded his system as he opened it and started to read the details. Male, late twenties, and leader of a street gang, which he'd managed to organize well over the last few years. So well that he had it running like a well-oiled business with several different branches. Drugs were a given, of course, but not just on the street. This aficionado had branched out and was dealing to high-end customers, and doing rather well using technology to his advantage, with his clients placing orders online and having them delivered after they'd paid via a secure online facility... all on the dark web of course.

He had girls working for him too. Not street girls either, although he probably had those to bring in cash on hand, but he also had sites set up where women were on display for whoever the fuck had enough money to pay for them, and, again, they paid online and the women were delivered to them for a set amount of time, overnight in some cases. Or, and this was scary in Lazarus' mind, for 'parties.' One or two of these women, and that was a term he used loosely as some looked very young indeed, were delivered to these guys for a 'party.'

Fuck. How many could be at that kind of gig? He didn't want to think about that. He didn't want to think about a whole hell of a lot of what this bastard was up to, but the worst was what he came to next: the wee ones.

The lassies so young that they should be at home still playing with dolls and watching cartoons instead of being sold off to the highest bidder.

But that's what he was reading now on the screen in front of him. His jaw clenched, his fury burned, and his beast wanted out to play.

"What's your fucking name, you dirty bastard?"

He scanned the rest of the info. *Raylon Barnes*, with a nice image of a guy in a smart suit. When he looked closer however, he could spy the top of a tattoo on his neck, just barely visible against the crisp white shirt. What appeared to be the gangs' *brand*, a crown with the number five through it. With his address right there too. One that caused him to raise an eyebrow because it was nowhere near the projects he expected it to be. Didn't Clive say this guy was a gangbanger? So what the fuck was he doing with an address just a few streets from where he was sitting now?

One that he knew would cost him a damn fortune because he owned the penthouse apartment in the building right next door. An apartment that had a nice rooftop area complete with a Jacuzzi, bar, and, more importantly, easy access to the building with the address he was looking at right now.

For him anyway. A human... not so damn much.

Glancing at the time, he saw he had several hours before his meeting at *Monarch*. Plenty of time to deal with this scumbag. He doubted he'd have more than a few henchmen around him, and he could handle them no problem; with his enhanced speed, they wouldn't know what hit them.

His inner darkness started to slither around inside, eager to get to work and release itself. He could feel it as his beast relished the thought of *playing* with this damnable piece of garbage who breathed the same air as the innocents he blithely sent to hellish and torturous places. Not for much longer. His dark hunter was being released, and Raylon Barnes' time was up... he just didn't know it.

Yet.

Lazarus reached into his pocket, his fingers roaming over the cold steel within as he pictured where it would be very soon. The image of Barnes' blood dripping from the blade vivid in his mind while he tortured the man responsible for so much pain and suffering.

"You're going to find out what it means, *Raylon*. Find out what pain is, what suffering is like, and I'm going to enjoy educating you in the fine arts of torture."

He rose with one thought only: Extinguish this destroyer of

innocence in the most painful way possible. That's if he didn't have a fucking army surrounding him; he hoped Clive's intel was right. He hoped this fucker didn't have a horde of low-life bastards with machine-guns guarding him.

That could put a whole different ending to this mission. A completely different outcome. One where he ended up with a thousand rounds of ammo inside him and *Barnes* got away intact.

"Guess I'll have to trust you, Clive." He shrugged. "Life would be boring otherwise."

He cracked his neck, prepared to head off into Hell if necessary.

DarkHunter

CHAPTER FIFTEEN

LAZARUS WAS in his penthouse in no time, and the first order of business was changing his clothes into something more... suitable. Just in case he was caught on any security cameras.

Dark jeans and a matching hoodie was perfect for the job, with black nondescript boots and several of his favorite daggers secreted about his body. He was ready to pay a visit to Raylon Fucking Barnes. The bastard who sold girls so young they should still be playing with damn dolls.

A growl rumbled up from his chest, a cold chill sweeping over him at the images that swept through his mind of a tiny dead and broken body with a fucking *brand* on it. Quickly followed by visions of glorious windswept hills leading to a small village ravaged by marauders, blood covering the ground with bodies littering the area. And another small body, one he knew well. One with hair like spun wheat and the brightest smile in the whole goddamn world. But he could no longer see her like that. His memory of her tainted and destroyed so he could only remember her broken, bloodied, and with her throat slashed wide open while she cried out in terror.

And he'd been helpless to do a fucking thing to stop it.

A wail erupted from him, up to the night sky, and he hadn't even realized he'd made his way outside. His fist slammed against his chest, over and over he pummeled himself while the memory tormented him and his beast battled to be free to hunt and slaughter in retribution for things that happened so long ago. Ones that haunted him and chased him through the centuries.

"When? When will I be free?" he whispered to nobody but the past.

His anger took over, as it always did. Grief and anguish fading as his darkness slithered up his spine to quickly quash it. His inner beast his only ally to help him quash the heartache that he would otherwise drown in. His focus now on his mission: Destroy Raylon Barnes and his inner circle.

Cut the head off the beast and then Law Enforcement could deal with the rest. If they didn't, then he'd do it himself. He'd destroy the whole lot of them. One by one if necessary.

Lazarus checked out the area, ensuring there were no outside cameras visible. If there were, he could simply use his enhanced speed to be a blur, or use a route that would not be captured. It wasn't his first rodeo, so to speak, so this wouldn't cause him a problem. Getting into the building, or even gaining access to the apartment, would be easy. To him anyway.

There was a short distance between the buildings, a mere twelve feet or so, which was no problem for him. As soon as he saw no cameras, he jogged toward the edge of his private area, leapt up onto the wall, and continued on over to the next. It was a few feet to the door that led downstairs and, again, he checked for security measures. None. Shit, he was glad he didn't live in this building. He'd be asking for some improvements to be made if he did.

Keeping his senses alert, he made his way down the stairs to the top level and, once there, he quickly located the internal stairs. He knew they were the best bet for not being seen, especially at this level. People who lived here would use the elevators, not the stairs, but he checked first just in case. Standing still and using his enhanced hearing for any heartbeats or footsteps, he heard nothing but silence. Just as he expected, so he quickly leapt down the two levels to where his target's apartment was.

Checking the hallway, Lazarus spied two well-dressed guys standing outside a door at the end of the corridor. Dark suits with white shirts. Their attempt to pass as legitimate security was offset by the designer trainers and the fact their shirts hung loose instead of neatly tucked in. He could also clearly see where they had their guns tucked into the waistband of their pants. No self-respecting security detail would have them there instead of in a shoulder holster.

Pathetic and unprofessional, but it was what he had expected to find.

He had to get past these two wannabes and into the apartment without causing a commotion, not wanting to draw the attention of the neighbors. Shouldn't be too difficult. A swift knife to the back of the neck of one, then he could sweep in and grab the other before he knew what was happening. Truth was, they didn't look to be the brightest bulbs in the box. The way they were lounging against the wall, smoking and chatting when they were obviously supposed to be defending their boss.

They obviously thought they were safe in their posh surroundings. They'd grown lax in their duties and didn't expect anyone to attack them here in their ivory tower, but he'd soon show them the error of their ways. His beast was eager to be let loose, and once he gave it free rein, they'd realize they were far from safe... even here in one of the best zip codes in the city.

Lazarus checked the area again, blade in hand, and stilled. A security camera caught his attention in the corner at the end of the hallway. Damn. If it was manned and saw one of the men downed, then the alarm would go off and he wouldn't have the time he wanted to spend with Barnes.

"Change of plans," he murmured softly, tugging his hood lower to cover his face as he stepped out and started to walk quickly toward the apartment.

They weren't aware of him at first, he'd taken at least fifteen steps before one even said a word.

"Hey, who're you? Whatdya want?"

He ignored him and carried on, speeding up but not too much, not wanting to catch the attention of anyone watching on the security-cam.

"Motherfucka, you better answer or I'll shoot yo ass."

Jeez, he actually talked like that? Really? Lazarus barely stopped himself from answering. He'd almost reached them. Slowing down, he murmured, "I've been sent with an urgent message for your boss. It's about some agent in the FBI who's onto him."

"What? What fuckin' FBI dude?"

He was there! Close enough to see the whites of their eyes and that's all he needed. Lazarus stooped and, turning his back to the camera, lifted his head and harnessed his power. His top lip curled back to sneer as they both saw it, stumbling back to hit the wall and reaching for their weapons.

"Don't," he commanded. "Do not move your hands."

Their hands stilled mid-air, their mouths half open and their faces were just as he liked them... filled with fear. "You'll do exactly as I say from this moment on, and if you don't, I'll force you to take your guns out, put them in your mouth, and pull the trigger. Do you understand me? Nod your head once if you do."

They did as he commanded, not that he expected anything else. His compulsion worked on every human he'd used it on, and most other Supernaturals.

"You're going to open the door and take me inside and, once we're inside, you will stand still and do and say nothing unless I instruct you. Do it now."

Lazarus stayed close behind them as they turned and did his bidding like a couple of automatons, the door opening into a small reception area where they stopped and stood like statues.

"Where's your boss? Point, don't talk."

Two arms shot up to lead him down the corridor on the left. "How many guards does he have?"

Both hands turned with four fingers pointing to the ceiling. Not too bad. Five in total, including Barnes himself. Unless they had silver bullets, or were lying in wait for him, he should be all right.

Lazarus sped down the hall. The thick cream carpet aided his approach to the almost-closed door where music and sounds of several men talking filtered out. They weren't near to his position so he chanced a glance inside, spying two lounging on a large black leather sofa on the far side of the room with their backs to him, with one in a chair to the side. A wet-bar was off to the left and that's where two others sat, drinking. All of them were lounging, with no weapons in sight. Didn't mean they were unarmed, only that they weren't in their hands at that point.

His eyes roamed over them again and he zeroed in on the lone armchair; Raylon Barnes. His target was the one sitting alone. Good. That made it easier for him.

Removing several knives, he hefted them in his hands, checking out the distances and positions of his victims. A blitz attack would be best. Giving them no time to react. So that's what he did.

Lazarus slipped through the opening in the door and sped into the large room, his body a blur to the human eye as he wielded his weapons. His first casualties were the two men on the sofa.., tossing his throwing knives with ease as he darted behind them. The blades landed on target, digging deep into the base of their necks and causing them to jerk once before their heads flopped to the side.

"What the..." Raylon sat forward, staring at his goons and wondering what the fuck had just happened to them as Lazarus carried on.

Speeding up, he dashed toward the two who sat at the bar, slow to react to their friends being killed. Their eyes were wide, but that was all the time they had before Lazarus was doling out their own demise. His daggers protruding from their chests, rammed so deep their hearts exploded and they slumped to the floor with crimson seeping out to stain their pristine white shirts. Shocked surprise the last look on their dark faces as they slipped from this world to the next.

Lastly, he reached Barnes, who'd finally realized he was under attack. His hand reaching for a weapon at his back, but Lazarus was already snatching it free and tossing it aside before backhanding his face and sending him slamming back into his chair, dazed and with blood dripping from his mouth.

Lazarus picked up the gun, wiped it free of his prints, and then flung it away in disgust before turning his full attention onto the man who sat staring up at him with defiance, loathing and a hint of disbelief on his face. Barnes looked around at the corpses of his cohorts then back up at him, his chin jutting out insolently.

"Who the fuck do you think you are? You've just signed your death warrant, you stupid fuck."

Barnes' bravado was quite something under the circumstances. His men lay dead all around him, yet he still tried to intimidate him. His voice was loud and only wavered slightly at the end. His eyes flitted to the bodies on the sofa then back up to Lazarus, who allowed his fury to show clearly as he snarled down at him.

"I'm your retribution for selling young girls to anyone who wants them for playthings, you sick bastard. I'm here to show you what happens to men like you, who think they can move out of the ghetto and live in a nice place like this and believe they're above the law. You're not. I don't care about the law. I care about justice and punishment, and that's what I'm here for; your punishment."

"What the fuck do you mean? My punishment? Who're you to—"

"Shut up." Lazarus pointed a finger at his face. The anger that had been rolling around inside him now past a boiling point. "Don't move a muscle and you might live for a few minutes longer."

Barnes squinted at him, opened his mouth, then thought better of it while Lazarus darted away. Again using his Vampiric speed to retrieve his weapons and, before his prey could make a dash for freedom, he was back standing before him, four deadly blades in his hands, dripping with blood.

Raylon's eyes locked onto the weapons, or rather the crimson that now dropped down onto his perfect thick cream shag pile carpet. The blood seeped into the fibers slowly as the blood was already congealing. Lazarus shook his head, sighed, and bent down to hunker on his knees. He was now at eye level with the gangbanger, who was pretending to be a businessman with his hand-made suit in his expensive apartment, the façade was almost believable.

Until you looked closer and saw the ink showing above the collar of his shirt and peeking out from the cuffs. Add in the sleekit look in his eyes... Aye, that was the word. A good Scottish word his mother would use for someone who was sly and untrustworthy. A damnable bastard in other words, and that was exactly what Raylon Barnes was.

Lazarus swiped the blades across the carpet to clean them, causing Barnes to wince and his eyes to narrow with a look of disgust flitting across his face. Lazarus wasn't sure whether it was because the sight reminded him his friends had been slaughtered, or he was offended that his precious carpet was now destroyed and stained by their blood. By the way Barnes' nose wrinkled, he thought it was the latter. Fucker. He more than likely didn't give a fuck about anyone other than himself.

Once he'd finished, he tucked away three of his weapons, hefting one dagger in his hand, and rose to tower over the man who'd wrought such misery to so many. His beast tore at his insides, eager to get to work.

"This is the time, and the only time, you get to make peace with whatever god or whatever it is you want to talk to." Lazarus spun the blade around, wondering where he'd start on Barnes. His face? His torso? His fucking balls?

"God? You think I pray to a god? Are you crazy?"

"To tell the truth... Yes, I probably am. More than a little, but that's another story." Lazarus grinned, his lips turned back in a grimace, which was more maniacal as his eagerness to start this fuckers punishment grew with each passing second.

"Just what are you doing here? Killing my men and standing with that knife like some madman. Are you going to kill me too? Is that it?"

"What the fuck do you think? Of course I am, but before I do, I'm going to have some fun. Fun for me but not for you. I'll use my dagger here, which is extremely good at skinning people, and yes, you heard me correctly. I'm just deciding where to start. Your face, chest, but then I'm thinking I'll start at your fucking balls. That's more apt, I think, for what you've done to so many young girls. Yes. I think that's where I'll start."

Barnes' eyes were spinning around all over the room, obviously looking for an escape now that he realized his predicament. Horror was evident in them, his hands shook on the arms of the chair, which he now held onto with a death grip as he refused to look up at Lazarus. His Adam's apple bobbed as he swallowed, looking off to the side.

"Do it."

"I will," Lazarus ground out. "Don't think I won't. I'll take great pleasure in hearing you scream, but the thing is, men don't scream and scream and scream. They do at first, but then the pain is so extreme that they simply lose their voice. The movies don't show that though."

"I said, do it! Now! Hurry the fuck up!"

Lazarus frowned, wondering what the hell he was saying... what the?

And then there was the sound of gunfire exploding. His shoulder jerked, his thigh too, white hot pain igniting inside him. The next two shots went wild, blasting into the bar and shattering bottles and glasses, but then another slammed into his back as he was turning around... to find a boy. A young boy standing behind him with the gun he'd tossed away earlier.

And he realized his mistake. He'd asked the goons earlier how many fucking men were inside. Men! How could he know there'd be a child here? A boy who couldn't have been more than ten or eleven. The whites of his eyes were huge as he held the gun with two shaking hands, his lips trembling and terror in his eyes.

Barnes shot up, grappling him from behind. Fucker. Not a chance.

Lazarus whirled around, elbowing him in the face viciously and snarling with glee when he heard bones crack, and Barnes went down like a sack of potatoes. That left the boy. A damn boy. He had to deal with him. He had no fucking choice.

But how? He couldn't kill a kid... and he *was* a kid. What choice did he have?

CHAPTER SIXTEEN

RIGHT NOW, the child was just standing there, trembling and shaking, with the empty gun in his hands. His eyes were wide and glazed with shock and fear. Lazarus could scent it all around him; the smell was thick in the air as the boy quaked in his shoes.

Lazarus was injured, three bullets inside him, but he had to deal with the boy and then Barnes. Quickly. The shots would've been heard and the cops would be arriving soon. He had a decision to make and he had to do it now. No time to think… just act.

He walked over to the youngster, who shrank back until he could go no farther, stopped by the huge entertainment system. Lazarus leaned down and removed the gun, wiped it clean and dropped it before making a decision. The only one he could.

He called his power forth once more to compel the child. Hell, what else could he do? He couldn't kill him, he wasn't *that* far gone. Not yet anyway.

"Where were you and what are you doing here?"

"I was in the bathroom and I was to be initiated into the Crowns and get my brand tonight. After that, they were going to send me out on my first job, taking drugs to the projects."

Shit. Not happening.

"Do your parents know about this?"

"No! My ma would kill me if she did, but we need the money. There's just her and me and my two sisters. She works two jobs and she's never home. I wanted to help, and they said they'd pay me for doing stuff for them."

"Anyone else know about this?"

"No. I was too scared to tell."

"Okay. You'll go straight home and you will forget about this. You'll forget you met these fuckers or that you even spoke to anyone to do with this gang. You will never have anything to do with any gang again. You'll work hard at school and help your mother any way you can. Do you understand me? You will not have anything to do with drugs or the Crown Five gang. Understand?"

"Yes."

"You never saw me. You never held a gun. You were never here. Go home now. Take a cab, here's some money, and when you get home and get out of the cab, you won't remember the journey, you were just playing outside. Go. Now."

The lad took the cash, turned, and walked away.

"Wait."

The boy stopped dead.

"What's your name and where do you live?"

Without turning around, the boy replied. Lazarus filed away the information, not quite knowing what he'd do with it. Not tonight anyway. It was something for another time. Another day. When he could think more clearly and didn't have three damn slugs hurting like a bitch inside him.

"Okay, you can go now, but pull your hood up and over your face. Don't talk to anyone on the way out, and make sure your face is covered so nobody can see you."

Lazarus exhaled as he watched the small underfed child continue on and disappear out the door and into the hall, anger and fury at what he'd been forced to do here by his circumstances, his poor life, by Raylon fucking Barnes.

His fury was now running like lava through him as he turned back to face the low-life who had ordered a child to fire a gun into his back. A boy who'd been forced into making a choice he never should have had to make, one that had led him to be in the apartment and ordered by Barnes to do something no child ever should have to, to kill a man.

The boy didn't know he was a Vampire. He only knew he held a weapon and the leader of the gang was ordering him to murder him. The child was terrified and aware he had no option but to carry out Barnes' order.

One more stain on the fucker's soul. One more crime to add to the long list he was already guilty of. One more sin he was going to pay for. Just not at his hands. Not tonight. Raylon Barnes would die for his misdeeds. Lazarus would make sure of that, but he no longer had time to stay and *play* with him. He could no longer allow himself the pleasure of torturing the man who'd caused so much pain to others. His end would be quick. Too quick. As he walked toward him and saw him lying unconscious, Lazarus couldn't help the roar of frustration that tore free.

The bastard wouldn't even feel the end. His last moments would be lost and he wouldn't feel them or the fear he deserved for what he'd done.

Lazarus kicked Barnes savagely in the face, demolishing it and leaving it a bloody and gruesome mess before he dropped down to his knees and finished him off. A swift stab to his chest, his dagger piercing the fucker's heart once, twice, three times, for good measure before he slit his throat ear to ear and right down to the bone.

"No coming back for you." He wiped his blade on the suit jacket that laid askew, then stood, the sound of sirens coming closer with each passing second. "Time to go."

He jogged down the hall and came across the two henchmen still standing in the entranceway. No point in silence now, the cops were already on their way. But he wanted to check something; although, he knew the answer.

"Have you killed an innocent person for Raylon Barnes? Answer truthfully."

Both of them answered together, a flat monotone yes falling out of their mouths.

"More than once?"

Again they answered in the affirmative, and their fate was sealed.

"You'll walk into the living room and stand right next to each other. Once you're there, you'll take your guns out and you'll count to ten together. Then you'll raise your weapon and shoot each other in the head. Do it now. Go."

They turned and walked away slowly. Lazarus gave neither of them another thought. Instead, he pulled his hoodie up and over his face before he opened the door and checked the hall. Clear, although, he could hear the elevator making its way up, and he doubted it would be long before it arrived. He wasn't sure if it was internal building security or police inside, but he wasn't waiting to find out.

His back hurt, burning hot, his shoulder too, but his thigh felt like someone had stuck a river of lava inside it. Lazarus turned his head to check the floor and was relieved there was no signs of his blood left behind. He could feel it starting to drip down his leg though, and he knew he'd better get out of there fast. Not just because he didn't want to be seen, but he couldn't risk leaving evidence of a Vampire being smack bang in the middle of this bloodbath.

They didn't have the same DNA in their blood like humans. It couldn't be tracked back to him, but it would raise questions. Too many.

Making sure to clean the door handle, he slipped out into the hall and sprinted for the stairway, his figure a blur of movement that no camera would ever be able to catch. Once inside, he carried on up, not slowing until he reached the safety of the roof. His injuries now screaming for relief that would not be forthcoming. Not until he reached the sanctity of his home. Once he slammed the fire door closed, Lazarus once again cleaned any surface he'd come in contact with before he limped over to the edge of the building.

"Shit." He gazed longingly at his own rooftop, so near, but his leg was now throbbing painfully and he wanted nothing more than to force the slug from his body to allow himself to start the healing process. But he couldn't. Not here where his blood could be found.

Pulling his energy inside and forcing himself to step back from the edge, Lazarus shook his head and snarled. "Just do it."

Forcing himself to run toward the chasm between the buildings, he used his uninjured leg to propel himself up and over the gap, landing heavily on his own rooftop. Down he went when his wounded thigh crumpled beneath him and he tumbled ass over head to land in a heap next to the bar with a thud. His breath whooshed out of him and his head knocked against the edge, causing it to split open and his blood to seep down into his eyes.

"Fucking great." He moaned as he reached up to grab a bottle of whisky, opening it and taking a slug before he hauled himself upright.

Now he could feed and heal and get these damn bullets out of his body.

Walking back inside, he gulped down some more whisky before heading to the kitchen and seeking out his stash of donor blood, he'd need that to heal. On his way, he noticed the time and realized he'd forgotten about another meeting he had planned for the evening with Ralf Sawyer.

The Wolf whose daughter had gone missing in Monarch.

He'd been so focused on Ariana Harmon that the reason he'd used to get her to their appointment had slipped his mind. She was getting under his skin and he didn't like it. Not that it would interfere with what he'd planned for Ralf. That was later, but still, it irked him that he'd forgotten about it.

Grabbing several bags of blood and a plastic rubbish bag, Lazarus made his way through to his bedroom, already drinking from the first. Stripping off his clothes and bundling them up into the garbage bag to be disposed of later, he walked naked through to the bathroom, throwing the empty donor container he'd finished into the trash and turning on the shower before checking out his wounds in the mirror. As expected, the gunshots had entered exactly where he thought, causing gaping holes and blood to now soak his body.

First order of business was to force the projectiles out, and that was going to hurt. It had to be done though. He lifted another plastic packet to his mouth and sank his fangs inside to drink it down, feeling his body grow in strength with each mouthful he swallowed. *Get it over with.* He thought as he looked over his shoulder into the mirror, focusing on forcing the projectiles out of his body and gritting his teeth as they started to move through his muscles and sinew.

Pain, agony, and white hot fire shot through his body as they slowly made their way out; so slowly he cursed aloud, leaned forward, and concentrated harder. He needed these fuckers gone. The faster the better, and he was determined to do it now. Closing his eyes, he directed his power inside, converging it to each one of the slugs and aiming it to the mangled pieces of metal and... and... they shot out of his body to clatter to the tiles, covered with pieces of his flesh and blood.

Picking them up, they joined his bloody clothes to be disposed of safely. Never to be found or to link him to the events of the evening. Especially the murder of Raylon Barnes and his henchmen.

Lazarus released a pent-up breath and walked to the shower. He had to get cleaned up and ready for his meeting at Monarch. He wondered what suit he'd wear. Of course he'd be dressed to the nines, top of the line hand-made suit, and he might even wear one of his expensive watches. Hell, yeah. He'd go all out to portray his businessman position; an extremely rich man who'd pay whatever it took to get what he wanted. And she couldn't turn him down. Not when he showed her what he wanted her to do. How could she?

But more importantly, he couldn't wait to see her face when she walked in and saw him waiting on her. That would be a huge fucking surprise, and an opportunity for him to gauge her response to seeing him again.

How would she react? Hell, how would *he* react? He wasn't entirely sure about *that* either, especially with the way his beast was prowling around inside him, unfulfilled from his earlier *liaison* with Raylon Barnes. It hadn't gone as planned, and his dark hunter hadn't even been slightly gratified with the way things had ended so fast for the bastard. A quick end had not been the way it should have gone. His beast had been denied its prey and its kill, which left it still skulking around just waiting for the opportunity to escape and wreak havoc.

Lazarus would need to be careful. He'd have to keep a tight rein on his emotions, and his beast. Lock it down tight for fear it would rear its ugly head and show itself to Ariana. Hells fire, he couldn't allow that to happen. She might turn tail and run for the hills. Or worse... attack.

Flight or fight.

From what he'd learned so far about her, she didn't come across as the flight kind of woman. Fight appeared to be more her style but, if that happened, it would be the end of her. There was no doubt she was an accomplished combatant, but against him? Against his beast? Against his dark hunter?

No fucking contest.

"Control it. Control the fucking beast," Lazarus muttered over and over while he readied himself for the face-to-face that had his heart beating faster and his blood rushing through his veins.

CHAPTER SEVENTEEN

LAZARUS' skin felt like it was going to rip apart. His beast was itching to break free, and he was fighting to contain it. Damn. He should never have gone to Barnes' place earlier. That had been a huge error of judgement on his part. He should've waited. Thought it through more. Not been so fucking eager to get the job done.

It hadn't gone to plan and his dark hunter had not been assuaged. It had not been released to wreak vengeance on that fucker. Now it was prowling inside him like the caged monster that it was. And he was battling to control it.

"Soon. I'll release you soon. Just fucking stop." He gritted his teeth and held onto the edge of the bar. His head felt like it was in a vise, the pressure had been growing over the last half hour while he'd been trying to go over the file for his meeting. The words and images blurring together until he'd given up and started to pace, his hands running through his hair in an attempt to ease the discomfort. "I need you to stop! She'll be here soon, and I need to fucking think!"

It slithered around just beneath the surface, snarling and angry, but finally it eased off, settling down just enough for him to focus and take in a deep breath. And just in time too. His enhanced hearing picked up the sound of the main door creaking open, then the sound of heels clicking. His appointment had arrived, and he had only a few minutes until she was right there with him.

"Thank you," he whispered.

Running a hand over his hair to settle it back into place, Lazarus checked his reflection in the mirror over the bar.

Straightening his tie, he then sat down at his chair where he'd set out his paperwork. He leaned over the files and made himself look as if he was going over them, while his eyes were glued to the mirror to watch and wait for her entrance.

He heard every footstep she made as she drew closer, his ears honing in on her heart to measure her response when she first saw him. Or rather, when she realized who it was her meeting was with. Would she know immediately? Or would it take her some time to figure it out? Would she be confused at first? Of course she would. Hell, there was no way she could know that he'd be sitting here waiting on her. What would she do? Would she remain professional? Or would she turn around and storm out? There was no way to know until the moment they met.

He couldn't stop his own excitement from building inside him as he heard the last door opening. He'd been waiting eagerly to see her again face-to-face since she'd escaped from his clutches so effortlessly. Especially after the video Acelin had procured for him. Ariana was no ordinary human female. He'd known that from the moment they'd met, but watching her battle against a man twice her size and beat his ass... that proved it a hundred fold. There was something about her that drew him to her and had caused him to spend money to get all the information he could on her. Why? He couldn't answer that. Yet.

Click click, her heels sounded closer and closer. Only one more flight of stairs and she'd be on the same level as him. He'd kept the lighting low enough for her to see her way, but he knew she'd more than likely not see him well enough to recognize him until she was much closer, and that was exactly how he'd planned it. Lazarus wanted her near him so he could see her up close when that happened. He wanted to scent her response.

Here she came. Her feet were the first things he saw. Encased in black stilettos and silk. Interesting. He half expected trainers and jeans. Was that stockings or pantyhose? A vision of her rolling stockings up her legs sprang to mind. Damn, that was a nice thought. She click-clacked down the last few steps to reveal a dark grey coat, which was open to reveal a red shift dress beneath it and a matching scarf hung loose at her neck. She held a black briefcase in her left hand. Ariana's long hair was swept up behind her and when she stepped off the stairs to turn and come his way, he saw it was in a chic French knot. Her make-up was almost non-existent, almost but not quite. His keen eyesight picked up a dusting of powder on her face and eyes, and she wore mascara that enhanced her lashes, making them look larger. Her lipstick matched her dress, red. Her lips were luscious and ripe for kissing, teasing, nipping. His eyes were drawn to them like a fucking bee to honey.

Shit. He couldn't help but wonder what they'd feel like beneath his. Would she surrender willingly? Hell, no. She'd put up a fight; no doubt about it. But it would be worth it, wouldn't it? His beast growled in his head, not with anger but something else... hunger.

While his mind wandered, she'd crossed the area toward him, her steps faltered and her heart rate had started to speed up. The skin between her eyebrows puckered as she closed in on him until, finally, he knew she grasped who he was. Her face lost color briefly before her cheeks reddened and her back straightened. She'd made a decision and closed the distance between them. Her last few steps were quicker until she stopped right behind him, her breaths fast and furious.

Lazarus could smell her sweet aroma all around him, it was delicious. Her indecision, her split-second of fear, and her ongoing anxiety, but she carried on until she was almost upon him, and that's when he sat up and turned around, pasting a look of surprise on his face.

"You? What the hell are you doing here?" he asked with a quirked brow and a tilt of his head.

Ariana's heart was stampeding like a herd of horses in her chest, but she held her head high with a haughty look on her face. Her eyes raked over him from head to toe. Taking in his immaculate appearance from his hair, which he'd just recently fixed, down over his face and to his silk shirt that fit his body snugly, visible with his hand-made suit jacket open. She continued down his thighs to his feet, which were encased in shoes that cost a damn fortune, and she knew it.

She looked back up, slowly, coming to rest back on his face with an icy glare. Those ruby red lips pursed together before she spat out like a goddamn gun, not pausing for a breath. "I could ask you that same question. Is this some kind of joke? Are you up to something? Did you do this to get me here, Lazarus Báis?"

Lazarus raised his hand and slammed it onto the paperwork on the bar, hard. Ariana jumped. "No. I certainly did not. My assistant made the appointment and I wasn't aware of who would be arriving. Only that the person was the best to do the job that's required. It's of the utmost importance, and if you're that person then you'll get the fucking job. Plain and simple. Are you? Up to the task, Ariana? Can you help? Because if not then turn around and leave and I'll get someone who can. Don't waste my time with stupid accusations."

Lazarus stared hard into her eyes, watching and waiting. He'd fired back at her with both barrels, teasing her with snippets of information but also insulting her talents. He was banking on her finding it irresistible to refuse. Her heart still beat like a drum, but she didn't waver and didn't move an inch. He knew she was making a decision and his own heart was matching hers as he willed her to stay. He wanted her to come closer, sit next to him, and... Shit. He didn't know what the fuck he wanted. But he knew what he didn't want, and that was for her to leave.

"What exactly is it that you need?"

Lazarus almost smiled. He had to fight to stop his lips from turning up but he managed it, only just.

"It would be better if I show you what's happened and then we can discuss what's required. But first I need you to sign a NDA." Her eyes widened in shock, but she walked over as he pushed a contract toward her. "This is not up for discussion, Ariana. What I have to show you is... delicate. I can't have the information being broadcasted. It could be dangerous. So you either sign this and see what I need you for... or you walk away."

He knew she would. After what he'd found out about her, the mention of danger had her eyes lighting up. That was all it took for her hand to reach for the pen he held. Ariana quickly read over the document, then signed on the dotted line on the two copies; one for her and one for him.

She held out the pen, which he retrieved, his fingers briefly touching hers and *there* it was. Right fucking *there*. A spark ignited between them, and she felt it too because she jerked away so fast she stumbled, her hand grabbing the back of the stool next to him. His beast growled again, hungry for more, and so was he. He wanted to taste her, every last inch of her before sinking his fangs deep inside her to drink down that precious negative blood of hers, but she refused to acknowledge anything. Instead, she placed her briefcase on the counter and slid his copy over. Her voice was like ice, cold and business-like, her brow arched.

"There you go. Now do you want to let me in on what's so *delicate* that I had to go through that?"

Fine. If she wanted to act like nothing had happened, he could play that game. Lazarus patted the seat next to him. "Here, get comfortable; there's a lot to go over."

Ariana eyed the closeness of the chair before she joined him, having to hike up her dress to climb up on the stool. Fuck, her thighs were gorgeous and he was now certain she was indeed wearing stockings. Would he be able to focus on the job at hand? He had to. She wasn't getting under his skin.

"So?" she prodded as his eyes lingered on her body a moment too long.

Pulling the papers free, he set out pictures of Keena Sawyer when she'd entered Monarch with her friends, and one of her on the dancefloor. That was all he'd managed to pull from the security feed, but he knew there'd be more. He just hadn't figured out how to locate them.

"This is Keena Sawyer. She's a Wolf and that's a picture of her in this very club. Her father, Ralf, is an employee of mine and he's asked for my help."

"I assume she's gone missing?" Ariana leaned in, focusing hard on the girl, her brow puckered as she gazed hard at the picture.

"No, she's dead. Murdered. She was abducted from here and she's dead."

"What? She's dead? When? Where was she found? What are the police saying about it?" Ariana shot back, sitting upright and turning to look hard at him.

The first thing he noticed was her face had lost all color. The second was the tremble in her hands, which she'd clasped tightly in her lap. Third was the scent that now seeped from her: fear. What the hell? Why was she reacting so much to the news of a girl she didn't even know?

Before he knew what he was doing, he reached out to hold her hands, steadying them. "Are you all right?"

"I'm perfectly fine. Tell me about the girl." Wrenching her hands free, her top lip curled back in a sneer while her hand stabbed at Keena's image.

"The police aren't interested in Supernaturals, Ariana. Never have been and never will be. I want your help. We have security cameras in the Club and, according to her friends, she was last seen talking to a guy who I suspect must be another Supernatural..."

Ariana's hand shot up to halt him. "What? Why? Why does he have to be a Supernatural?"

"Because, Ariana, Keena is a Wolf Shifter. She's strong and fierce. If a human took her, they'd soon find that out. She'd be able to defend herself against them, even a gunshot wouldn't stop her. The only logical explanation is another being who's stronger than her... hence another Supernatural. I'd suspect a Vampire, one who's old, ancient. We're much stronger than a Wolf, and she'd be easy pickings."

"I see." She frowned, and he could almost see the cogs in her brain going to work. "And how do you know she's dead? Couldn't she have just gone off with this guy? Met him and, you know, went for some fun, or fell in love?"

"No. Wolf Shifter families have a bond, a link, and her father, well, that link is gone. He knows she's dead. He's devastated and he's asked me for help. I intend to do what I can. I will not allow anyone to hunt in my establishments. I'm going to find them and end them. It's that simple. Now you know how *delicate* the situation is, Ariana. You can walk away now. Or stay and help me. The choice is yours."

There. He'd laid the gauntlet down. Now he'd see whether she lifted it.

Dark Hunter

CHAPTER EIGHTEEN

LAZARUS WATCHED and waited as Ariana's dark brown eyes were drawn over and over to Keena's picture. She drew her plump bottom lip between her teeth, nibbling nervously on it while she scrutinized the image of the young woman who'd been snuffed out of existence. Her hands once again trembled. What was going on that affected her like this? Then she reached over, her index finger trailed over Keena's face before she turned to him, her eyes now steely and her chin jutting out.

"I'm in. What is it you need from me?"

Once again, he had to force himself to remain calm, trying not to show how happy he was at her decision. Instead, he merely inclined his head in a brief nod.

"Thank you. My assistant tells me you're the best in your field." He lied easily. "What I need is to try and trace her that evening and see who it is exactly she left with."

"Your system keeps logs for that long? Normally places record over after a few days." She asked him with an arched brow and a tone of voice that told him she was surprised he had access to the information she needed.

"Don't sound so surprised, Ariana. Things happen in my places that I like to keep a handle on. I pay a hefty fee to ensure I can access information for up to three months. The answer to your question is yes, we have access to the night in question, but how do we get what we want without trolling through the entire night?"

"Leave that to me." She smirked over at him, tapping the side of her nose. "I have a program that I can use, but I can't tell you about it. It's one I've been working on and it's not released yet.

It's similar to face recognition but it's like a worm I release into a system. I can set it to find someone and it will go in and find every image of Keena in the time slot we give it. As I said though, it's not released and I can't give you access to it."

He wasn't sure he'd heard right. If he had, then she was onto something worth gold. She could make a fortune off this if it worked.

"Have you tested this? Do you have a patent? Or one pending? Are you in discussions with anyone yet?" He fired off his questions as the enormity of what she'd revealed hit. She could make a fortune, but so could he. He owned a tech company. Fuck, he owned several, and if he could get his hands on this... they could print money.

Ariana laughed, the sound tinkling around them as her eyes lit up. She was excited and the sight was glorious; it changed her entirely. She was gorgeous to him before, but now? He wanted to fuck her right here. Take her in his arms and... Stop. What the hell was he thinking?

Ariana was nodding, her hands flying all around as she talked, and he zoned back into what she was saying.

"Of course I've tested it. Multiple times, and yes, I've got a patent. I'm not an idiot. But no, I've not discussed this with anyone yet. It's too new and I'm also nervous about who I hand this over to. I've worked my ass off on this and I want it to find people like Keena, hopefully before something bad happens to them. I'm not interested in handing it over to the military. That's not what it's for."

"I see." He could. But it would limit their production. Although, Law Enforcement worldwide would still be a huge sell. "We can talk later about it. I own several companies that could help you, but of course I would never do anything you don't want to. However, that's for the future. For now, we have to focus on Keena and her movements that night. More importantly, if we can narrow down the time she left. If we can get that information, I can possibly find out what vehicle she got into and trace the owner."

"Trace the vehicle and owner?"

"I have contacts I can use for that."

"Nice contacts to have, or I could help there too." She didn't make eye contact. "Although, we wouldn't talk about how I got the information. Now, back to Keena. I'll need access to the system and I think you should add more cameras to the club. I'm just saying, if this is something that concerns you, then you should have extra cameras to cover more areas. It would help if anything else is going on, or comes up. I can help with that too. It wouldn't cost much. I've not gone over your system, but I'd bet there are dead areas in the club. There are always dead areas and anyone who is out to do bad things, they check this shit out and use them to their advantage. But, first things first, when do you want me to start?"

"Right now, if you're available." Lazarus stood and waved toward his office. "I have an office here that we can set you up in, and Keena's father is coming in later. I'm giving him a new job and I'd like you to meet him so he knows we're doing something to find the fucker who hurt his daughter."

Ariana slid off her stool, her body taut and not in keeping with the way she was dressed like a high-powered business woman. She looked more like the woman in the video, someone ready and able to take on an enemy, and he smelled the unmistakable aroma of anger rolling off her as she stabbed a finger toward Keena's image.

"Hurt? Don't you mean murdered? Someone abducted this young woman from here then killed her. I intend to find out who that person is and help you, now what did you say, end them. Those were your words, right?"

Her voice was low, not high-pitched like most women when

they were upset. Ariana's was filled with cold fury, and she was staring at him with eyes filled with anger. But what she'd just said? That was not happening. Absolutely no fucking way was she getting involved, but if he allowed her to think she was... that would keep her happy. For now.

"I'm employing you for a job right now, Ariana. That's why you're here, and that's what we need to focus on. We can't do anything else without that information. Let's get you set up and started. Time is of the essence because we have no idea if Keena was the first, or if they've got any others, Ariana. For all we know, they've got their hands on other young women, humans or Supernaturals. We have no way of knowing until I get to the bottom of this."

The change in her was instant. Her face lost color and her body trembled and shook. Her hands bunched into fists at her sides as she took a great gulp of air into her lungs while she closed her eyes. She stood there like that, with her heart, which had only a few moments ago been beating almost normally, now careening out of control as beads of sweat appeared along her forehead and upper lip.

"Ariana? Ariana, are you okay?" Lazarus stepped closer, reached out, and touched her shoulder to shake her gently.

Her reaction was violent and shocked the fuck out of him.

One arm rose quickly to shove his away while the other pulled back in a defensive motion, ready to punch him. Her legs had automatically moved too; however, in her stiletto heels and her tight shift dress, she was limited in what she could do. No matter, he was quicker and stronger, his reflexes lightning fast. Lazarus rushed in, crowding her and wrapping his arms around her to pull her into his body. Holding her in place and refusing her the ability to hurt him, or herself.

It was the out and out scent of fear that had hit him and caused him to react. It was all over her, seeping out of her pores and covering her completely. She was soaked in it. Utterly, completely immersed in it.

"Ariana! Stop. You're safe. Stop it."

She struggled for a few seconds more before she stilled, the fight left her as quickly as it had arrived. Ariana's body collapsed against him, but only for a second until she stood straighter, her voice muffled.

"I'm fine, please release me."

Lazarus did so, but slowly. He opened his arms and stepped back to check her over. Ariana's cheeks were scarlet and she refused to look him in the eye. It was obvious she was embarrassed, but he was desperate to know what the fuck had happened. Or what had set her off.

"What happened?" he asked quietly.

She didn't say a word. Instead, she made a show of straightening her dress.

"I asked a question, Ariana. What the fuck just happened?"

Still she remained silent, and this time she reached up attempting to fix her hair. She failed, so she released it to allow it to hang free.

"Hells fire." He turned and strode away then back. Hands on hips as he faced off with her again. "Do you want to help me out with this? If you do, you'll explain yourself."

Her head rose and there it was... that haughty look with her eyes blazing with fire again as she glowered over at him. "I'm fine. I merely had a moment of... upset."

A moment of upset? Was she fucking kidding him? She'd had a full on melt-down, and he was no closer to knowing the reason.

"Are you shitting me? You freaked out, and don't you try to say different. Why?" he pressed her, taking a step closer to crowd her with his body and waiting to see if his proximity would garner another reaction.

It didn't. Her hands shot up to push him away with a strength he was aware she had. He'd seen it in the video he'd watched, over and over, of her fighting that ogre at her Krav class. Her eyes flashed with anger, her jaw clenched, and her fists bunched in front of her. Did she expect him to attack?

"I said I'm fine. Can we get on with this or not? I thought you were eager to get started."

His eyes flicked to her hands and she immediately relaxed them, dropping them to her sides. Was she trying to hide her fighting abilities from him? If so, that ship had sailed. He was well aware of what she was capable of, even though she was hiding behind the façade of a well-dressed business woman.

Lazarus would play her game, for now.

"I'm just worried about you." He reached out to her and she backed up, refusing to allow him to touch her.

"No need. I apologize for my... lapse. It won't happen again."

He watched as she drew strength from somewhere, an armor being pulled around her, and her entire demeanor changed before his very eyes. What he now saw was the woman he'd seen in the video. One who was a lethal weapon and who was scared of nothing. Ariana's head lifted, her eyes held no emotion whatsoever as she reached over to pick up Keena's picture.

"Let's get started. Keena deserves some justice, don't you think?"

He did. Of course, he fucking did.

"Indeed, follow me." He turned and led her to his office, the clicking of her heels behind him reminding him of what was above those damn shoes, her legs encased in silk stockings.

What was worse was the fact his beast was acting strange. Again. It wasn't acting like it had earlier, as if it wanted to tear someone apart. No, it was sniffing around and growling inside his head in a most peculiar manner. He'd never experienced anything like it before, and it was most unsettling. Lazarus was on edge when he opened the door, holding it wide to allow Ariana to enter the room, and the fucking animal surged to the edge of his brain and almost broke free, right there when she was beside him.

Lazarus stumbled back, turning his head away while Ariana carried on into the room. His fangs sprung free and he knew, without a damn doubt, his eyes would be fiery red. *What the fuck?* He fought to push his inner demon back as it grappled within him... but why? It didn't want to kill her; that much was clear. He could feel it slithering around inside his skin, writhing in his head with a yearning to get nearer to the woman who was now in the office setting up at his desk.

He could hear her shuffling papers around, moving chairs and rolling one with wheels nearer to the desk, her breath sounding so fucking loud in his ears... and her heart beat? That was like a damn drum being blasted through the sound system. It reverberated in his head, causing his hands to shoot up to cover his ears and shake his head. And all the while her scent lingered around him, like she was still standing right next to him. Right. Fucking. Next. To. Him.

"Lazarus? Where are you?"

She asked from the room quietly, but it sounded like she was roaring at the top of her voice. What the hell was happening to him?

"I'll be right there," he ground out around his elongated teeth, his hand shot up, fingers tracing the razor sharp canines. Hell, he had to pull himself together. Fast.

"Fucking behave or she goes," he snapped out, not sure who he was talking to. Himself, his beast, or the damn universe. All he knew was he had work to do, and he couldn't do it if he was losing control. Of his fangs. His body. Of his fucking mind.

CHAPTER NINETEEN

A MAGIC WAND. That's what it was like when his fangs disappeared and he was once more in control. Lazarus took a deep breath to settle himself. What the hell had just happened? "Lazarus! Are we getting started on this or what?" Ariana shouted again, her tone sharp.

"Yes," he answered from right next to her after speeding to the office.

She jumped away from him, her hands shooting up to ward him off. Again with the automatic defensive stance. Her training kicked in without her having to think about it. She'd been taught well, and he doubted she'd be caught off-guard often. Not by a human anyway.

"You shouldn't do that," she grumbled, pulling a seat closer to the desk and sitting down. "Could you set up your computer for me so I can get started?"

"Sure." He smiled, doing as she asked before going to the bar in the corner. "Want anything?"

"If you've got an energy drink, that'd be good, and some nuts."

"Ariana, I'm a Vampire. I don't eat nuts," he reminded her as he fished around, looking for her drink, finding one, and bringing it over. "I've got donor blood in the fridge if you'd like to try it?"

The look she gave him was full of disgust. Her nose crinkled and she shook her head as she snorted derisively. "I think not. Who the hell would take you up on that offer?"

"You'd be surprised," he answered solemnly.

Ariana stared at him, her fingers pausing over the keyboard.

Her mouth opened then closed, his eyes drawn to her ruby red lips once again, causing his stomach to tremble and his groin to clench with desire.

"I think you're toying with me," she finally breathed out, turning away to type furiously.

That didn't help him. Not one bit. The sound reminded him of her heels which, in turn, brought to mind her silk encased legs.

"Believe what you want." He sidled up behind her, leaning in close to look over her shoulder. "I see you've located the security feed already."

Her perfume was light and fresh, not overpowering; it was one that enhanced her own scent, enticingly so. It drew him in like nothing before ever had. His nostrils flared of their own accord to garner more. More. He couldn't get enough of her inside. The bouquet was tantalizing and so fucking tempting, it was driving him to distraction.

"Of course I have. This is the easy part."

Her mocking tone brought him out of his fantasizing, and there was no doubt that's what he was doing. Or rather, that's where it was headed. In no time, his mind would've gone straight to the bedroom, and he dreaded where that would've ended.

He was already having trouble controlling himself. If he allowed his mind to wander along those lines? No. Not a good idea. Not today.

"Okay, so how long will all this take?" Lazarus moved away, grabbing his drink and slugging it down in one gulp.

"Give me the date and I'll locate that in the database. Once I have that, I'm afraid I have to go home and get my little toy, which I'll use to locate Keena on that night. Once I return, I'll set it up. It could take hours to get all the information. It could be tomorrow before we have it all."

"Tomorrow? What will you do? Remain here or set it running and come back?"

He saw her balk at his words. Spotted indecision rush over her face and settle into her entire body. Ariana looked at the screen, then glanced at Keena's picture, then back up at him, nibbling that fucking lip again. Shit, she better stop doing that or he was going to pounce on her and show her exactly what it was like to bite a damn luscious mouth.

"That depends and, to tell you the truth, I've not decided yet. I did have plans for later, but I might be able to cancel them." She glanced away to the screen. "Let me get the date separated from the rest of the data, and then I'll go and get what I need."

This put him in a difficult position. If she decided to stay, what would he do? He could, of course, remain the entire time because he didn't require the rest as she did. But if he did that, she would question why he wasn't asleep when dawn broke, like she would expect him to be. He would have to come up with something before they came to that, but what?

Her fingers flew over the keyboard as he thought on the conundrum, her face a mask of concentration. He was enjoying watching her work when his phone rang in his pocket, interrupting him. His first thought was to ignore the call, but when she flicked an irritated look his way, Lazarus fished his cell out, saw Clive's name, and thought he should answer.

"What's up?" he answered non-committedly while he walked away from Ariana to the other side of the room, sitting down on the sofa.

"Laz! Did you see the news? It's all over it. Fuck! It's a bloodbath."

"I'm not deaf." Lazarus didn't want a certain female hearing what his FBI contact was talking about, but the way he was yelling... she just might.

"Sorry, but it's all over the news. At first I thought it might've been you. Then I realized that it happened early and, well, he wasn't *treated* the same as your usual suspects so I guess it wasn't. That means you don't have to do it, and you needed to know because you couldn't go over there and get in the middle of things with the place crawling with police and god knows who else."

"I've no idea what you're talking about."

"You know who was killed, and so were his men. No witnesses. The fucker had paid the guys on security in his building to disable the camera on his floor. Stupid idiots are up to their necks in trouble now because they took his money and there's dead bodies all over the place with nothing on their feed. They'll lose their jobs, but they could end up doing jail time."

"Is that so?" Lazarus kept his answers short and generic. The last thing he needed was Ariana knowing what was going on, but this snippet of information meant the boy hadn't been caught on camera. That was good news.

"Yes, but the best news is that fucker is out of the game, and so is his right hand man, as well as his guards; the gang will be in turmoil with no leadership. I'm going to go in to work and get some guys on this. I want to round up the rest and see what we can do about putting them away for anything we can pin on them. If we can do that, then the ring that's dealing with these kids should collapse, and that's the main thing. That's the only fucking thing I care about tonight. I just needed to let you know not to go anywhere near him."

"Thanks for the heads up." Lazarus hung up quickly, a smile playing across his lips at the thought of the boy escaping without being caught, and that Clive hadn't tied him to the slaughter.

"Everything all right?" Ariana asked quietly. Her fingers still typing as she looked over at him.

"Aye, everything's just fine. Just a friend passing along some information I needed."

"Okay, well, I'm just about set here." Her fingers flew over the keys for a few seconds more before she finished with a flourish and rolled her chair back. "There, I've managed to pinpoint the time-frame we require. Now I need to go and get my little magic trick, and then I'll have to come back and upload it. After that, I'll have to configure it and do some tweaks so it's set to hunt down Keena's images, and then it'll be a case of waiting."

Lazarus watched as her face flushed with excitement, her eyes sparkling and her hands moving animatedly as she spoke about her work. She also moved her hair around, a lot. Her hand reaching up to run her fingers through her long locks over and over as she talked. It was like looking at a completely different person to the one he'd first met that night she'd ran into Fortune, or the one he'd watched beating up on a guy in her Krav club. This woman was another person entirely.

"You enjoy your work, don't you?" he commented when she finished, and her cheeks flushed redder, her eyes falling to the screen in front of her.

"I do," was all she said, mumbling it as she reached for her coat, which she'd slipped off to hang over the back of her chair. "I should go. The quicker I get what we need, the faster we can get the information."

"Did you drive here?" He knew she hadn't. He knew everything about her, and Ariana didn't own a vehicle.

"No. I got a cab. It's fine. I won't be long."

"No need. I'll take you." He looked her up and down, grinning. "You might not be dressed for the ride though."

She gave him a raised eyebrow but remained silent as he rose and strode out of the room with her at his back, those heels clicking furiously as she tried to keep up. Lazarus wound his way through the dimly lit club, past the bar, through the door at the end, and into the hallway. Ariana kept up, although he knew it had to be hard for her with those stilettos on her feet, but she didn't utter a word of complaint or voice her concern when he turned into another hall that held no light whatsoever.

He heard her speed up, her body almost touching his, and he slowed his pace, causing her to bump into his back and stumble. Lazarus whirled around, lightning fast, his arms grabbing hold of her before she fell. "Are you okay?" he asked with feigned concern.

Ariana's breathing picked up, her heart beating like a staccato in her chest with her hands scrambling against his body to break free. "I'm fine. I just don't have the eyesight of a Vampire. Some lights would help me."

Lazarus held her for a moment longer, her body feeling good in his arms, before he released her. "Sorry. I forget that others don't see as well as I do. It's not far now; here, take my hand."

"I'll be fine," she snapped back, tugging her coat around her and holding it tightly in front of her chest.

He could see her clear as day as she stood before him. Her chest heaving and her eyes as wide as she could get them as she fought to see in the darkness. He could also see the red glow on her cheeks... was she blushing? Or was it anger?

"Take my hand, Ariana. I don't want you going over on your ankle and injuring yourself. We don't have time to visit the emergency room tonight."

Lazarus watched as she battled with herself, and there, she did it *again*, drawing her deliciously plump bottom lip between her teeth and nibbling it until he felt his groin tighten in his pants. Fuck. She had to stop doing that. Although, he doubted she was aware that he could see her as she sucked it, bit it, then sucked it some more before releasing it with a soft *pop*. The noise barely there, no human would've heard it, but it reverberated in his ears and his eyes were glued to her mouth until she finally moved an arm, releasing her fingers from the death-grip on her coat to reach forward.

Anticipation built quickly inside him as he waited, a scarce second beat, while he stretched his own to grasp hold of her delicate hand in his. But, at the last moment, she snatched it away, his beast growling in frustration inside him.

"Why don't you turn around and I'll hold onto your jacket. That will ensure I don't trip over."

Damn it! Trust Ariana to come up with a viable solution that ensured she didn't have to actually touch him skin-on-skin. One he couldn't argue with and not come across as an asshole.

"Sure," he replied, doing as she asked and trying to sound as if he wasn't... what? Angry, upset, pissed off? Probably all three, and all because she'd pulled away from him.

He was acting like an idiot and, for the life of him, he still couldn't figure out why.

Ariana grasped hold of the tail of his jacket, and he set off again, slower this time so she wouldn't trip over herself. His earlier ploy hadn't worked, but she was in for a surprise when they got outside. He couldn't wait to see how she reacted.

Would she bolt? Would she refuse? Or would she be excited?

Only time would tell.

Dark Hunter

CHAPTER TWENTY

ARIANA SHOOK HER HEAD, staring at his prized motorbike with hands on her hips. "Are you kidding me?"

"What?" he asked, tugging on his helmet and securing it beneath his chin.

"It's a motorbike, Lazarus."

He turned, looked at it, then back at her. "Oh my god, so it is. What's your point?"

She waved a hand up and down her front, then pointed to the bike. "I'm not exactly dressed for *that*."

"This is fast, Ariana. Very fast. And I can drive it unlike any human can. I can get you home and back before a cab. Are you coming? Or not?"

He honed in on her face, her reaction to his words, every little nuance her body was giving out and he saw her eyes give her away; her pupils dilating were the first sign. Quickly followed by an increase in her heart rate, and it wasn't fear. No, definitely not. The scent rolling off her was pure adrenalin. Ariana was excited, and she was doing a piss poor job of trying to hide it.

"How am I supposed to get on that thing?" She took a step toward him, her heels echoing in the alleyway.

"Hike up that pretty dress of yours and slide on up behind me. I'm sure you can manage that. Can't you?" he teased her, pressing the remote in his pocket which caused the engine to roar to life and Ariana to jump back, eyes wide as she looked at him then back at his magnificent piece of machinery in surprise.

"How did you do that?"

"Magic." Lazarus slung his leg over and settled himself on

the seat before patting the space behind him. "Are you coming? If so, you'll need this. "

Lazarus held out a helmet before he revved the engine for good measure, loving the sound, and when he turned to look at Ariana, it appeared she did too because she was now headed his way with a twinkle in her eyes. She stopped beside him, grabbed the helmet and put it on, then she reached down to pull up her dress, but she stopped when she saw him watching her every move, just when the hem was reaching the top of where he thought her stockings were... damn.

"Eyes front," she ordered with a brusque and firm tone. One that sent shivers running down his spine and caused his beast to slither around inside him once more.

He did as she asked, slowly, and only when he had did she mount the bike, settling behind him. She sat well back, leaving space between them. That would never do. Not with what he had in mind.

"Ariana." He turned to spear her with a cold stare. "You have to hold on and hold on tight. That's if you don't want to die. I've already told you I'll be using my Vampire abilities to drive this baby. So... do you want to die?"

Her heart thudded wildly as she slid forward, closing the inches that separated them. No words said as she wrapped her arms around his waist, clasping her fingers together to hold on firmly.

"That's it." He gave her a brief nod. "Don't let go, no matter what, and trust me. I know what I'm doing."

Finally, she responded, her voice barely a whisper as he turned away. "You better. I've got things to do later. Remember, I'm human, Lazarus."

"You'll be fine." He chuckled while he revved the engine. "I'll make sure of it."

Kicking the stand, Lazarus reveled in Ariana's nearness and

shot away down the alley, heading for the main road; her sharp gasp as he did causing him to grin wickedly. Her scent surrounded him as he neared the opening, basking in it, inhaling it, and ingraining her unique aroma inside him so he'd know it anywhere, anytime; he'd be able to find her wherever she went.

Kicking his abilities into high gear, Lazarus sent them outward, his ears picking up everything on the road ahead, which they were seconds away from joining. He could feel Ariana's apprehension when he barely slowed down, sliding out onto the tarmac and careening into the traffic. The drivers' horns blasted behind them as he sped away, darting in and out of the vehicles in their path, his speed making them appear as if they were standing still. All the while, Ariana clung to him with her breaths whispering along his neck.

It wasn't until he reached the first set of red lights he realized his mistake; he hadn't asked her where to go. Fuck. He looped around, away from her place, speeding away for another couple of minutes until they came to another set of lights, which changed to red on their approach.

"Ariana, what's your address?" He looked over his shoulder, hoping he didn't look as flustered as he felt. "I forgot to ask. I'm afraid I was a little eager to show you what this little thing can do."

She looked around her, frowning. Damn it, had she grasped they were already en-route to her home? She gave him her address, asking if he knew the area.

"Yeah, I think so. Hang on."

She then snuggled back into him as the lights changed and he sped off, switching lanes to take the next left and back the way they'd come. Lazarus focused back on getting to her home, fast. Giving her the ride of her life and using every inch of his abilities to do so. Taking risks no human ever could and riding his bike to the limit of its capability, and then pushing it past it to get more out of it than he'd ever gotten before.

He laughed out loud when she yelped as he roared between two semis with barely enough space to do so, her heart thundering wildly in her chest. But he'd bet his last fucking dollar that it was excitement causing it, and not fear. Ariana was no ordinary woman; that was for damn sure. He'd never met anyone like her before. Not in the long centuries he'd lived. She was unique, intriguing, and she was getting under his skin in more ways than one.

When they finally arrived in her quiet street, roaring around the corner and slamming to a stop, she was still holding tightly to him like he was her lifeline. Her breathing coming in short, sharp gasps.

"I think this is your stop, Ariana." He smirked over his shoulder. "Did you enjoy the ride?"

She unclasped her fingers, one by one, and sat back, taking off her helmet and raising a brow before she gave him a hint of a smile. "What do you think?" Then she pushed his head back around and dismounted. "I'll be back shortly."

Ariana disappeared up the path and into her home, leaving him with thoughts of what he'd like to do to her if he managed to get her back to his place.

The first thing would be to slowly remove those silk stockings. Possibly with his teeth. Hmm, would she agree to that? Hell, if she didn't he could always restrain her. Even if she didn't agree to the restraints, he could still use them. He just needed to use compulsion on her to get what he wanted. And what he wanted was Ariana on his bed, spread-eagled and at his mercy.

Or did he?

Would it be better if she was fully alert and fighting him? Fuck. His cock started to harden in his pants at *that* thought, and his beast made a sudden appearance, prowling around snarling and pawing inside him, eager to be let loose. "No you don't." Lazarus forced it back, again.

What the hell was wrong with it tonight?

"What's wrong with what tonight?" Ariana asked right beside him, causing him to jerk like a mannequin whose strings had been pulled taut.

Had he just said that aloud and not even known? He must have.

"Nothing, just thinking aloud."

Ariana had changed. She no longer wore her dress, but worse... she'd lost the stilettos and stockings. She stood before him in a black polo and black leather jacket, which had a bulge at the front, possibly a laptop? She now had on jeans, which hugged her so tight he wondered how she could breathe, and as his eyes lowered further, he saw her feet now encased in black boots, which were laced all the way up the front and stopped just below her knees. Damn, boots instead of heels and stockings. Then again, as his eyes worked their way back up, she looked deadly and hot like this too. Fucking hell, was there nothing this girl could wear that didn't make her attractive to him? He still wanted her in his room... and he definitely didn't want her under his compulsion this time.

No, he wanted her as wild as she looked right now.

"What? You didn't think I was going to ride back on that thing in my dress? Did you?"

He didn't reply. He couldn't. If he did he'd say something completely inappropriate.

"Lazarus, can you please stop looking at me like you're about to have me as your next meal?"

Lazarus tore his eyes from her and revved the bike, managing to growl out, "Are you ready?"

"Yes." She put on her helmet and mounted behind him,

sliding up and hanging on with no need for him to say anything more. Her hands linked around his waist and, as soon as they were, he shot off. Quickly and loudly roaring away from her home. Her body wrapped around his back and her scent all over him, driving him insane.

If the ride to her place had been fast, the one back was even crazier. He took the quickest route he knew and risks he shouldn't have. He wasn't sure if it was to impress her, or if it was to get them there as fast as he could before he lost control. He'd never know because, before long, they slid to a stop behind Monarch, with Ariana breathless behind him, gasping into his neck.

Ariana peeled herself from him and jumped off before she tore her helmet off. The long braid of her hair fell free, to hang over her shoulder, as she stood glaring at him, her nostrils flaring wildly. "What the hell was that? You were driving like a lunatic."

She was right. Of course she was. He'd been desperate to reach the safety of his club so he would be released from the agony of having her so close to him. The torture of her touching his body, having her scent invade his senses and taking him to dark places he wasn't sure he would be able to stop himself from acting upon. Every second she was next to him, that her breaths touched his skin, was sending him insane. Totally and utterly crazy. He was one second away from losing control.

Completely and utterly losing it, and he wasn't sure what he would do if that happened. Would he take her right there in the alley? Would he taste her lips? Taste her pussy? Taste that fucking blood of hers that was screaming out to him right *now*!

He was craving her like he'd never before craved anything, or *anyone*.

"Answer me, dammit!" she screamed at him, her voice echoing through the alley.

And all he could do was stare at her dark beauty. Her glorious fury as she ranted at him with fire in her eyes and no fear whatsoever. Ariana was in no doubt he could kill her. Snap her neck in two seconds flat. Drain her dry in moments. Yet still she faced off at him with her head high and her dazzling eyes, which he couldn't tear his own from.

"If you don't answer me, Lazarus, I'm gone. You hear me? I'm out of here and you won't see me again."

The words jolted him like an electric shock. Gone? No. He couldn't allow that. She couldn't leave. That thought had his belly rolling around like an ocean in a storm, and, if he could, he would've thrown up right there.

"I apologize. The call I got earlier was... upsetting. I allowed it to get to me and I'm sorry." He lied so fucking easily, but he had to. He couldn't have her going. "Someone I know was killed."

It wasn't all lies. Not exactly.

"What?" Ariana's body slumped, her face shocked, and she took a step toward him. Shit. No, that's not what he needed right now. He wasn't in control, not yet.

Lazarus held a hand up to stop her. "I'll be fine, but I'm sorry for my behavior. I tend to do things in the *extreme* when I'm upset. I know this doesn't help, but I assure you that you were in no danger."

Lies, lies, lies. He'd been close to... what? Lazarus wasn't sure exactly, but Ariana most certainly had been in danger. Not from a motorcycle accident. But from *him*.

"I'm sorry about your friend, but you shouldn't drive like that. Well, not with me on the bike, if you please."

"Noted." Lazarus kicked the stand down and got off, removing his helmet slowly. "Can we forget this and get back to work?"

"I'm not sure I'll ever be able to forget that ride, but yeah, let's get back to work."

Ariana gave him a lopsided smile, one that had his heart doing strange things inside his chest and had his beast slithering around uneasily. This woman was having an effect on him, and he wasn't entirely sure what or why. All he knew was he was going to figure it out.

One way or another, and Ariana was going nowhere until he did.

CHAPTER TWENTY-ONE

LAZARUS COULDN'T KEEP his eyes off her as she went to work, her fingers flying over the keys on the laptop she'd brought along as she'd refused to use his computer. "I'm sorry, Lazarus, but my software is mine and I'm not uploading it to yours. I'll use my own equipment. Nobody else touches this."

He'd agreed. Of course he had. He'd no choice in the matter if he wanted her help, which he did. If it meant they found out who took Keena, but also if it kept Ariana here. So he sat down on the sofa with a glass in hand and tried to pretend he was relaxed while she worked.

When staff knocked on the door to ask him questions, she barely reacted, raising her eyes, scanning the intruders, and dismissing them before carrying on. Lazarus got the distinct feeling she only checked them out for one reason: to gauge if they were a threat.

When she saw they weren't, she went back to work. He was sure that was the only reason she paused in what she was doing, and, after the fourth time, he finally walked over and sat on the edge of the desk to test his theory.

"Ariana, the staff here aren't a threat to you, and I assure you nobody will get anywhere near you while you're with me."

He watched as her fingers paused, her eyes flitted to his, one brow arched. "Is that so?"

"It is."

"And why did you feel the need to say that?"

"Because, Ariana, every time one of my staff comes in here, you check them over like you're expecting them to attack you. You look at them like... I don't know how to explain it," he paused, because he did know exactly how she was checking them out but he didn't want to give anything away. "I'm not sure what to say other than you know what I mean. You've been pausing each time and making sure that they're not a… threat."

"Have I?" Ariana pursed her lips together and sat back, crossing her arms.

He knew she was playing a game. They both did. But he wasn't joining in.

"You have, and we both know it. I'm just saying that you're safe from anyone attacking you, for whatever reason, when you're with me."

"Fine." She returned to work, ignoring his presence completely.

He stayed there for another ten minutes until there was another knock on the door. Damn. It was like Grand Central Station tonight.

"Who is it?" he barked out, fed up with the constant stream of people.

The door opened just a crack and a head poked in. "Sorry to bother you, but you said to come tonight, sir."

Ralf Sawyer.

"Ralf, of course. Come in."

Ariana jumped in her seat, turning around so fast that her chair skidded on the floor as it rolled back. Her face lost color for a moment and then her cheeks pinked up, her eyes locked on Ralf as he entered, closed the door, and strode toward them.

"Sorry, are you busy?" The man was huge, his body bulging in the suit he was wearing.

"We are." Lazarus rose to shake his hand, turning to wave toward the desk and Ariana. "I'd like you to meet Ariana Harmon; Ariana, this is Ralf Sawyer. Ralf, Ariana is helping me with our problem about Keena. She's a bit of a computer genius and she's going to help me get more information on the night Keena was here."

Ralf's face shadowed with anger then pain, his jaw clenching before he responded. "Thank you. I know you said you'd help, but, to be honest, I wasn't sure you meant it. I mean, you're a busy man with all your businesses and I didn't know what you could do to help."

Ariana got up to join them, her hand tiny in comparison to Ralf's when she held it out to shake his. "I'm pleased to help, Mister Sawyer, and I'll do whatever I can to get to the bottom of what happened to your daughter."

"Ralf, call me Ralf." He shook her hand gently before releasing it, looking down at her with relief flooding his face. "I can't tell you what this means to me. It's been horrific knowing that she's... gone, but having nobody to help me find out what happened to her or find those responsible. She was a good daughter, a good person. She didn't deserve this."

Ariana's face clouded over with a look Lazarus couldn't quite put a name to, but the closest he could get was one he knew well. It was one he saw reflected in the mirror when he received certain files from Clive. She looked away briefly then back, and it was gone, replaced with a tight smile, covering up her true nature?

"I've got some tricks up my sleeve that I'll put to good use." She turned to nod to the desk. "I'm confident I can get something for us to make a start on finding out what happened that night."

A rumble started in Ralf's chest before it fell out of his mouth. It was a sound that startled Ariana, her eyes shot to Lazarus as she stepped away from the Shifter, her stance automatic and defensive. But it wasn't made with any kind of threat from the man. It was one of pain, suffering, and loss.

"It's all right, Ralf." Lazarus moved in to reassure Ariana, but also the man. "I told you I'd find out who was responsible, and I will. Now, why don't I get you introduced to the Head of Security here and he can find you a position. He's a good man and I'm sure you'll fit in well with his team. They're made up of Wolves, Vampires, and I think he has a Witch too, but I'll let him clue you in on everyone and all the details."

"Of course, and thank you, sir. I can't say how much I appreciate you giving me this opportunity and for helping me with... Keena," Ralf's voice hitched, his head falling forward and his hands clasping in front of him. "Will you keep me in the loop about what you find? Please?"

"You're welcome about the job, and of course I'll keep you informed, Ralf. If I need help on this, you'll be the first one I'll call." Lazarus wasn't making empty promises either. If he required back-up, there'd be no better man to use than the father of the murdered girl. His fury at the people behind this would ensure he'd do whatever it took, and that's someone Lazarus could use.

"I'll do whatever you need. Whatever it takes," Ralf growled out through clenched teeth. "My Keena deserves nothing less."

"I know that." Lazarus led him away, feeling his pain and his rage while Ariana watched with a guarded look he couldn't read.

When they made it to the office door, Moose, his Head of Security, was waiting on them. His shaved head glinting in the strobe lights, which were now flashing wildly as the club came to life, and the Shifter's intelligent brown eyes ran over Ralf from head to toe and back again. Lazarus saw him take in everything about the man before he stuck out a hand in welcome.

"I'm Moose, and I'll be your boss. I see you're a Shifter, so you should be able to handle yourself, but in case you can't, I'll be putting you through your paces. I want you to come to some classes with me so I can make sure you know how to deal with things properly, especially if Vamps get out of hand, and also humans... you have to be careful with them. They break easily; we can't have that. They're paying customers and we can't have it getting around that we hurt them. So are you okay with that?"

"Of course. I'm Ralf, Ralf Sawyer, and I'll do whatever you want for me to prove I'm good enough for your team. Years ago, I was security for our Pack, but that dealt with other Shifters and Supernaturals. It was a long time ago though, so I could do with a refresher course, especially when it comes to humans. Thanks for the opportunity, Moose, and for your time in teaching me."

"If you're on my team, then you're my responsibility. Come with me." Moose turned and walked away with Ralf on his tail.

Lazarus shook his head as Dina, one of the waitresses, gasped beside him. "Wow! That's the most I've heard Moose say in... forever."

"Aye, he's a man of few words, usually." Lazarus turned back into the office, knowing Ralf was in good hands. He'd done what he'd promised and got the man a new job, now he had to find his daughter's killer.

Ariana was back at his desk, eyes glued to her screen, but she glanced his way when he closed the door and walked toward her. "He's intense."

"He's a Shifter who knows his daughter is dead but doesn't know the details of where or why. Any father would be upset, Ariana, but a Shifter? His instincts are screaming inside him to tear the person responsible apart, and I don't fucking blame him. There's too many people getting away with shit, and killing Keena isn't something I'm letting go."

His tone was cold. He knew it, but he couldn't help himself. Not when the girl had been taken from one of his clubs with such ease and snuffed out of existence to leave Ralf wondering what had happened to his daughter. Add in that his *meeting* with Raylon Barnes hadn't gone well and he'd not been able to exact his proper retribution on that fucker, he was wound up tight as a drum. Not to mention the effect Ariana had on him earlier. Aye, that added to the way he was feeling and, right now, he was in a foul mood. He wasn't even attempting to hide it.

Ariana's lips pursed together as she stared at him. Her dark eyes scanned him for long seconds while he glowered back at her, daring her to argue with him. He wasn't backing down from his stance on the matter. He'd find these fuckers and he'd deal with them in his way. She could like it or damn well lump it.

"So." She cocked her head to the side. "What you're saying is that you and Ralf are going to go after these people and what? You're going to stand by and allow him to, what was it you said? Let him rip them apart? Is that what you're planning? What if they're human? Do the same rules apply?"

Lazarus snorted, turned away, and strode to the bar to pour a fresh drink. "What's better? Handing them over to the police to see if they can make a case against them?"

Ice, lots of ice clinked into his glass before he poured in his whisky, but he kept his back to her, waiting on her response. The one that came wasn't what he expected. Her laughter surprised him. Hard as flint and cold as the ice he'd just held in his hand. Lazarus spun around to find Ariana tapping a pen on the desk.

"They fuck up more than they put away, we both know that." She raised the pen to point it at him. "So you decide who lives and dies? Is that it?"

"I didn't say that." He had to be cautious here. She couldn't know what he did. She couldn't know his secrets. She couldn't know anything about him. "All I said was, in this case, it's pretty clear what happened, or so it appears. If I follow up and find out that it *is* as it appears, then Ralf deserves his justice. He deserves to avenge his daughter's death, and I won't stand in his way."

Ariana pushed her chair away, rising to pace back and forth while tapping the pen repeatedly on her free hand. Her face was inscrutable, closed down and impossible for him to read as she walked back and forth. "I see. So if Keena was, indeed, taken from here by a person, or persons, who did her harm, and that information is uncovered, you and Ralf intend to do them harm. Correct?"

Shit. He'd opened his mouth and put his foot in it. She was going to back out of helping them because she'd be liable of a crime for aiding and abetting in said crime.

"Ariana, I didn't say that. Not exactly. It was hypothetical," he tried to backtrack quickly. He needed her help to find out what happened that night and, more importantly, who the hell Keena had left with. If he didn't get that information, they'd be at a dead end.

He might be able to get it from other avenues, but it would take longer, much longer, and he wasn't in the mood to wait. Not when Ariana could get it to him faster... and there was the other reason. He admitted it. He wanted to work with her. See her. Be in her presence.

Ariana whirled around, pointing the pen at him accusingly. "Don't. Don't lie to me, Lazarus. I hate lies."

She walked toward him, stopping right in front of him and looking up into his face while tilting her head to the side. Her eyes were dark pools filled with difficult to read emotions, and he was tempted to use his abilities on her, force her to do his bidding, but he didn't. He saw her brain working as if she were wondering the same thing. A moment later, she asked.

"You could force me and then wipe my memory. Couldn't you? If I said I wasn't going to help you. You could do that."

"I could, but I wouldn't. Not with you, Ariana."

There. He'd said it, and he didn't know why. He *should*. He normally *would*. He still *could*. He was a master liar. He could do it and she would never be the wiser, but... he wouldn't.

Why? Quite simply, he had no clue. What the hell was the matter with him?

Ariana's eyes stayed on his, questioning, probing, asking, but he had no answer. "I think I believe you, Lazarus. Why the hell I do, I can't say and I hope I don't regret it. I'll continue to help because I believe Keena deserves it, and some people deserve more than a life behind bars for their crimes."

She turned away but, before she did, he saw a glimpse of... something. It was a darkness that lurked beneath the surface, a pain she was hiding deep inside... but what? What had hurt her so deeply that she'd help him in such an endeavor? Another layer he'd have to unravel, to peel back and find out more about Ariana Harmon.

"Thank you, Ariana." He followed her back to the desk, where she fell into the chair as if she had the weight of the world on her shoulders.

"I'm afraid this is going to take longer than I'd thought." She pointed to the screen. "Here, let me show you what I mean." He went over and sat in the chair next to her. "So the lighting in the club is poor, obviously, and I've input the details of what Keena was wearing that night, together with her image for face recognition. We've hit a snag because there are two other girls who look very similar to her who are in the club, see?"

He did. There, on the screen, were images of two other young women who were uncannily like Keena. His enhanced sight, even with the bad lighting, saw they had different eye colors, and their hair was obviously not the same shade. But to others looking, they were extremely similar.

"Shit, they could pass as her. I can make out different eye color and their hair is off and their tops aren't the same. But, hell, they do look alike."

"Exactly. The program is picking up their images too." Ariana sighed, stabbing her finger at the screen. "It's slowing things down. I'm sorry, but this is going to take until tomorrow,

Lazarus. The lighting in the club is pretty bad; if it were better, we'd be able to speed things up."

"Don't worry about it. It's better than what we had yesterday. At least we have something to work on." Lazarus caught a glimpse of Keena. A still image of her with her friends at the bar.

She was smiling as they waited to be served at the bar. She looked happy and... alive. Leaning in, he took in every detail of the picture, checking to see if he could catch a clue to what had happened to the happy girl he was seeing in that moment. He saw nothing that could tell him why she'd be dead soon... was it hours? Days? He wasn't certain, but that beautiful and vibrant life was snuffed out, and he was going to find the person responsible.

"Are you all right?" Ariana asked quietly.

Was he? The answer to that was no. He wasn't.

"Aye, I'll be fine when we find the people responsible for this." He reached forward and ran a finger over Keena's face.

"We will," Ariana whispered softly. "Now, if you don't mind. I have something planned for tonight. I need to go. I'll take this with me and..."

Lazarus rose, shaking his head. "Sorry, but I can't allow that. This is security footage from one of my establishments, and it stays here."

"What? No, that's my property and has my new..."

"Ariana! This isn't up for discussion, and I can assure you I won't steal your invention. If I wanted to do that, I would have already. It would be easy enough for me to do, as you've already pointed out. I could compel you and then wipe your memory. I'm extremely interested in working with you on developing it. That is still on the agenda, but that's for later, not now. Your laptop will be safe here in my office until I come back from dropping you off, and then I'll keep it with me until you come back."

Ariana shoved her chair back and stepped away, her face like thunder. He could feel her struggle with what he'd said, but what could she do? Fight with him? That wouldn't go well, either with words or if she attempted it physically. Neither would work and she knew it. She kept her back to him, taking deep breaths in, over and over while her hands clasped into fists at her sides. She was obviously used to getting her own way.

Tough. So was he, and he always won. She'd have to get used to that.

"You better not drive like a lunatic this time," she snapped over her shoulder. "Or you'll regret it."

The way she looked at him, with a steely glint in her eye and the stance in her body, like she was about to launch herself at him, he had no doubt she meant it. The point was though, did he want to find out what happened if he pushed her too far?

CHAPTER TWENTY-TWO

LAZARUS MADE his mind up when they got outside. He couldn't risk having her hanging onto him the way she had on their previous ride. Ariana was affecting him in ways no other female ever had but, more importantly, she was causing his beast to act up too.

With the fiasco with Raylon Barnes earlier, he couldn't take any chances with it tonight. No. He'd have to be careful and not push it any further tonight. He'd already pushed her with the revelation of what his plans were regarding Keena. Revealing anything more of himself was not on the cards.

"I'll drive like a normal person on the way back. You don't have to hang on like you did before. I promise I'll be good." Lazarus started his bike, giving her the go-ahead to mount.

"I doubt that," she muttered as she got on, hooking her fingers loosely at his waist.

Good, that was perfect. There was enough space between them to stop him from going... what? Crazy? Nuts? Mad? Probably all three, but at least now she wasn't wrapped around him and her breath wasn't caressing his skin. That had been a perfect torture. One he'd been spellbound by and one he wanted to relive over and over again... and run far from at the same time. He couldn't risk it. Not again. It would drive him utterly insane. He'd lose control of himself, and if he did that he wasn't sure what he'd do.

Would he take Ariana? Like, take her... not fuck her. Although, that was something he'd dearly love to do, but she'd fight him tooth and nail. He'd no doubts about that, but he wanted her. He craved her. He fucking want to... stop. He had to stop thinking about her or he'd do something stupid, and they had a job to do first.

First?

You're going to do something after? He wondered to himself as they drove toward her home. His chest constricting with that thought careening around in his brain. The possibilities were endless. What? Where? When? Why?

No!

She was helping him. Helping Ralf. Helping Keena. What the hell was wrong with him?

You're a hunter. You're a monster. You know it, so why deny it? You can't escape it. You can't escape your past. You can't escape what made you. You can't escape what you are. You've tried before... and failed. Give in and do it. Take her. Take what you want. Take what you crave. Do with her what you want... you know you want to. You know you will!

"Shut up!" he yelled, speeding up to zigzag in and out of the traffic.

"Lazarus! Don't you dare! Slow down." Ariana's hands tightened on him, shaking him hard. "Lazarus! You promised me."

Her voice filtered through, somehow, and he did. The bike's engine quietened as they reduced speed, his head spinning around to see where they were. Thankfully, they were mere moments from her house. "Sorry, I'm not used to driving like an old man."

"Not funny," she mumbled as he pulled off the main road and onto her street, relief flooding through him.

He pulled up onto her drive and he didn't kill the engine. He took her helmet, looping it over his arm. "What time will you be back tomorrow?"

"Is six too early?"

"That's fine. I can pick you up if you need?" He looked away, still feeling unsettled.

"I'll be out in the afternoon, so I can just swing by afterward."

"Okay, I'll see you at six. Thanks for your help tonight, Ariana."

He finally looked up at her, and he shouldn't have. Not in a million years should he have looked up. With the moonlight shining behind her like a halo and her head tilted to the side while she gave him a hint of a smile. Hells fire. No. That was the last thing he needed right at that moment, with his resolve unravelling and his restraint almost broken. He was about to leap from the bike and snatch her into his arms when she turned on her heel, striding quickly away.

"My pleasure," she threw over her shoulder as she disappeared into the darkness.

Pleasure. That word shot through him like a bolt of red hot lava. Fucking hell. Trust her to use two simple words that were anything but... not in his mind anyway. He'd have to find a way to expend some of his pent up energy or he'd explode. Thoughts of Ariana laid out before him ran through his mind, a soft moan escaping him with his head falling forward. Her hair would be free from the braid, splayed out on fresh white sheets, her soft skin there for the taking. His tongue would lavish every damn inch and he'd take his time as he savored her taste before sinking his fangs deep inside her.

Lazarus could almost taste her right there and then; her unique aroma still in his nostrils. Shit. Where could he go now? He had to go somewhere to get rid of his hard-on and to get Ariana out of his head. A human wouldn't be acceptable tonight. He needed something *more*, someone who could stand up to what he was going to dole out... and he was ready. Right this fucking minute. He'd have to find a club for his kind, or Shifters. Aye, a strong Shifter would be able to deal with him tonight, and they were red-blooded and sensual as hell. He knew just the place.

Backing out of the driveway, Lazarus turned the bike and sped to the end of the road, turning and roaring away.

ARIANA DASHED INSIDE, turned, and placed her head on the door, gasping for breath. "Damn it," she managed to get out, her fist slapping her thigh.

She was rattled, and the reason for that was still sitting in her driveway; Lazarus Báis. The man had gotten to her and she had no idea why. But it had to stop. Now. He was dangerous, hell, he was a Vampire with the ability to compel her to do whatever he wanted. Not to mention he could kill her in one second flat. And what had she done? She had walked into a meeting, and not only had she stayed, but she'd agreed to help him, handing over her new invention.

"What the hell, Ariana? What are you doing?" She reverted to talking to herself when she was extremely upset, like she had all those years ago. No, she couldn't go back to that. She was better now. She didn't need to do that. Did she?

She watched through her spyhole as Lazarus' head fell forward. What was wrong with him? Was he having as much trouble with the *situation* as she was? *No. Don't be so stupid. He's loaded. A millionaire. Just look at him. He could have any woman he wanted and he's, he's, a Vampire! Get a grip on yourself. You've got a mission to do tonight; do it.*

And she did. Evan Smythson. He'd gotten away on the night she'd first met Lazarus, but she'd vowed he'd pay and he would. She'd planned on making that happen tonight, and she would. She needed her weapons, some blades to cut him in just the *right* places so he could never do to any other women what he'd already done to others. That would be justice for his crimes. She had her plans and she'd stick to them. She'd put Lazarus Báis out of her mind, until tomorrow at six anyway.

Ariana turned away from the door as Lazarus backed down her drive and sped away. Good. That's what he needed to do. Leave. Leave her alone so she could do what she had to do, which was to dole out some justice to Evan Smythson.

She let out a long, pent-up breath, knowing that the Vampire had left and she was no longer tempted to go outside and invite him in... for what? A drink? A kiss? No. She hadn't done that ever. Not since... No. She wasn't going there. She couldn't. Her hands bunched into fists before they could start to shake, before she could go down that rabbit hole. "You've got this."

"Got what?"

The voice sent ripples down her spine; she must be imagining it. Her brain wasn't working properly. Not with everything that was happening with Lazarus.

The alarms! Her brain fired off into a million pieces as she remembered opening the door, darting in, and turning to watch Lazarus through the peephole. She didn't turn off her alarm systems. No. It couldn't be happening... not again. Not ever again.

Her training started to kick in, but before her synapses could make her body move, something huge slammed into her from behind, sending her crashing into the wall in front. Ariana screamed as loudly and as wildly as she could, with one thought in mind... survive.

"Lazarus! Help me!"

If she couldn't fight off this fucker, she prayed he was close enough to hear her. He had super hearing, didn't he? This guy was huge, his body pressing against her so hard she could barely draw a breath, then she felt them... two things. A butt of a gun at her head, and something hard pressing into her from his groin.

He slammed her head into the wall, hard. "Shut the fuck up, your boyfriend's gone. He can't help you."

Terror filled her. Nothing she'd ever felt before could compare to how she felt in that moment. She couldn't deal with this, not again. Her brain froze. For a few seconds, she couldn't think, couldn't breathe, couldn't do anything. Not until he snarled and his words slammed into her brain. She made the decision to do the only thing she could. What she'd been training for ever since those dark days.

She'd fight until her last breath. No other option was viable. None. *Courage strengthens. Fear Weakens.*

"Fucking move and I'll shoot you. Nobody will hear a thing 'cause I'm using a silencer." He snorted out a laugh before carrying on, his voice right at her ear, his breath foul and smelling of cheap whisky. "Not in your head, bitch. I want you alive. But it'll hurt, I'll make sure of that. So let's get this straight. I'm in charge. Hands behind your back. Now."

She couldn't move her hands, they were squashed in front of her body, but, when she could, she definitely wasn't complying with his demands. Behind her back so he could immobilize her? Not happening. He could hurt her all he wanted, but the last thing he'd do was tie her up. Her face ached from being smashed into the wall, and she could feel blood sliding down her skin, but so what? She was alive, and what had she been taught? If you're conscious and alive, you can fight. *Courage strengthens. Fear weakens.*

So, Ariana, this is it. This is the moment you've dreaded, but it's also the moment you've trained for, so fucking use it. Use every last session with each trainer and fucking fight. Fight for your life, but, Ariana, fight for more than that. Fight for your fucking sanity.

"Okay, just don't shoot me," she whispered, playing along and adding a whimper to her voice for good measure.

She thought of her position. Where was her nearest weapon? If it was nearby, she'd go for it. If not, she'd improvise. She'd been taught how to do that; it was time to see if all the talk worked. Could she really use anything around her to kill someone? Or was it all bullshit? If it was and she lived through this, she'd be asking for her money back; that particular course in Israel had cost her an arm and a leg.

Her eyes swiveled to the side. Hallway, but not near enough to the console table to reach the dagger in the drawer, and nothing else was close. Okay; think, Ariana, think. His hand tangled in her braid, wrapping it in his free hand to pull her head back, and before she could do anything, he slammed her face into the wall again. She couldn't stop the scream that tore from her as agony ripped through her, blood pouring from her nose, and stars appeared before her. She was disorientated and woozy when he tugged her away, her hands shot to her face briefly before she reacted to her new-found freedom.

Now, Ariana, now! Fight. Do it before he can restrain you!

Terror washed over her at the thought of this hulking man having her at his mercy. She couldn't allow that to happen. What would he do to her if she were tied up? She couldn't even think of the many things he'd do. She'd been there before and knew she wouldn't survive again. *Courage strengthens. Fear weakens.*

She spun around fast, his grip on her hair barely holding her back as she raised her arm, using every ounce of her strength, and aimed for his face with her elbow. He saw it coming at the last minute and tried to dodge out of her way, but he was slow to react and her blow connected with a resounding crack to his cheekbone. His eye burst into a halo of red, blood spurting everywhere, and he released her braid, staggering back with a curse. Ariana moved in, ready to attack with a flurry of blows, anywhere she could land them, but he had other ideas. The gun raised toward her so fast her stomach lurched when she looked down the barrel of the silencer.

This was it, the end. She knew it because she wasn't standing there waiting to be hobbled by that fucker so he could hurt her over and over, to do with her as he wanted. Not here in her own home. Her safe haven. She would not allow that. She couldn't live through that, not again.

"You'll pay for that, bitch."

She'd made her decision. She was okay with it. Her heart slowed down and she smiled over at this piece of shit who'd invaded her home, her sanctuary. Her soul settled inside her as she lifted her head and spat at him, readying herself to attack and knowing she'd take the bullet square in her chest.

An explosion of noise to her left shattered everything as pieces of wood fell all around them and the angriest bellow she'd ever heard filled her home completely.

"Get the fuck away from her! Don't you dare hurt her!"

Lazarus. It was Lazarus' voice, but it was all around them, completely and utterly filling her house, and it wasn't just words... it was a *command*. Her attacker's face went slack, his feet moving slowly backward until he hit the wall behind him, and there he stood. His eyes wide and wild with terror. The next moment, Lazarus was in front of her, his face white with fury, but his eyes were red with flames burning brightly inside, and he had the largest fangs she'd ever seen protruding from his mouth.

"Ariana! Fuck. You'll be all right. I'll get you help. Just hold on."

She couldn't believe he was here, but she was relieved he was. He'd just saved her life.

"I'll be okay." Her legs wobbled, but she tried to stop them. She wasn't weak. Never was she weak.

His arms shot out to hold her before he turned to the man still stuck to the wall opposite, a snarl erupted from his throat. "Do you know this guy?"

Ariana looked at him properly for the first time, gasping as she recognized him. "You! You bastard!"

"I take that as a yes." Lazarus pulled her to his side.

"I fought him at one of my martial arts classes and beat his ass." Ariana knew he'd taken it bad, but this? He must be insane to have gone this far to get her back for something as stupid as defeating him in a fight.

"I'll deal with this. You need to…"

And that's all she heard. Her legs began to shake and her sight darkened. The last thing she felt was Lazarus' arms tighten around her as he caught her when she fell. Safe. She felt safe. In the arms of a Vampire.

Dark Hunter

CHAPTER TWENTY-THREE

LAZARUS SKIDDED TO A HALT, hearing a scream in his head. Was that Ariana? He'd been too filled up with trying to escape from her, his mind full of images of what he wanted to do with her. To her. Things he shouldn't be thinking, feeling, and if he didn't get away from her fast... He'd act on them.

He'd sped away from her to get distance between them and now he'd slammed to a stop, her voice in his head. *"Lazarus! Help me!"*

Panic. Fear. Terror.

He felt them all in those three words. What the fuck was happening? Who was there? Who dared to make her feel like that?

Lazarus peeled his bike around, cursing himself for driving so fast when he'd left; it would take him minutes to get back. Minutes before he'd be able to reach her. Help her. Fucking save her from god knew what, or who. But whatever it was, was in for a shock; he'd kill them for daring to touch her.

His bike skidded around a semi, clipping the truck and causing the driver to honk the horn loudly. Lazarus ignored him while he regained control, whipping between two cars and around another, cutting it off. The driver didn't have time to react, he was speeding so fast, desperation filling him because Ariana hadn't made another sound. She hadn't shouted for him again. Did that mean she was all right? Or had her situation grown worse?

He'd watched that video over and over. Seen her fight like a demon; she could handle herself. For her to scream like that meant she was in trouble. Fury ran through him, white hot, boiling fury. Whoever had caused that would pay, but he had to get there. Now.

He scanned ahead, checking the traffic and saw it was backing up. "No fucking good," he cursed, spinning his bike off to the side and jumping the curb to cut through a parking lot, through an alley, and out onto a backstreet. When he arrived there, Lazarus continued down it until he reached another main road, flew across it without a thought for any other traffic, and off into another small alley he was certain led to Ariana's. It took him another few minutes to arrive at the end of her street, but when he did, he raced to her house, slamming on his brakes and leaping from his bike while it was still moving. It rolled on until it fell over onto her drive while he used his Vampire speed to careen toward her door.

Lazarus raced for the door, harnessing one of his many powers. He didn't give a fuck who saw him as his hands formed an orange ball of energy, which he released a second before he reached the large oak door. It shattered before him, sending pieces of wood to explode inside, leaving nothing in his way. The sight before him caused his beast to soar to the fore and his heart to turn to stone.

Ariana was bloodied and bruised, facing the barrel of a gun wielded by the fucker who she'd fought in her Krav class. The brute of a man she'd beat, who'd taken it badly. So badly he'd obviously come seeking revenge.

Lazarus brought forth his compulsion, forcing it toward the thug to stop him in his tracks and back him against the wall, visions of his past coming to haunt him. Instead of Ariana, he saw his mother. Instead of the man she'd fought in her class, he saw marauders dressed in filthy furs with ancient swords dripping in blood. The flashes of images rushed around in his head for long seconds until Ariana's eyes turned to him, dark pools of chocolate filled with pain and set in her pale face, which had blood and bruises marring her beauty. She was on her last legs, he could feel her strength draining from her with each breath she drew, every beat of her heart, and it was only a matter of moments before she collapsed.

He raced toward her, his eyes taking in her injuries. "Ariana! Oh fuck. You'll be all right. I'll get you help. Just hold on."

She bravely answered she'd be okay, but he knew better. She was on the verge of collapse. He turned to the cause of her pain, asking if she knew him. He was aware she did, but he couldn't reveal that fact. Her anger when she realized she did was fast and furious, but it didn't last. He knew it wouldn't. He could feel her fading. Feel her body shutting down, and he was there when she tipped over into darkness and into his arms.

"I've got you." He carried her into her living room before he pulled out his phone, calling for back-up. He had to get her back to his place, or to one of his places, so he could help her, but he also had to have her door fixed, and then there was the matter of the fucker in her hall.

He was going to deal with him personally. He pulled his phone out and dialed, impatiently waiting for it to be answered. "I need you to get Ralf and two cars and come to the address I'm going to text you. Straight away. It's urgent."

Lazarus didn't wait for a response. He didn't need one because he knew the man he'd spoken with would already be moving before he'd hung up. It would take twenty minutes, maybe less, to reach him, so he went to check to see if the neighbors had been alerted with the commotion. He didn't want the police showing up. Not with what he had planned.

The sleepy cul-de-sac Ariana had chosen to live in was dark and silent when he slipped outside. Quietly making his way to the middle of the road, Lazarus cocked his head to the side, concentrating hard as he listened for any telltale signs that any of her fellow citizens had been woken by the disturbance. Or worse, were wide awake and heard everything and were already on the phone to report it. He honed in on everything around him, but all he could detect was some snoring from nearby houses, and a few pets roaming their homes restless with his presence so close by. Their owners were none the wiser that a deadly Vampire was outside, but their beloved dogs and cats were nervous and scared. One let out a whimper while another growled a warning; a brave dog trying to guard its home.

However, he couldn't allow that to continue. It might alert the owners that something was amiss; he had to put a stop to that before the animal grew braver and louder. Lazarus turned toward the home housing the pet, throwing a vicious snarl its way, together with some of his supernatural power, and quickly heard the beast whine in surrender before silence ensued. Once more he listened for any signs anyone had heard what had gone on, but there were none. He returned to Ariana's, so fast that one moment he was in the street and the next he stood before her tormentor.

The fucker who dared to lay his hands on her. The man who'd marred her beauty. The bastard who'd left her bruised and broken and unconscious, and who he was going to deal with in his own way. His beast pawed inside him, eager to get started, impatient to dole out retribution for his crimes because he was certain Ariana wasn't his first victim. The stench rolling off him testified to the caliber of the man standing before him. He was rotten, through and through, and he deserved the punishment he was about to receive.

Terror stared back at him when he looked deep into his eyes. "You dared to come here, into Ariana's home, with the intention of hurting her. But that wasn't all you had in mind, was it?" Lazarus flicked his wrist. "Answer. Tell me what you had planned. You cannot lie to me. You are under my compulsion, asshole. You can try all you want, but only the truth will come out of that mouth."

Eyes darted left and right, looking for an escape, for help, but no one was coming.

"I was going to tie her up and... and..." He stopped, gagging on his own tongue as he attempted to avoid revealing his intentions.

"Speak the truth now or I'll start by skinning you alive. I'll do it slowly. You can't begin to imagine the pain you'll endure, and I assure you that you'll talk within seconds."

"I was going to rape her for what she'd done to me. For shaming me in front of everyone. She's just a woman and she... she..."

Lazarus' fist shot out to slam into his belly, causing him to double over, with a cry of pain shooting out of him. "Silence. Do not utter another sound or I'll cut out your tongue."

White hot rage was burning inside him, his fists bunched at his sides as he tried to contain it. Lazarus felt pain deep within his chest, an agony he'd felt once before, long ago when he was but a mere child witnessing a horror he'd locked up tight in the recesses of his mind. The palm of his hand shot up to cover his heart. "No," he whispered; he couldn't allow those memories to escape.

Not now. Not here. Ariana was hurt and in need of his help. If he relapsed now, all hell would break loose.

"You...you're the cause of this." He growled, descending on the man once more. "What's your fucking name?"

"Ricus Bouer," he stammered.

"You were going to kill her, Ricus Bouer, after you raped and beat her, weren't you? You couldn't leave her alive. Not when she could identify you. Your only option was murdering her. That was your plan, wasn't it?"

Terror shot through the man. The scent of it leeching out of his pores to waft around him in a disgusting bouquet that betrayed him before he had a chance to open his mouth. Bouer's eyes swiveled to the left and right as if he expected a savior to suddenly appear from thin air. His body trembled so badly his teeth rattled, and his answer was a disgusting snivel, drawn out of him only because of Lazarus' compulsion.

"Yes, I couldn't do anything else. She knew who I was."

Another shot of pain ran through Lazarus as a vision of this dirty beast following through on his plan ran like a grotesque movie in his mind. Of Ariana lying in a heap and of Bouer standing over her with his gun pointed down at her. Hatred sprang forward at the same time as he did, his fangs in full view and producing a groan from the fucker pinned against the wall.

"You won't hurt her, or anyone else, ever again."

Lazarus could have easily ripped his throat out. He could have gone in for the kill and made it more *personal*, but the thought of tasting this man's tainted blood caused his stomach to turn over in disgust. Instead, his hand shot forward so fast his victim never saw the manner of his demise coming, his fist crushing Bouer's chest in the blink of an eye and carrying on until he reached his still beating heart. It didn't remain that way for long. The power of his punch obliterated it, leaving nothing but a bloody mess behind. His arm was out and he'd stepped away before the corpse had hit the floor. Ricus Bouer was gone.

The sorry excuse for a human would never hurt anyone else, but, more importantly, he'd never lay a hand on Ariana ever again.

Why was that important? Rather, why was that *more* important? He didn't have time to think about it. Not now. Car doors slammed outside. Police? He sped to the remnants of the door to check but was relieved when he saw two familiar figures heading his way; Moose and Ralf. Help had arrived.

"What do you need?" Moose came right to the point,

scanning the demolished door while Ralf remained behind him, silent.

"This is Ariana's place. I'll keep it short. I'd left when I heard her shout for help. I returned to find her injured and an intruder with a gun who was intent on rape and murder."

Ralf surged forward, growling viciously. "Is she all right? Let me at that fucker. I'll rip him apart."

"Stop." Moose's hand shot out to bar Ralf's way. "I assume you've dealt with things?"

"Indeed." Lazarus waved them inside. "I need you to get rid of him and to make her home secure before morning so the neighbors are none the wiser that anything went on here. Can you do that?"

"Of course. The body isn't a problem; I'll make sure he's never found. As for the door, I can get that fixed with the company we use. It'll cost, of course, getting them out at this time of night, but I assume that's not an issue." Moose looked around, spotting a rug in the living room. "Ralf, go get that to wrap him in."

"Charge it to my personal account; use this." Lazarus handed over one of his cards. "And if you can ensure the place is cleaned thoroughly afterward."

"I'll deal with it."

"Knew you would, Moose."

"Is she okay? Ariana?" Ralf asked, looking around.

"She's out cold right now. Concussion. He beat her before I got back and her face was bruised and bloody. With the traces on the wall, it looks like he smashed her against it, more than once. He took her by surprise when she got home and the fucker had the drop on her with the gun."

Ralf growled again, obviously angry. "She's a nice girl, Ariana is. The way she's offered to help with Keena... Well, I'm shocked this happened to her."

"Me too." Lazarus couldn't begin to describe how he was feeling. Upset didn't come fucking close. "Are the keys in the cars? I'm going to take her back to my apartment over the club and watch out for her."

"They are," Moose said, but Ralf was frowning.

"You're not taking her to a hospital?" Ralf questioned.

"No," Lazarus shot back, too quickly and with a bite to his tone. "She'll be safer with me."

He didn't tell them who the guy was, or the reason for the attack. Their eyes fell to the body and back to him. Moose nodded. "Probably best. I'll get a couple of the guys to stay downstairs, just in case there's any trouble."

Lazarus couldn't say no. He'd implied there was a threat to Ariana's safety; Moose's offer was reasonable. "Thanks," was the only acceptable thing he could say in the circumstances.

"I'll stay," Ralf offered. "It's the least I can do. If there's two of us, we can take turns to have a couple of hours rest later in the day. That's all we'll need."

"I will too." Moose tipped his head. "I can't have my boss and his lady friend in danger and not hang around, now can I?"

Lazarus didn't say anything. He couldn't. He had no come back. He turned on his heel and went to Ariana, who was still out cold. He could hear her heart beating strongly and her breathing was normal; his keen senses telling him it was the knocks to her head that had caused the problem. Concussion was a fickle thing though; she could wake up and be fine. Or she could remain unconscious and be in serious trouble if she didn't receive medical help.

There was another solution, but he wasn't thinking of that. Not yet anyway. It wasn't one he'd used on a human for... ever? He couldn't think of a situation where he'd done it before. Or anyone he'd risk it for. Ariana? Maybe, possibly, perhaps... but not here. Not with witnesses to something so... drastic.

CHAPTER TWENTY-FOUR

LAZARUS SCOOPED ARIANA UP, cradling her against him. Her scent engulfed him, overwhelming his senses and almost knocking him on his ass.

She was tantalizing. Sweet. Absofuckinglutely sending him and his beast insane. A growl rumbled in his chest, or rather it was more of a whine. A goddamn whimper of... what? Need? Fuck. He was losing his shit. "Get a grip," he mumbled down into Ariana's blood soaked hair... and *that* wasn't a good move.

Not when he got a lungful of her glorious crimson, which set his synapses on fire. His skin felt like it was being eaten by a million hungry ants, and his fangs were desperate to sink into her pale skin and finally sample her unique...

"Are you all right?"

Ralf's hand landed on his shoulder, jolting him out of what he was on the verge of doing, feeding on the injured woman in his arms. Damn, he was an animal. A fucking lowlife monster for even thinking of violating her in such a way, but that's just what he was. Wasn't it? A damned monster.

"I'm fine," Lazarus ground out. He whirled around but refused to meet the Wolf's gaze. "I'm taking Ariana back to my apartment now."

"She looks like she needs a Doc."

"I'll take care of her," Lazarus snapped. "You do what you're here to do, Ralf."

Lazarus didn't wait for an answer. Striding to the door, he checked there were no prying eyes before going to the vehicle at the bottom of the drive and placing Ariana gently in the back seat. She didn't make a sound. Her breathing was steady, so he quickly got in, started up, and drove away, knowing Moose would do what was required before leaving.

He tried to focus on the road but found it harder with each passing minute. Not only was Ariana's scent everywhere, driving him insane, but he was filled with a fury that was building inside of him, like a volcano about to erupt with a spectacular explosion. He should've known there was a threat inside her home. He should've sensed there was someone else there. He should've heard something sooner. He should've gotten to her faster. He should've *saved* her.

He should've smelt that fucker's foul stench the moment he'd arrived on her drive. It was every-damn-where, all around her property where he'd prowled before taking out her security and breaking in. Lazarus could *see* it clearly in his mind now. Too late, asshole, too fucking late. Instead, he was focused on his own fucking *feelings,* and that was why she was lying in a heap behind him. Bloodied. Bruised. Unconscious.

And with his beast prowling around inside him angry, furious, and leaving him feeling like his head was about to explode in a glorious eruption of blood, brains, and gore. Hell, Lazarus would welcome that right now. Anything to take away the emotions that were overwhelming him, causing him to feel things he'd never experienced before. No. That was a lie. He had. He'd just locked it away.

Inadequate. Weak. Pathetic. They were just a few words to describe how he was feeling. "No!" he slammed his fist on the steering wheel, forcing them away... again.

He was strong, capable, and powerful. He'd had a moment's lapse. That was all. He'd ensure Ariana was safe and healed. He'd make up for his mistake, and they'd get back to work. But a vision of her terror-filled eyes shot into his mind; the scent of her fear cloying in his throat, causing him to gag. "Fuck, Ariana, what happened?"

She'd beat that guy's ass with no fear, no dread whatsoever, so why was she in such a state of terror when he'd arrived? She'd been ready to fight him again. He'd seen it in her, but the scent of her distress and panic was everywhere, and something had caused that. Something had happened to her that he didn't know, and he *had* to find out what.

The lights from Monarch shone brightly ahead. The queue to get in was longer than ever, even though it was the early hours of the morning. Hell, for once, he wished the place was quiet. The door to his apartment was in the alley, but not that far back from the street or prying eyes. He'd have to be careful and fast if he didn't want to be seen carrying a body through the door. It would be easy enough to park, unlock the door, and have it open before retrieving Ariana. Then he could use his enhanced speed to get inside. It would be fine. He wouldn't be seen and nobody would call the police and have them knocking on the door, asking why he was carrying in a woman's body in the early hours of the morning, right?

When he pulled off the main road, he saw two hulking bodies at his door. He slammed on the brakes and shoved the vehicle into reverse before one stepped into the light and held a hand up to wave him forward. He saw they were part of the Club's security team. Of course, Moose had called ahead and arranged for his men to be here in case he needed help. Or if there was any trouble. After all, he'd hinted there might still be a danger to Ariana.

Lazarus drove slowly forward and parked as close to the door as he could before getting out and handing the key to the nearest guard. "Open up so I can get her inside."

The man, a Wolf, merely did as asked while the other stood at the rear of the vehicle with his eyes scanning the area for any threat. The added bonus to that was his hulking figure hid them from view of the street. Lazarus leaned in and his breath caught in his throat when he saw Ariana's blood-soaked face, but he steeled himself, pasting a hard look on his face as he hauled her into his arms and made a dash for the door with her cradled against him.

Her soft body was limp and frail while he sprinted up the stairs, the door closing behind him once he made it inside. In no time at all, he'd reached the inner door, which he fumbled with but managed to get opened, and he backed into the large entrance before deciding where to put Ariana. The logical place was his bedroom. So that's where he went. The fact it held the most comfortable bed and surroundings didn't factor in his decision. Of course it didn't. It was because he knew where everything was in his room, rather than the guest room. Wasn't it?

When he placed Ariana down onto the plush comforter, he saw the state of her clothes, blood-stained and torn. As well as her pale face, which was covered in dried blood and swollen with bruises. A loud growl startled Lazarus, causing him to jump away from the bed until he realized the sound had come from him. Whether it was anger or something else, he wasn't sure, but it had been him who had made it all the same.

"Get to work," he mumbled, tugging the boots off her feet while he tried not to look upon her damaged beauty. Once he'd removed her jeans, jacket, and shirt, he realized he'd made the error of not bringing some of her own clothes with him; he did the only thing he could think of, retrieving one of his white shirts and placing it on the bed before going to get a bowl of warm water and a cloth to clean the dried in blood from her as best he could.

When he returned to the room, he stopped at the edge of the bed, his heart stampeding in his chest as if he had a herd of wild horses running madly inside him. His breath caught in his throat at the sight of Ariana's pale beauty lying against his dark red covers. She looked fragile and delicate, when he knew she was anything but. He'd seen her strength, saw the way she'd battled against the ogre he'd killed earlier, but in this moment in time, that wasn't the Ariana before him. This Ariana was someone else. This Ariana was fragile, but also the most beautiful thing he'd seen in his entire life.

Her face was pale beneath the bruises and blood. Her nose looked broken, maybe her left cheekbone too, but still her damaged splendor was magnificent. It called to him deep down inside. Pulling at something buried so far down that he wasn't sure where it was. What it was. He had no name for it. All he knew was... Ariana was his, or would be. Somehow. Someday. Someway.

Come hell or high water... Ariana Harmon was... what? Meant to cross paths with him? Meant for him? Meant to be with him? Fuck if he knew what was going on, but he would. He'd figure it out. Figure *her* out. Figure everything out.

She moaned, her head rolled to the side and she moaned again. He moved so fast he was amazed he didn't spill the water he was holding. "Shh, it's okay, Ariana. You're safe."

"Lazarus." She opened her eyes once, then they closed and she dropped back into oblivion.

His name. She'd known it was him and she'd said his name. Lazarus' guts clenched as he went to work, gently washing her clean before managing to dress her in his shirt and gently lifting her and placing her beneath the cover. Then he cleaned up the room, removing the blood-soaked towel and the water, which was now a murky burgundy with the aroma of her A Negative surrounding him until he forced himself to pour it away. His eyes locked on the liquid until the last remnants dropped down the drain... but not the scent.

It lingered all around him. In his nostrils. Ingrained in his soul from that first encounter in *Fortune*, and now even more so.

"What are you doing to me?" He stared at himself in the mirror, not sure who he was seeing because the man peering back didn't look quite like himself.

Lazarus leaned in, scrutinizing his reflection. His skin was as pale as it normally was. Perfect as usual. His eyes were... a noise from the bedroom broke his concentration. One that normal ears would not have heard, but his? He heard it clear as day. It caused him to dash from the bathroom and straight to Ariana's side; her body was stretched out straight, taut as a drum skin, and the noise he'd heard were her teeth clenching together.

She was having some kind of fit, or worse. He wasn't a medical doctor, but he could see she was in trouble and he now had a decision to make. Take her to a hospital, or help her himself. That was a big decision. Huge. One he'd never done before and one he'd vowed never to do.

Ever.

Was she worth breaking the solemn vow he'd made so long ago? Could he go against everything inside him that was screaming so loud he felt like his head would implode? Was Ariana Harmon worth it? Would he do this? *Could* he do this?

Lazarus stared down at her as her body started to spasm, her head fell to the side, and blood seeped from her mouth where she'd bitten through her tongue. Lazarus took a step toward her, then another, not able to drag his eyes from the trickle of blood that now ran down the side of her mouth; a river of scarlet against her ashen skin. Mesmerized, hypnotized, enthralled by that tiny stream of red, he stopped by the side of the bed. His hand reached forward and one finger stretched to capture just a drop. Just one drop was all he wanted. All he craved. Just a taste.

His finger was there, right *there,* when Ariana's body arched off the bed and it went into a full seizure. The bed started to shake with the force of what was happening, and it jolted Lazarus out of whatever fog he was in. "No time." He dropped beside Ariana, snatching her into his arms to stop her from causing herself any further harm.

The decision was... he either helped her, or she died in his arms.

DarkHunter

CHAPTER TWENTY-FIVE

IT WAS neither simple nor easy. The decision. But it was one Lazarus had to make with Ariana's shuddering body held tight against him.

How could he make such a decision with no time to think? Time to sort out in his head what would happen if he went through with this. Time to decide if this was what he wanted. Time to choose if he could do this, if he *should* do this. Time to process the ramifications of his actions if he went through with this. Just fucking *time*!

But he had none or, rather, Ariana didn't. She was failing fast. Her seizure had passed and she now lay limp in his arms, but that didn't mean she was better. Hell no. She was worse. Much worse. Her heart was slowing down. Her blood now pumping sluggishly through her veins, and with each passing second, it grew graver. He knew she'd be dead within minutes if he did nothing.

It was the head injury. Must have been. He thought briefly while gazing at her bruised face. *Humans... so fragile.*

Ariana moaned, the sound feeble and weak, but it was enough to jolt him into action. He was out of options. "Do you live or die, Ariana?"

Those were the choices. "Choose," he whispered into thin air.

A simple decision. Only it wasn't. There was nothing simple about this. About the woman in his arms. About the secrets she kept. About the way she drove his beast insane, and calmed it at the same time. About the fucking insanity she caused inside of him. No. There was nothing simple about this at all... yet there was.

Could he let her go? Here and now. Could he allow her to slip away from him and die? Could he do that? Never see her smirk again when she was so obviously keeping things from him? Never see those eyes full of fire and reminding him of the whisky he loved? Never see... No! His belly felt like someone had thrown a lit torch inside, fire was eating him up inside and his beast howled in pain at the thought of Ariana being taken from them. That wasn't happening. Lazarus would not allow it. Could not allow it to happen. Ever.

Decision made.

Lazarus shuffled up so he sat on the bed with his back against the headboard and Ariana across his lap with one arm around the back of her neck. Her face was chalk white and her breaths were slow and shallow. With no more time to waste, he brought his free wrist up to his fangs and slashed a deep and vicious wound across it. His blood started to flow and he quickly placed it against her mouth to allow it to drip inside. She gagged and choked as his thick crimson dripped inside, flowing down her throat, but he held her firmly, forcing her to take the only thing that could save her life: his Vampire essence.

Twice he had to stop and cut his wrist open again when the wound healed over, but he didn't care. All he cared about was getting enough inside Ariana to heal her, especially when there was more than he'd like slid from her mouth, down over her face, and covered her skin like a monstrous mask of crimson. Finally, he managed to get enough inside her to satisfy him, and he allowed his injury to remain closed and waited with his eyes glued to Ariana for any sign that she was out of imminent danger.

Seconds ticked by with his blood drying on her pale skin, hardening to cake her silky softness with a burgundy chalk. To anyone else she would look horrific, terrifying even, but to him she looked gorgeous, perfect; because while he gazed down on her grotesque beauty, he saw the bruises on her cheek begin to fade. Slowly, but it was a start, and a sure sign that his essence was getting to work on healing her. Added to that was her heart beat was now stronger… and steady.

Lazarus exhaled a pent-up breath he hadn't known he'd been holding in. But he had. He'd been terrified he'd waited too long before helping her. Scared he'd thought too much about it and had taken her to the brink of death, and maybe tipped her over with not enough time to bring her back without having to do the unthinkable, turning her into a Vampire.

That was a step too far. Even for him.

He waited a few moments longer until Ariana was breathing normally before he slid from beneath her to go and get a clean shirt and another damp cloth to clean her once more. When he returned, he stood and gazed down at the woman who'd forced him to do what he'd vowed never to do… share his blood.

What would happen now? He'd heard the stories from other Vampires. Many of them had shared their tales of minds melding and having a bond with the human they'd allowed to feed from them. Accounts of being able to know how the person was feeling, while others said there was nothing at all. Some said they passed on some of their strength, and when the humans had abused it, they had to end them. Others had more colorful stories that sounded too far-fetched to believe but… were they? Hearsay, gossip, fairytale, or truth? Or was it a mix of all of the above? Lazarus couldn't know. Not now. Not until Ariana was awake and healed completely, and maybe not even then. It could take days or weeks before he knew what would happen.

Would it change her? Change who she was? He was filled with a darkness like no other Vampire alive… or rather dead. But he was *different* to any other. He'd been changed before he became a Vampire; so would his essence be unlike others? Would it then be such a leap to think his blood could do something unusual to Ariana? Fuck. He hoped not, but he didn't have a choice. He was all out of options... live or die. There was no fucking other choice.

"What will be will be."

Lazarus whirled around. His skin prickling. "Mother?" He spun around, looking in every corner of the room for the woman he knew would not be there. She'd died many centuries ago, right in front of him. But that was her voice. Clear as day; he'd heard her as if she were right by his side.

Shaking his head to clear it, Lazarus whispered, "Indeed. What will be will be, Ariana."

He went to work removing any signs of his blood before he changed her out of the stained shirt and settled her back beneath the cover.

Stealthy footsteps coming up the stairs to the apartment had him at the door in seconds. His hand on the doorjamb to bar entry. When he opened it, he found Ralf on the other side with a small suitcase and a look on his face that told Lazarus that the Wolf was worried. Why?

"What's wrong?" he asked straight away.

Ralf looked confused for a moment before he held the suitcase out to him. "Nothing's wrong. I'm concerned about Ariana. Is she okay?"

Of course. Ariana was around the same age as Keena and Ralf would be feeling... protective.

"She will be. What's this?"

"I noticed you left without taking any of her things; I packed some of her stuff. Not a lot, just a couple of changes of clothes." Ralf shrugged. "Are you sure she's okay? She looked like she needed a hospital earlier."

"Thanks for this." Lazarus placed the case behind him. "I'm certain she'll be fine. She just needs to rest, Ralf. Did everything get fixed at her place?"

"Yeah, everything is sorted and the *garbage* has been removed. Moose has passed that onto a specialist to deal with. There's a new door being fitted now, and they'll drop off the new keys once they've finished."

"Good. You can both go home. I'll be fine."

"Nope, we're staying. We said we would and we will."

"Fine, but you don't have to. I think he was working alone, and he's gone."

"'Think' being the operative word; we'll stay until we know for sure." Ralf turned and started back down, pausing. "If Miss Ariana wakes and needs anything, just let me know and I'll get it for her."

"I will, and thanks, Ralf; I appreciate the help tonight."

"No problem, and Moose said to tell you that your bike has been taken care of. You didn't leave the key and it was banged up a bit; he had it taken to your personal garage. He said you'd know where that is."

"Shit. I forgot about it and yeah, I'll work on it when I get the chance."

Lazarus closed the door, annoyed that his prized bike had slipped his mind and his men would be downstairs for the remainder of the night for no good reason. He could tell them to leave. Make up a reason. Lie. He was good at that, but he couldn't be bothered. Truth was he was tired. Not something he normally was; maybe it was all the worry about Ariana? Maybe it was... Fuck, it didn't matter what the hell it was, but the thought of having Ralf and Moose downstairs while he had a nap and Ariana was out cold brought him some kind of peace.

But when he returned to the bedroom, taking a seat in the armchair in the corner, he felt anything but peaceful when thoughts of what might've happened if he hadn't made it to Ariana in time ran rampant inside him. Or worse, his mind went into overdrive wondering if Ricus Bouer had anyone helping him and if they'd come after Ariana next. After all, what had he planned on doing once he'd killed her? Was he going to leave her body in her home for the cops to find? Or was he going to call someone to come help him dispose of her and clean up the mess?

Lazarus cursed to himself as he realized he should've questioned the man more, gotten more details before ending his life... but anger had gotten the better of him and he couldn't hold himself back from destroying him. Taking his life before he had the answers to the questions now running a damn marathon in his brain. The fucker seemed to have planned things well; surely, he'd have had things in place for afterward.

If the latter meant she was still in danger, mortal danger, Ariana could be in the sights of someone out for revenge. Someone who he wasn't aware of. Someone who could be worse than Bouer, more deadly and with an axe to grind. Especially if they realized their friend was dead. And they would. Anyone with two fucking brain cells would know he was going out on a *mission* such as this, and not returning? Yeah, they'd know he was gone and not on a damn vacation. They'd be certain their buddy was dead and they'd come looking for the reason: Ariana.

CHAPTER TWENTY-SIX

SHE'D NEED PROTECTION, until he was certain she was safe and there was no threat. Or until he'd dealt with anyone who surfaced and came after her. Lazarus' beast prowled restlessly inside him while he sat in the dim corner with thoughts of faceless men stalking the woman in his bed running through his head. His attention split between watching Ariana and deciding what course of action to take.

The fact he'd take action was already decided. His beast would give him no rest otherwise. It would drive him mad until it knew she was safe. *Yeah, right. Blame it on the beast.* He bunched his hands into fists, refusing to acknowledge anything else. Even to himself.

His head snapped up when he noticed a change in Ariana. Her breathing had evened out. He heard the unmistakable sound of bones healing while she lay immobile, with only a soft moan escaping her once or twice in the process before she lapsed into silence once again. He couldn't stop himself from leaning forward with his elbows on his knees, hoping she was on the verge of waking but she didn't. She remained silent and out cold as dawn broke. The shutters on the windows kept out the light, but he knew. Minutes turned into hours, with him watching her chest rising and falling beneath the covers.

He couldn't get her safety out of his head. It ran over and over in his mind. He'd have to watch her and guard her in case anyone came for her. It was him who had killed that fucker, so it was his responsibility. But he had businesses to run, and what if she saw him during the day? He didn't want to let that cat out of the bag, and Ariana was no fool. She'd be even more alert after this latest attack. Fuck. What could he do? Or rather, who could he use? Who could he trust? Who wouldn't she see?

Acelin Keeling. The Witch would be able to watch her when he couldn't, and he'd be able to protect her, using his magic if a threat appeared. Hell, he could even ask Acelin to use a protection spell on Ariana. It would cost him. But it would be worth it.

Decision made, he went in search of a laptop. Finding one in the living room and bringing it back to his room to fire it up, he sent the Witch a message that his services would be required once again. He told him what would be needed, but he didn't have a time and it would be at a moment's notice with payment commensurate for the inconvenience.

Lazarus left the machine on the floor beside him, then settled back into the chair, hoping to get some rest. Rest which refused to come.

Three hours later, his eyes hadn't left Ariana and he'd received one message from Moose, saying that her door was fixed and asking if he needed anything. His response was three words: thanks and no. Ariana continued her deep sleep while he watched over her. With each passing hour, he started to grow concerned. Had he given her enough of his blood to heal her or not? Did she have an underlying injury he hadn't picked up on? No. Impossible. He would've sensed it.

So why wasn't she awake?

Another four hours went by and Acelin replied with a figure, which wasn't as high as Lazarus had expected but was still above his normal rate. He paid immediately. Then he replied with his target: Ariana. Giving Acelin details that she might be in danger and to use any and all means necessary to keep her safe. The Witch replied instantly with one word: understood.

When Ariana turned over onto her side, Lazarus sat forward, eager to see her open her eyes, but she didn't. Instead, she curled a hand beneath her cheek and settled down into the pillow and remained sound asleep. Her breathing was different now though. It was more gentle and soft, as if she were napping and not unconscious and fighting to recover from serious injuries.

Lazarus lifted his head to inhale her scent, taking it in to process it fully for any changes giving her his blood might have done. Bam! It slapped him full in the face when her sweet aroma touched his nostrils, his mouth opening to taste her fully. Ariana's tantalizing fragrance had driven him insane from the moment he'd met her, but now? Now her bouquet was... was... divine in the extreme.

Whatever had happened over the last few hours had altered her, but it wasn't so much that she didn't smell like *her*... she did. But it was enhanced tenfold, and there was something else added to it, infinitesimal, something miniscule but that changed her heady perfume so it now called to him like nothing he'd ever encountered before. Lazarus felt himself being pulled forward from his seat, his body sat eagerly toward her, his tongue licking his lips in anticipation of... No.

He would not be drawn to her like a fucking newly turned Vampling. He refused to be weak. She would not control him. Nobody controlled him.

Lazarus slammed back into the chair, breathing raggedly in an attempt to control himself. The realization that his essence had changed Ariana crashing down on him like a ton of bricks. "What have I done?"

What you had to. His beast replied angrily.

Ariana would've died, but now he knew the price of her life. He'd have to fight the draw to her every damn day.

He could do it. He was Lazarus Báis; cold, hard, dangerous, and strong. Nobody would be the cause of weakness to him. Nobody, no human, and especially not a fucking woman. He'd work with her just long enough to find out who took Keena, and then that'd be the end of it. He'd send her on her merry way and limit any contact with her.

No! His beast snarled. "Yes!" he snarled right back.

He'd fight his beast. He'd fight this pull. He'd fight Ariana. He'd fight tooth and nail because he would not bow down to anything, or anyone, that would make him weak. Ever. Not ever again would he allow anything inside to cause him pain. Cause him to *feel*.

"What the hell? Where am I, and what the fuck am I wearing?"

Lazarus' head snapped to the bed where Ariana was sitting up, looking around. She looked... glorious. She didn't look injured, and she didn't look frail. In fact, she looked strong and pissed off as she glanced around the room, then down at the shirt she wore. His shirt. Fucking hell, she looked amazing in his bed, but it would be the one and only time he'd see her there so he remained silent and allowed himself this time to roam his eyes over her. Set this image in his brain, because it wouldn't happen again. She'd leave and they would never repeat this. He would not allow it.

Her chest heaved as she huffed out a breath, the material straining over her breasts while her fingers played with the expensive material. Ariana frowned, shaking her head before she lifted her eyes and looked around... and caught sight of him. "Hey, you enjoying the view? And why am I in your bed? I assume it's your bed, Lazarus, or are we somewhere else?"

She spat the words out like bullets. Her eyes full of fire as she sat back against the headboard. Lazarus stayed where he was, his face cold and aloof. "Indeed, it's my bed, Ariana."

"You better not have..." She stopped, her cheeks, which had been full of color just a moment before, suddenly paled. He knew that memories were coming back.

Bad memories. Ones he hoped might not return. But it

appeared they were and it was showing in her face, her body, as she started to shake, her hands, as they tightened on the covers, her eyes, as they widened and locked on his, and her lips, as she caught them between her teeth... to stop herself from crying out perhaps? And the scent of her fear seeped from every pore to engulf Lazarus. Soaking him in her utter terror and, before he knew what he was doing, he'd flashed to her side.

"You're safe, Ariana. You don't have to worry; you're safe."

He hadn't meant to move, and he hadn't meant to say a word... yet he had. Why? Why the fuck had he done that? She meant nothing to him. Nothing. She was a means to an end. Nothing more.

Her arms wrapped around herself and her eyes closed tightly. "It wasn't a dream. It happened. That fucker! What happened to him, Lazarus? Tell me what happened to him?"

Lazarus' arms moved to take her into them before he snatched them back a second before she opened her eyes. They were now full of anger as she glowered at him. "He won't bother you again, Ariana. I can promise you that."

"I see." Her chin jutted out. "I'm glad."

So few words for what he'd just told her; that he'd killed the man who'd attacked her.

"Why am I here?"

"Your place needed... fixing." Lazarus shrugged, not knowing a better way to explain. "I'm afraid I demolished your front door when I arrived, and my men needed time to sort things and clean up the *mess* I left behind. You were also injured so I brought you here."

"I see." She looked down at the shirt she was wearing. "And this?"

"Yours were... soiled." He pointed to the case that Ralf had brought. "There's some of your things in there."

"Fine." She frowned again, lifting her hands to her face and feeling everywhere, her nose especially. "What's going on, Lazarus? I broke this. I'm sure I did, so why is it okay now? How long have I been out? In fact, my entire face feels healed, and I know it was bashed against the wall hard enough to do damage. I thought my cheek was broken too. What the hell's happened?"

The moment had arrived. What would he tell her? The truth? Hell, no. But what? Lies obviously, but what?

Before he could say a thing, she started again. "I don't just feel okay. I feel wonderful. I feel better than that. I'm feeling fighting fit, Lazarus. Strong and, hell, I can't describe it but I think I could run a damn marathon right now, and that's just wrong. Not after what's happened. Tell me what you did. Right now."

Now was the time to decide, and he had to make it believable. Ariana was smart. He could compel her, of course he could. But where would the fun be in that?

"Magic." He looked her straight in the eyes and carried on. "You were more badly injured than you thought. You had a head injury, which would've required hospital treatment. If I took you to any hospital, well, we would've had to tell them what happened. That wasn't an option, not after I'd dealt with the cause of your injuries. So the only option open to me was using other means."

Her mouth fell open in shock. Her hands still roamed over her face, her fingers probing for signs of her injuries for long seconds before she replied, "Magic? Will I have any... I don't know... side effects or anything?"

"No. You'll be fine. As you say, you're fighting fit now. All you needed was rest afterward, and now that you've had that, you're perfectly okay."

All the while he'd sat next to her, the hypnotizing scent of her had been teasing him mercilessly. It had been invading him, mind, body, and fucking soul. He'd been fighting to stop his fangs from breaking through his gums, and he'd wanted to snatch her into his arms and rip his damn shirt from her to feast his eyes on her body beneath. See her breasts, which were heaving beneath, and see her flat muscled stomach that led down to...

"Lazarus... Lazarus... what's wrong with you?" She prodded his chest, breaking him free of what he was on the verge of doing.

He slid off the bed, marching to pick up his laptop then heading to the door. "I've got things to do. You can use the shower and, when you're ready, we can get back to work."

Ariana said something else as he left, but he didn't listen. Didn't stop. Because if he did, he wasn't sure what he would do. Her face, her body, her fucking delicious blood was driving him to the brink of insanity, and he needed to get some space between them before he lost it. Lost his self-control. Lost his damn mind. Lost himself completely to Ariana Harmon.

DarkHunter

CHAPTER TWENTY-SEVEN

Ariana stared open-mouthed after Lazarus as he stormed away, bemused and angry in equal measures. He'd ignored her when she'd asked what was wrong, and the way he'd been looking at her... Damn. It looked like he'd been about to eat her up... whole.

She shivered, her skin covered in goose-bumps, but she wasn't sure if it was fear or something else. The intensity in his eyes had been... unsettling, for sure. But something else too. Something that had her heart beating far too fast and her belly clenching in ways it hadn't done. Ever. Her thighs had clamped together, and she'd wondered what the hell was going on with her body's reaction to him. To his closeness, to his impossibly dark blue eyes, which appeared to darken even further while he was looking at her with that strange expression on his face, and then there was his hair.

What the hell had he been doing with that? It was gloriously dark, shiny, and usually perfectly in place, but just then? Nope. It had been shaggy and sticking out all over as if he'd been running his hands through it over and over. Then there was his clothes. Usually flawless, but just now? They were crumpled and dirty. She was certain there were blood stains on his shirt too. Definitely not what she expected to see. Had he been in that chair the entire time since they'd arrived? How many hours had that been? Ten, twelve, more? What time was it? Hell, she had no idea what day it was.

Had he been watching over her while she healed? While she lay asleep in his bed? Had he been worried about her?

No. That was ludicrous.

Ariana sank back into the lush bed. One she'd never felt so comfortable in. Damn it. Where did he get this thing? It felt like heaven, as if she were lying on a cloud. It was so soft, she didn't want to move... until a vision of Ricus Bouer sprang in front of her. She could smell his foul breath as it wafted over her cheek; she could feel his body as he pressed her against the wall so hard she couldn't draw a damn breath. Could feel her nose break as he slammed her head viciously, the pain lancing through her once again. Her hands shot up to cover her face as she scrambled from the bed. Her head swinging around frantically with terror and, before she knew it, she let out a scream.

Her hand shot to her mouth to stifle it. But it had slipped out before she could stop it. Her heart was thudding a cacophonous rhythm in her chest, and her breath was stuck in her throat. All the old fears she's fought for years to overcome had come tumbling back in, and, for a brief second, she'd allowed it. But she wouldn't allow it. No. She. Would. Not.

It was a second. Just a second. But that was all it took. The next thing she knew, she was snatched so fast her breath whooshed out of her lungs. Strong arms held her against a rock-hard chest, which she tried hard to break free from. She kicked wildly with all her strength, trying to free her arms so she could attack with everything she had. She would not go down without a fight. Never again would she allow that to happen.

"Ariana! Stop it. You're safe! *Ariana!*"

That voice... she knew it. Didn't she? It wasn't an enemy, was it?

The steely grip lessened and she took the opportunity to break free and attack. Her fists flying to hit... nothing.

"I'm over here," the voice said quietly. "I expected you to attack and I didn't want to have to restrain you again."

Her head whipped around the room to land on Lazarus Báis.

The Vampire stood in the corner of the room, staring at her with a strange look. His head cocked to the side and his eyes hooded with... what?

Ariana's heart still thudded like a train, and she fought to regain control of her breathing. She wasn't entirely sure what the hell was going on with him, but the way he was looking at her, as if he wanted to devour her whole, made her shiver.

"I'm fine." She wrapped her arms around herself to hide the fact her hands were shaking uncontrollably. Fine? She wasn't fine. Far from it. But she wouldn't admit that to anyone, and definitely not to *him*.

"You screamed. That doesn't sound fine to me."

He took a step toward her. One step, and she shuddered. Her entire body reacted to him, and she had no fucking idea why. Her skin suddenly felt hot, as if the temperature in the room had shot up, but she knew it hadn't. If Lazarus weren't standing right there, she would've ripped the shirt she was wearing clean off.

His lip curled up in a smirk. His eyes roamed over her from her face down, and then back up. Damn it! She felt as if he'd just undressed her with his eyes, and if she'd felt warm before, she now felt boiling hot. Beads of sweat appeared on the back of her neck and the top of her lip. She wanted to reach up and wipe them away, but she refused to move, unsure of what he would do if she did.

Why had that thought popped into her head?

He continued to watch her. His azure eyes now so dark they reminded her of the blueberries she'd eat at breakfast. They remained locked on her with such intensity that she wondered what was going on inside his head. What the hell was he thinking to have him look at her like that?

His brow rose, quirking as he swept his eyes over her in a long, slow regard. Her body reacted once again. Betraying her mercilessly when her nipples pebbled into hard peaks, pushing against the material of her bra. Her skin warmed further with a blush creeping up her throat. She had to end this. Now. Before... what? She didn't want to find out.

"Are you okay, Ariana? You look a little... flustered," Lazarus asked in a voice that dripped like warm chocolate.

Wait? What? What the hell?

He gave her another smirk. One that caused her to bristle with anger, and, even though she was *flustered*, she drew a deep breath in and straightened her shoulders. Shit. She shouldn't have done that. It caused her breasts to push forward and her nipples to chafe against the material of her bra even more. Damn it. Lazarus' smile widened further, which infuriated her even more.

"I'd like to get cleaned up. As you said earlier, we've got work to do," she said it as coldly as she could, but she heard the tremble in her voice, and so did he.

Lazarus' brow arched, his chin tipped up, and his eyes bored into hers. "Are you sure you're okay? I can stay here if you're nervous?"

"What? No, that's not necessary. I'll be fine," she blurted out straight away. The thought of him sitting here while she was naked, just a few feet away, had her sweating buckets. Ripples ran down her back, and her belly was doing somersaults. If she didn't get him out of the room soon, she was going to puke right in front of him. Her guts were in knots now. This little game he was playing was getting to her. And he was playing with her. No doubt about it.

"Okay, Ariana, but if you need me, I'll be close. Just call." He turned toward the open door, paused and looked over his shoulder. "As you just found out, I hear everything that goes on in the apartment and I'll be at your side instantly if you need me."

She couldn't answer. Her breath was caught in her throat

until he left, leaving the door wide open. She sprinted to it and shut it, leaning up against it with her breaths coming in short, sharp gasps, wondering what the hell had just happened.

Ariana didn't know. She had no idea but she felt... strange. Not quite herself. It had nothing to do with her mini panic attack either. That had rattled her, for sure it had, but it was more than that. She wasn't sure what the hell was going on with her, or Lazarus, but with each passing second, she calmed down, taking in long gulps of air until she felt better. And she realized that Lazarus had been right, they had work to do. The entire day had been lost, or more, she wasn't entirely sure how long she'd been out. A day where she should've been working on finding out what had happened to Keena.

Instead, she'd been here with *him* and he'd done... what? Magic. Or something else? What else? It must have been magic because she was healed. Her nose, her face; she had no broken bones, no bruises, and she felt strong. Definitely not like she should have after being beaten. And Lazarus had said she'd had other injuries, more severe, that required hospitalization. He wouldn't have lied about that. Would he? Of course he would. But why would he? There was no point in him lying about that.

So he'd had her injuries healed. She should be grateful. Instead, she was questioning him and his intentions. *He saved your life.* Yes, he did. And he killed the fucker responsible for hurting her. Why was she overthinking this? Why did she still doubt what he'd told her?

Because of the way he just looked at you. Because of the way you feel right now; your body doesn't feel right. Because everyone lies and you know it. Because you can't trust anyone. If you do, it could be fatal. Don't let anyone in, Ariana. Never let anyone in. It makes you weak. Weakness can kill you, Ariana. Don't be weak. Be strong; always be strong.

Ariana lifted her head, jutted her chin out, and nodded to

herself. She knew what she had to do. Focus on the job at hand, and then walk away. Get away from *him* and never look back. No matter what. It didn't matter that he caused her to *feel* for the first time since... that horrendous time in her life. Since *forever*. It didn't fucking *matter*. Nothing did, other than getting him out of her head. Out of her life.

Get your head back in the game, she thought, unbuttoning the shirt as she walked to the bathroom and picking up her suitcase on the way. *Do the job and walk away.*

Simple. No. But she'd do it because it was the only way to survive, and she *was* a survivor. She'd do what was necessary. She'd done it before, and she'd do it now.

Survive.

Then she'd do what she was supposed to have done before that bastard Bouer had interrupted her plans. Why she'd insisted on going home. She had something that needed finishing, and now she felt fine, back to normal. No. She felt better than that. Her body felt full of power and stronger somehow, but no matter. She had unfinished business to take care of: Evan fucking Smythson.

That low-life had a reckoning coming, and she was it. He'd gotten away from her once, but he wouldn't escape her again. She'd get him soon; tonight, if she had her way. She could work with Lazarus for a few hours and then slip away to finish the job she'd started. Evan Smythson would soon be in a world of hurt, and she'd be the one doling out the pain.

All she had to do was ensure the Vampire left her alone to do her job. Easy? Probably not, but she'd manage it. Somehow.

CHAPTER TWENTY-EIGHT

LAZARUS PROWLED AROUND THE APARTMENT, listening to every breath Ariana drew into her lungs, every step she took, and every damn thing she did.

He knew when she turned on the shower; the vision that brought to him almost sent him running back to the room to join her naked body under the cascading water. He could almost feel his fingers as they caressed her bare skin, her breasts, her nipples, the ones which had hardened earlier and caused her to blush like a fucking schoolgirl before him. He could sense her thoughts inside him now, and it was driving him mad. Although, he couldn't quite hear her, not like some he'd heard about. Earlier, in the room, he could certainly sense what she'd been thinking.

The draw to her had been stronger than ever. Pulling him and his beast like a fucking magnet. It had taken all of his willpower not to rush to her and drag her into his arms, crushing her to him and devouring her. He could almost taste her lips against his. Feel her skin against his. The touch of her breasts as they slid against his chest, her thighs opening to grant him access to her warmth... but he couldn't.

He saw in her eyes the fear. The spark of interest was there. She felt it too. The draw between them; the pull to him was just as strong. But he could feel something deep inside her that was undeniable, terror. Ariana was hiding something. Something that was locked up inside her. Hidden. Concealed. Buried. Lazarus could feel it, sense it, knew it was there, but what it was? That was still a mystery. He'd find out. He'd get to the bottom of it.

Ariana's secrets would not be kept from him. Not for much longer. Lazarus was certain of it. For now, though, he had to steel himself against the emotions attacking him. He had to stop himself from being weakened by the pull to Ariana Harmon; she was a distraction he couldn't afford. He would not allow any woman to have any kind of control over him. He'd never felt anything for anyone. Not since he was a child. Not since that fateful day when he retreated to the darkness. And he wasn't about to start now.

Ariana Harmon would not be the woman who would be his downfall, the one to distract him from his work, and the one to get under his skin. She would not.

His beast whined then snarled loudly inside him. Lazarus ignored it. He would not allow it to rule him. He refused to give it the power to lead him down a path that could weaken them.

"I'm ready." Ariana pulled him out of his inner argument.

She stood at the door, dressed in jeans and a jumper with her hair lying over her shoulder in a damp braid and her chin jutting out defiantly. Her entire body language was telling him she was ready to get to work, and she wanted to keep her distance. That was fine with him.

"Are you going to change?"

She waved a hand at him and he realized he was still wearing his blood-stained clothes. Blood from Bouer and Ariana. His shirt was wrinkled and he bet he looked a mess. "I'll be five minutes."

Lazarus used his Vampire speed to whisk away, leaving Ariana standing alone with her eyes wide and her hair flying up with the velocity of him passing by. It took him four minutes to have a shower, dress, and return to be by her side, dressed immaculately in one of his hand-made suits.

"Ready to see if your program has any results?"

She jumped, her hand shooting out to ward him off. "Jeez! Don't do that."

"Are you ready?" he asked again. Cold and distant. Refusing to allow her scent to affect him. That sweet and tantalizing aroma, which was already seeping inside him and causing him to lean toward her.

Lazarus turned away, striding to the door without saying another word. Ariana scrambling behind. "Of course, I'm ready. I'm the one who's been waiting on you."

"Let's get going then. We've got work to do." Lazarus was already out the door and half-way down the stairs while Ariana mumbled under her breath as she followed.

He kept going until he reached the door and met two massive guards, who moved aside to allow them outside. One remained in front, and one behind, as they led them to the back entrance of the club deeper inside the alley. Ariana glanced around nervously from one to the other before they reached the door where the guards secured their entry.

As soon as the door closed behind them, Ariana grabbed his arm, tugging him around. "What was that all about?"

"You're safety, of course. You were attacked last night, Ariana. Or did you forget that?"

Her face paled but two pink spots appeared high on her cheeks, showing her anger a second before her words did. "Of course, I didn't. You're an ass, Lazarus. But what are they for? Are you expecting trouble from someone I don't know about? Bouer was working alone. He was a coward, and he came alone. He wouldn't have the guts to involve anyone else. I don't know why you've got guards unless you know something you're not telling me."

The club was open and, by the sounds of it, it was busy. Voices, thudding feet dancing, and music booming, all added to the noises assaulting Lazarus' ears, but it was nothing compared to Ariana's heart, which beat just a few inches from him but sounded like it was hammering in his head. He could hear her blood as it gushed through her veins so fucking loud, he had to concentrate on the words coming from her luscious lips. Added to that was her smell, which was overpoweringly strong in the confines of the hallway.

Then there was her touch. Her fingers were still wrapped around his forearm; her skin separated from his by two layers of material. Two thin layers, which suddenly seemed to have disappeared because the skin beneath her touch felt as if it were on fire. Her fingers felt more like a caress setting his senses aflame, and Lazarus was finding it impossible to think straight. Not when all he wanted to do was pull her into his arms, walk her back up against the wall, kiss those lips that were just begging for him to nip them, and fuck her senseless right here and now.

Lazarus could see it all in his mind. Every last detail. The way her head would fall to the side as she gasped when he thrust himself against her, feeling the hardness contained within his pants. Her eyes widening with just a hint of fear when his fangs dropped from his gums to scrape along her collarbone while his knee edged her thighs open so he could press himself against her core...

"Lazarus! What the hell is wrong with you? I'm talking to you. At least give me the courtesy of answering."

Ariana tugged on his arm before she swiped it away to cross her arms and glare at him, her nostrils flaring and her eyes full of fire as she faced off with him.

Lazarus took several steps back, putting distance between them as he tried to remove the images that lingered inside him. Ones he was fighting against. Ones that were so vivid, he fought to ignore them and push them from his memory so he could string two fucking words together without snatching Ariana and acting on the visions he'd had.

"Well?" Ariana shook her head before she stomped around him. "Damn it, Lazarus, I don't have time for this. I don't need guards and we've got work to do. You can call off your dogs and let's go and see if we've got anything we can use to find Keena's killer."

His eyes dropped to her ass as he followed, but he kept his distance from her. He wasn't sure what had happened, but he didn't want a repeat performance. He'd almost lost control. Ariana was making him insane. Or more so since he'd given her his essence. Foolish. Stupid. Reckless. The one thing he'd vowed never to do and now he'd done it and was already feeling the consequences. Ariana Harmon had gotten under his skin from the start. Now? Now he couldn't get her out of his mind, and he could feel her, sense her, *wanted* her like he'd never felt before in his very long life.

Fuck, it was more than that. Lazarus could feel something growing inside him. Had felt it the second he'd passed his blood into her. The moment she'd drawn in her first ragged breath afterward, when her heart had started to beat and pump her changed plasma through her body. He'd sensed the change. Felt it deep inside him and experienced a pull toward her, which he'd been trying to ignore, attempting to force aside and struggling to overlook. And failing.

There was only one solution. He'd have to stay away from Ariana Harmon. Limit their time together as much as possible because if he didn't... he couldn't be responsible for his actions.

"Jesus, this place is heaving."

Ariana was attempting to push through the heaving bodies, but she was having a hard time of it. The club was packed, and she was making little headway. Lazarus grabbed her arm, tugging her behind him, and took the lead. With his strength, he made quick work of clearing a path and got them to the office quickly. Diego was at the end of the bar and gave them a wave and his customary smile before they disappeared inside.

"You must make a fortune with this place, not to mention your other clubs." Ariana went straight to the desk and opened her machine.

"They are profitable and I have several here, with others all over the country, but I also have clubs worldwide. I don't limit my business to this type of income, Ariana. I have other interests too, including property, tech, and others. Too many to mention. I keep track of them, but I also have business managers who do the day-to-day running of most of the companies."

"You're quite the mogul, aren't you?" She glanced over at him briefly before returning her attention to the screen.

A second later, he heard soft rumblings from her stomach, realizing he hadn't attended to her basic human requirements. What an oversight. She'd gone through hell and he hadn't even fed and watered her. She was human after all.

"I'll get you something to eat. What would you like?"

"What?" She stopped, looking surprised. "I'm fine."

"You need food. What do you prefer?"

"If you insist. Chicken salad..." She paused, her brow puckering. "No, wait, that's what I'd normally eat, but suddenly I'm in the mood for pizza. No idea why, but I'll have a chicken topped pizza with a Diet Coke please."

"Coming up." Lazarus left to get the order himself. It would give him some respite from being locked in the room with her and everything that was still going on inside him. Some fresh air and some time to think would do him well. He had to think about how to minimize his time with Ariana. He needed time to think about how to deal with the ramifications of what he'd done and how it was already affecting him.

More importantly, how it would, or could, affect Ariana.

Would she be different? Would she begin to be drawn to him too? And what about other changes? He already knew she was strong, resilient, and a fighter, but would she grow more powerful? Had he made her even more lethal? Hell, there was so many things to consider and he had so little time to do it. He was doing a fucking pizza run so he could figure this shit out and give him some breathing space.

What was next? Therapy?

DarkHunter

CHAPTER TWENTY-NINE

WHEN HE RETURNED, Ariana was still huddled over her machine with her fingers flying over the keyboard. She didn't appear to hear him enter and barely acknowledged him when he gave her the food, going so far as to open the box and pushing it toward her. She reached over, snagging a slice with one hand while she typed with the other, but she didn't say a word. He went to the bar and poured himself a drink, sat down, and watched her while she worked.

She appeared to be able to eat, drink, and type all at once. Quite a feat in his opinion. Occasionally, her braid fell in her way and she would flick it back over her shoulder, where it would stay for a while before she would lean forward too far and it would flop back over; only for her to flick it out of the way once again. He continued his observation as he thought on what he'd decided while he'd been waiting in the queue at the Pizza shop.

First was what she'd said about the fucker who'd attacked her. Had she been right? Was he working alone? If she were so certain about that, then she was safe from further attacks. But could he take that chance? He'd decided the answer was no. He'd have Acelin watch her when he wasn't available, and if no threat materialized, then he'd call him off. But he'd rather be prepared than regret it later.

His second decision was limiting his time with Ariana on a one-to-one basis. The pull to her had always been there. From the moment he'd first set eyes on her, but now it was worse and he would not allow anyone to have such an effect on him.

Especially a woman. It was a weakness he was not prepared to permit into his life. He would not tolerate it. He could not.

Lazarus lived a dangerous life with secrets. Having anyone around would be impractical and unworkable. He couldn't do his special *projects* with someone else in his private space, with ears there to listen in on calls, or, worse, with Ariana's skills, she'd be able to access his emails. The files he received held details of his targets over the dark web. Hell, she'd be able to crack those in no time if she decided she wanted to. Ariana Harmon was too dangerous. Plain and fucking simple. She'd be a danger to his security. She'd be able to get information on him, and do what she wanted with it. In short, she'd make him weak.

No matter that she was gorgeous. No matter that her blood literally called to him like a siren. No matter that he wanted her more than anything in his life. No matter that his beast craved her. No fucking matter.

He would not go there. The decision was made. His decision. His choice. His life.

So damn simple standing in a pizza parlor. Not so much when he was sitting ten fucking feet from her.

Not when her scent was once again invading his senses. Not when she tilted her head to stare at something on the screen and he got a clear view of the pale skin on her neck, just where he'd sink his fangs in to drink down that sweet blood. Not when she licked her lips after she'd swallowed a mouthful of pizza. Not when the tip of her finger reached up to catch a drop of cola when it escaped the straw she'd been sucking on. Not when she smiled at the screen like a kid on Christmas morning opening their presents.

Fuck it to hell and back. Lazarus was lost in a haze of emotions he'd never encountered before, but one of them rearing its head was one he knew well: anger. Anger that this puny female was affecting him like this. Anger that she could topple his self-control. Anger that she could have his cock hard as a rock and she didn't even know it. Anger that his heart was steam-rolling in his chest because she'd smiled at a fucking screen. Anger that her scent was imprinted in him and he knew, he fucking *knew* that he'd die if he never smelled it ever again.

That he needed it to survive. Needed her to live. Craved her more than the blood he drank to sustain himself. Needed Ariana Harmon to fucking *live*.

"Lazarus, I've found her... and the guy when they were leaving! Come here, quick! Come here!"

Ariana waved her hand at him, her eyes glued to the screen. He jumped up, rushing to her side. Sure enough, there was a picture of Keena with a young man at her side. He had his arm around her waist and she was smiling up at him, or rather, it looked like she was laughing. Laughing. The image brought a surge of fury to him as he stared at it because he knew the young woman had no clue the bastard was taking her to her death.

"Do you have anything else? We need something more with him so we can see who he is, Ariana. I need to know who he is, and can we see anything outside? Did they get into a vehicle or what?"

She stopped and turned to look at him, her brow arched. "Excuse me? Who do you think you're talking to? Don't use that tone with me, Lazarus. I'm not one of your lackeys who you can boss around. I damn well know what we need and I'm doing my best. I've trawled through hours and hours of images to source what I've got, and the answer to your question is yes. I've got more. So just back the hell up and let me show you."

Lazarus was sure he saw fire in her eyes before she whirled back to the screen, her fingers going to work, and before he knew it, pictures started to slide across in front of him. Starting with Keena and the mystery man dancing together, and ending with a grainy shot of them outside. He leaned forward, looking over her shoulder and stabbing a finger at the picture.

"Where is that?"

"It's outside the entrance, and it's the last shot I have of them together, but it looks like they're headed to that limo. I've got one more shot that doesn't have them in it, but it does have the license plate."

"Do you have one of them actually getting in?"

"No." She sighed, shaking her head. "The cameras facing that angle aren't the best and they don't run all the time. They only take images every ten seconds, which is more than enough time for them to get inside a vehicle. But look, the door is already open and they're walking toward it. Why would they be doing that if they weren't going to get in?"

Lazarus looked again and, true enough, the back door of the dark limo was indeed open. His keen eyes saw a dark interior but nothing else, not a hint of a clue that would help them. "But you got the license in another frame, didn't you?"

"I got a license plate of a similar vehicle. I can't say for certain it's this one. But it was taken just ten or so seconds after this shot so... what do you think? I'd say it's this one, but it wouldn't hold up in a court of law, or if we took it to the cops."

Maybe not. But it was enough for him. He'd find out where the damn vehicle came from and where it went with Keena inside. He also wanted to know who the fuck the guy was. He was a good looking guy, with blond hair and an easy smile, but the way he held himself and the muscles he had told Lazarus one very important fact. He was a Shifter. Powerful, strong, and a match for Keena. Just as he'd suspected.

"I need the plate number," he ground out, determined to get the details as quickly as possible.

"Lazarus, it's late. Not sure if you've noticed, but it's almost morning. I'm tired and I'm sure you'll need to go to bed soon too.

Why don't we meet up in a few hours and I'll get you the details you need. I promise you I can do that."

What did she just say? Almost morning? Lazarus realized there was no music blaring and no noise of dancers enjoying themselves either. Hell, he'd been so engrossed in watching her that he'd tuned out everything else... for hours. He never did that. Never allowed himself not to be aware of his surroundings... yet he had. And not just for a few minutes, but for hours. Yet, again, Ariana Harmon had caused him to act out of character. The only saving grace was that they were in a safe environment.

"So that's okay? We can wait until tomorrow evening to do this?" Ariana repeated, her words causing him to clench his teeth to stop him from snarling.

Was she mad? Wait? No way was he waiting. He could get the information he wanted in minutes and be out hunting within the hour. He had no intention of delaying any longer than he had to, and he was just about to tell her so in no uncertain terms.

Ariana reached over, her hand landing on his arm and her dark chocolate eyes locking with his, her voice soft and pleading, "We can get Ralf in on this, show him what we've found and you can go after them together. He deserves to do this with you, Lazarus. He's her father. He needs to do this. He has to do this. Please."

And before he knew what was happening, he nodded. "Okay, Ariana. I'll wait. But I have to send a quick email, then I'll drive you home."

"Hold on, you're not taking me back on that bike again. Are you?"

"No." He didn't tell her it was in the shop because of the previous night. "I'll drive you in a car, don't worry."

He sent Acelin an email alerting him he was dropping her at

home and he had to be there fast to stand guard until she was picked up again the next evening, then he waited for a response. Ariana closed down her machine, stretching herself out afterward. While he watched, he wondered why the hell he'd agreed to her request. A touch, a fucking touch of her hand and he'd caved. Another frisson of anger reared its head, but before it could take hold, Acelin's response arrived, telling him he was on his way and would be there in ten minutes. Just as well. If he'd said anything else, Lazarus would've exploded.

"Ready?" he asked.

Ariana yawned, rubbing her eyes. "Yeah. Don't be upset if I fall asleep though. I'm exhausted."

He hoped she did. He prayed she did. Maybe that way he'd be spared the agony of having her next to him in the confines of the car. Maybe then he wouldn't want to drag her to him. Maybe then he wouldn't want to tear her clothes from her body and sink deep inside her while he tore into her throat to finally taste that blood of hers, which had been teasing him from the first second he'd met her.

Maybe. Or maybe not.

CHAPTER THIRTY

WHEN THEY LEFT THE CLUB, they were met by Moose and Ralf; both of them standing guard by the back door. Damn it. He hadn't told them they were no longer required.

"Boss." Moose tipped his head while Ralf checked over Ariana with a keen eye.

"I'm taking Ariana home, but you won't be needed."

Moose tossed him a set of keys. "For the new door."

"I can stay outside if it's needed," Ralf added, looking at Ariana then back at him.

"It's fine, Ralf, but can you pick Ariana up at six thirty tomorrow night and bring her here? Then join us in my office."

"Is it about Keena?" Ralf straightened up, his body exerting energy and his face lighting up while hope shone in his eyes.

"Yes, Ariana's been working all night, but we should have some information we can use by then."

"I'll be there."

"If you need me, I'm available," Moose added.

"I won't know that until we get to the bottom of what we've found. I'll let you know." Lazarus handed off the new keys to Ariana. "Let's go."

He wanted to get the drive over and done with. He was feeling... unsettled wasn't quite the right word, but he couldn't think of another. Too many things had happened that had changed his ordered world in the last twenty-four hours, and he didn't like it. Not one damn bit. The way he felt about Ariana was growing out of control. Even before he'd been stupid enough to feed her some of his blood he'd been obsessing about her, but now? Now he seemed to be tied to her by some invisible rope, and it was making him mad as hell.

Lazarus cracked his neck as he stomped away to the vehicle he'd used the previous night, hoping that whatever it was between them would fade away if he kept his distance from her. He could do that. He would do that. He had to do that. Because he sure as hell would not have any woman getting under his skin, far less into his home, or anywhere else. He was strong and he could resist whatever was going on between them. He fucking would.

"What?" Ariana tapped his shoulder. "You fucking would what?"

He carried on walking. Ignoring her for a second or two before responding. Damn it. He couldn't believe he'd spoken aloud. But he had, so he needed to say something that made sense of his outburst. Luckily, they'd reached the car so he unlocked it and looked over to her. "I'll find the ones responsible for Keena."

Not saying anything else, he got in and started it up, hoping she'd let it lie. And she did. When she joined him, she whispered, "I know you will," before she fastened her belt and curled up against the door. In moments, her eyes slid shut and she was asleep.

Lazarus wasn't sure if it was better having her lying helpless mere inches from him while he drove, or having her awake and talking to him. The sound of her voice would drive him crazy, but the soft rise and fall of her chest as she slept was also making him nuts. There was no end to his torture with Miss Harmon. Whatever was inside her was his cross to bear, but he wasn't going to bear it much longer. He had to break free from whatever it was about her that was affecting him. Even before the added complication of his blood inside her. There'd been something about her that had drawn him to her.

The craving inside him was growing out of control. He wouldn't allow it. Couldn't allow it. *She's ours,* his beast growled. "No." He smacked the steering wheel, denying it, denying her, denying everything.

"Hmm, what?" Ariana mumbled, rubbing her eyes and turning to him. "Is something wrong?"

Shit. He'd woken her and now she was looking at him, tired and a little bedraggled. Her braid had broken free in places, with strands of her auburn hair sticking to the side of her face while others fell over her shoulder. He had a passing inkling to reach over and run the errant locks through his fingers, to feel the silkiness against his skin. Would it be as soft as it looked?

"Lazarus! Eyes on the road, please."

She pointed out the windshield, scowling over at him. Hells fire. She'd been awake for a few seconds and she'd distracted him again. When he looked away, he was relieved to see they were nearly at her place. Just a few more minutes and he'd be able to toss her out and be done with her. For a few hours anyway.

"I'll be ready for Ralf, and I promise I won't talk about what we've already found."

"What?" he tuned back in.

"I said I won't tell him what we've already found out when Ralf picks me up."

"No, don't," he snapped.

Ariana let out a long sigh before she turned away from him. Her foot tapped furiously but she remained silent for the next few minutes. That was all it took to arrive at her house. Lazarus barely managed to keep his own sigh of relief inside when he pulled to a stop and Ariana jumped out quickly.

"I hope you're in a better mood tomorrow." She slammed the door before he had a chance to say anything.

Then again, he wasn't going to reply. He'd already shoved

the gears into reverse and was just waiting on her getting out of the way before he made his escape.

He'd hoped once she was gone, once he was alone without her scent to tease him, that he'd feel better. Feel more at ease. But he didn't. The drive home was anything but peaceful. His skin felt like it was on fire. His insides churned furiously as if he had some kind of stomach bug. A long ago memory of his childhood sprang to mind when he'd been ill and he'd puked for two days straight; his belly ached and he'd felt like his insides were rolling around like a nearby whirlpool. That was how he was feeling. But he didn't get ill. He was a Vampire and hadn't been sick a day, an hour, since being turned. So what the fuck was going on?

Maybe he needed to feed. He'd been injured after the fiasco with Raylon Barnes. What if he hadn't ate enough to heal properly?

"Aye, that's it," he mumbled as he parked behind Monarch, deciding to stay there. It was closer than his other places, and it was equipped with everything he needed, including donor blood.

He'd feed and rest. That's all he required. After that, he'd be all right.

Only he wasn't. The blood tasted off even though it was the finest and rarest types. He forced several bags down but didn't enjoy them, not one drop, and he had to chase them with his favorite whisky just to rid him of the sour aftertaste that lingered. Then he attempted to rest, and that didn't go well either because Ariana had been in the fucking bed; her smell was all over the sheets.

He'd tossed and turned until he'd given up and tore the sheets from the bed, leaving them in a heap in the corner and spending the next few hours prowling the apartment in a foul mood. Checking in with Acelin, everything was fine, with no sign of anyone being there. He'd placed a protection spell around the property, and also one that would take effect on Ariana when she left. It would attack anyone with any ill intentions against her. In effect, it would stop them in their tracks. Acelin told him it would keep her safe from anyone, or any*thing,* that tried to harm her, and it would remain for a period of three days. If he wanted it for longer, then he could re-erect it.

Satisfied that Ariana would be okay, Lazarus spent the rest of the night catching up with work. Everything from boring paperwork to online-meetings; even firing the head of one of his companies in Australia, who dared to question him on some improvements he wanted to implement. His second-in command got the promotion of his life right there in the conference call when Lazarus asked his opinion on his suggestions just prior to his sacking his boss. When the guy told him he agreed that what Lazarus had suggested would enhance development of their new prototype while his boss had tried to shut him up, Lazarus had blown his top and told him he was out of a job and his assistant was promoted.

He'd picked the wrong time to argue with him. Not that any time was the right time. The guy had been relatively new to the company, and he'd found out the hard way that Lazarus wasn't just a name behind his companies. He knew what the hell he was talking about, and you didn't fuck with him. "Okay, I'll leave this in your hands. Run with it and get those implemented. I'll expect an update on how things are going within the month."

"Of course, sir, and thank you. I won't let you down."

Lazarus knew the young man wouldn't. He'd just given him the chance of a lifetime.

After that, he finished off the mountain of emails he had and, before he knew it, the sun had disappeared and it was nearly time to meet Ariana once again. He showered and dressed in dark jeans, a black shirt, and a leather jacket, before returning to his office in the club, which was coming to life again with Dian giving out orders for the evening to several members of staff as he walked quickly by.

When he saw Ariana's laptop sitting on his desk, he couldn't resist opening it. When it powered up, he wasn't surprised to see it was password protected, and he was in no doubt that she would have it well safeguarded. No chance for him to get into it easily, and if he did, she would know about it. Not that he'd care if she did. But she and Ralf would be here soon, so it wasn't worth it for the sake of saving a few minutes. Closing it down again, he poured himself a drink and took up a position on the sofa.

Lazarus heard her long before she arrived. Her footsteps unique, and ones he'd know anywhere even when she wasn't wearing those fuck-me heels that click-clacked on the floor. His heart stuttered, just for a moment, before settling back down.

She arrived with Ralf right behind her. She walked in without knocking, her hair loose and flowing down her back, stopping just above her waist; it was like a cascading wave of dark chocolate with highlights of gold weaved through it. Then she looked over and shot him a smile, which would've lit up the darkest night. The darkest heart. The darkest damn soul, and Lazarus knew he was lost.

"Hi." She lowered her eyes, her thick lashes hovering around those eyes that were glorious, deep, and so fucking sexy.

Eyes... sexy? What the hell was he thinking?

"Good evening, Ariana. I hope you had a good night's sleep."

He stood up and went to her. How could he not?

"I did, thank you. And you?"

She moved slowly to the desk, but her eyes stayed on him. "I was working for most of the time. I had a lot to catch up on."

"You should've rested too." She tilted her head, frowning. "You look tired."

Did he? And why was she worried about him? Was she worried about him, or was she just making small-talk? And why the fuck did it matter?

"Let's get started." He glanced over at Ralf. "We've got work to do, and we should catch Ralf up on what we've got already."

Ralf surged forward, his hulking body moving with the ease of a Wolf and the speed of his kind. "What? You've already got information about Keena?"

He shot Ariana an accusing look, which she completely ignored while she logged into her machine, leaving him to explain.

"We don't have firm information yet, just images, but we're hoping to get something tonight that we can act on."

Ralf's jaw ticked, his chest heaved, and he looked like he was ready to explode. Lazarus couldn't blame him. Not really. His daughter had been abducted from the club he owned and had been killed. Hell, he'd be fucking furious. Nobody would've been able to stop him going ballistic if it were him.

"Okay, can you fill me in?"

Ariana turned to look up at Ralf, her eyes full of sadness and her voice soft, "This might be hard to look at, but it's images of Keena and the guy she left with on that night. It takes them right up to when they left. I've opened them up and you can scroll through to the end, Ralf. When you're ready, just let me know because then I need to do something to try to find out who took her. Okay?"

Ralf gulped before nodding, but he didn't say anything before Ariana made way for him. She left Ralf alone at the desk to scroll through the pictures of his daughter on the last night he'd seen her alive.

With one arm wrapped across her front, and the other

reaching up so she could nibble the skin on the edge of her fingernail, Ariana stood watching as the massive Wolf pored over the images she'd found of the only person Ralf had left. Of the daughter he'd loved. Of the girl he'd brought up and who had been taken from him. Had been ripped away from him by the guy she was smiling with, laughing with, dancing with... left with.

A growl echoed around the room. Ariana stepped back, away from Ralf. Lazarus placed a hand on her back. "It's okay," he whispered. "He's upset but he won't harm you."

"I know that," she shot back over her shoulder.

But her body betrayed her. She shivered when Ralf's beast whined with despair, followed by another snarl of anger. His head shook and his shoulders followed before he shot up, turning to them.

"Who is this fucker? I want his blood. I want his heart in my hands. I want to kill him and make him suffer. I have to for my Keena. I have to avenge her. She was my baby. The last of our line."

"We don't have a name but we have the vehicle they left in." Lazarus stepped forward. "Ariana managed to get the license plate, and that's what we're going to get tonight. She says she can find the owner's details and when she does, you and I are going hunting, Ralf."

Ralf lifted his head, looking down at him with grim determination. "Indeed we are. That guy won't know what's hit him."

"Right. Ariana, you're up."

Ariana gave a curt nod before stepping around Ralf's hulk to take her place at the desk. She cracked her knuckles, looking up at them. "Give me a little time and I'll have what you need."

"How?" Ralf screwed his eyes, looking doubtful.

"That… I can't tell you. I can give you a name and, hopefully, an address, but I won't tell you how I do that."

Ralf gave her a smirk and tapped his nose. "Okay, little lady. We all have secrets."

Lazarus barely held himself in check. Secrets. Yeah, Ariana had those in spades. Ralf didn't know the half of it. Getting them a damn name and address was the tip of the iceberg.

It took her only a few minutes, with Ralf pacing back and forth, before Ariana said, "Got it."

Ralf rushed back to her side, eagerly waiting for her to carry on. "Well?"

"It's a strange name. I've never read anything like this before… maybe it's foreign?" Ariana turned to them. "Tanith Kiden, but I can't get an address. No matter what I've done, there is nothing coming up. I'm sorry. I just can't get anything on this person. Shit, I don't even know if that's a man or a woman. There's something strange going on because with what I have, I can usually get more, even a copy of a driving license, but this time? Nothing."

Lazarus cursed and his heart sank. "Fuck."

"I said I'm sorry, Lazarus. I've tried every trick I have and, trust me, I have more than most in my arsenal. I'm telling you I can't get anything else. Just this name. Maybe if I work some more, I'll be able to get you more."

He realized she thought he was swearing at her. He wasn't. "That wasn't aimed at you. It was hearing her name."

"It's a she? Is she foreign?" Ariana asked.

Ralf looked between them, angry and confused.

"Yes and yes, but it's worse than that. I'm sorry, Ralf, but we're going nowhere tonight."

"What? Of course we are. You know her, right? We can find out where she is and go get answers from her. Find out who this guy is. We can still do that."

Lazarus heard the desperation in Ralf's voice, saw it in his face, in his eyes, but there was nothing he could do. Not tonight. Not unless they had a fucking army with them.

"No, we can't. Tanith is a Vampire, and she's a powerful one, with a small army around her. We wouldn't get anywhere near her, Ralf, and that's if we could get an address. There's obviously something more going on here than we first thought. We can't just go tearing up to her and hope for the best because the best wouldn't happen. Trust me on that. I've met her and she's a cold, hard, and dangerous bitch. We need to regroup, rethink, and find out what the fuck is going on. I promise you, Ralf, we will find out. I promised you that before, and I've not changed that. It just won't be tonight."

Tanith Kiden, here in his town and he didn't know about it. That fucking bitch. Dangerous, deadly, and with a heart as cold as ice. What was she up to? Nothing good, that was for damn sure. He had to find out what because wherever Tanith went, death and destruction followed.

CHAPTER THIRTY-ONE

"**W**HEN?" Ralf was furious, his face bright red as he spat out, "I don't know how long I can last before I hunt her down, Lazarus. My Wolf is begging for vengeance, and now I have a name; I'm not sure I'll be able to stop myself."

Lazarus was well aware of how Shifters reacted to these situations. A family member being murdered wasn't something they could sit back and take. He was certain Ralf would be fighting every instinct to go after Tanith. But he couldn't allow that. The man would be slaughtered if he did. That was an absolute certainty.

"You can't. I'm telling you straight that she has an army surrounding her. You won't get near her and you'll never get that guy's name, Ralf. You won't get Keena's killer. It would be futile to attempt it."

He had to stop the Shifter from attempting this. It was his responsibility. He'd started by promising to look into this, and now he'd teased him by passing on Tanith's name.

"I'm not saying we won't take this farther. We will. I'm saying we have to be careful how we do it. Leave this with me until I look into what she's doing here. Whatever it is will be dangerous and unlawful, that's a certainty, but I have resources I can call on to get me information. When I have that, then we can discuss how to proceed, but, for now, you have to trust me."

"Could I help?" Ariana asked quietly.

"Absolutely not." His head spun to her, his answer immediate and sharp. "You stay away from this. These are dangerous Supernatural beings you don't want to mess with. You don't look into this, Ariana. I've got my own people I can use.

You cannot, under any circumstances, have anything else to do with this."

Ralf backed him up. "He's right. It's too dangerous."

"Fine," she snarked. "I'll stay out of it."

The way she looked at him didn't make him feel like she meant it though, and that gave him a sick feeling in his gut. The thought of Ariana and Tanith within ten miles of each other caused a cold sweat to break out all over him. Shit. A fleeting thought of getting her out of town ran through his mind. Maybe he could get her out of the way until he figured out what the hell was going on. Or until he'd dealt with Tanith fucking Kiden.

"For the time being, everything is left up to me. Plain and simple. Ralf, can you let Moose know you'll be taking Ariana home, then go get the car parked out back and pick her up at the front."

"Sure, I'll be there in five."

Lazarus tossed him the keys and he left them alone. Ariana turned to him and shrugged. "If you need me, you know where I am."

"Of course, and I'll be in touch when this is over with about your program, if you're interested in working with my company on that. We can discuss it after all this has been dealt with."

"I'll see what terms you come up with, and that also gives me time to fine tune some bugs that showed up while I was using it here. But yeah, we can talk."

She gave him another smile, her plump lips lifting and her eyes lighting up. Lazarus felt the sun's rays shining down upon him exactly as he had that very first time he'd stepped out willingly as a daywalker. The feeling was so overpoweringly intense, he couldn't help but step toward her, to the light that called to him, closing the distance between them until he stood right before her.

Ariana's heart had sped up with each step he took, but he

couldn't stop himself. He knew she wasn't afraid. Not really. It wasn't fear that caused the staccato drum to beat inside her, and he was proven right when she popped up on her tiptoes and placed a quick kiss on his lips. It was the last thing he expected Ariana to do, and going by her surprised expression, she was just as shocked by her actions. Her hand shot to her mouth as she stepped back, tripping over her own feet as she backtracked to the door, but he couldn't forget the touch of her skin on his.

It was... magical. And horrific... because now he'd tasted her. Sampled her sweet mouth, her unique and wonderful flavor that was her, that was Ariana. He doubted he would be satisfied with just a hint of a caress of her mouth against his. He wanted to plunder her lips, her tongue, her entire being until she was completely his and only his.

"I'm sorry. I shouldn't have done that." Ariana turned and sped from the room, leaving him alone with his hand playing across his mouth where he could still feel the brief caress that had changed everything.

Lazarus was still there when Moose arrived a few moments later.

"Can I talk with you?"

"About?" Lazarus turned away, forcing Ariana from his mind.

"Ariana Harmon."

Damn. Looked like the universe wasn't playing ball.

"What about her?"

"When I was at her place the other night, I had a look around." Moose shrugged. "Sorry, but it's my nature to be thorough, and what I found was surprising."

Moose was a man of few words. Usually. For him to come to talk like this was unlike him. It was unusual. "Surprising in what way?"

"I couldn't get into any of her technical stuff, that isn't unusual as she's in the business and everything was protected, but the things I found around her home was unusual. She has weapons, boss, everywhere. She has them hidden in spots easily accessible for her to get to, in every room, and she has them in her bedroom too; some at her bedside table, and I even found a dagger beneath her pillow."

Lazarus had walked to the bar, ready to pour a drink, but on hearing this, he whirled around. "Weapons. How many and what type?"

Moose reached up, scratching his head. "A lot, too many to count, and there's a variety. She has a liking for blades, in all shapes and sizes. Daggers and throwing knives, she also has those stick things that are used in martial arts, kali or something, but they were worn and obviously used a lot. They weren't just for show. She has weapons in every room, in multiple places in the rooms, for easy access. In my opinion, it looks like she was scared of an attack and was trying to defend herself."

"It would appear so." Lazarus tried to digest the information, but as he did, his stomach felt like it was on fire. His belly clenched and a cold fury engulfed him.

Who was she scared of? Who had scared her so much that she'd bought an arsenal to equip her home like that? What had happened to her to make her like this? He'd seen snatches of that fear, seen her quiver and shake with it, but he didn't know why. He hadn't been able to find out what the fuck it was about.

"Thanks, Moose; I appreciate the information. I've got someone watching out for her and I'll keep that ongoing just in case there's any further threat."

"Just thought you should know." Moose turned and made to leave, pausing at the door. "She must be real scared to live like that. I've never seen so many weapons in a house before. She even had them in the bathroom. Who has weapons hidden in a bathroom?"

"Someone who's got reason to be terrified of something," Lazarus whispered, wondering what the hell Ariana was hiding, and how he could find out what it was.

First, he had Tanith Kiden to deal with, and he had to make a start on that. He knew where to go for starters and dialed his FBI contact, and friend. "Clive, I need you to check up on someone for me, and I'd appreciate if you could do it as quickly as possible."

"Hello to you too, Lazarus." Clive sighed.

"Sorry, but I've a lot on my plate. Can you help me?"

"If I can. What's the name?"

"It's another Vampire who I've just found out is here. She's dangerous, her name is Tanith Kiden. I need anything you have on her, including addresses, businesses, vehicles registered to her, her employees, everything, Clive."

"Damn, Laz, you sound worried. Does that mean I should be too?"

Lazarus thought about Tanith and the last time he'd seen her. She was stunningly beautiful but cold as ice. When Lazarus had rebuffed her at a charity ball and gone on to dance with another young woman, Tanith hadn't liked it. Although, Lazarus didn't know the girl well, or have any feelings for her, Tanith had sought her out and had ripped her throat out for pure spite and nothing else.

"Yes, I am worried. Everything about Tanith worries me. She's a deadly bitch with no heart who will kill with no thought. So, yeah, you and anyone else in the city she turns up in should be worried."

"Fuck, just when I was thinking of taking a vacation."

Clive taking a vacation? Yeah, right. Lazarus had known the man for decades, and he'd never known him to take more than a couple of days off at a time.

"What? You planning on cruising around the world or what?"

"I was going to ask you for some recommendations. You've been just about everywhere over your life. Hell, I might even go to Scotland. Your homeland is on my bucket list and I've got to get started on it or I'll never do anything before I go to the big guy in the sky."

Scotland. The Highlands... his home. He'd left centuries ago and didn't even have an accent now. He only went back when there was a *case* to be worked. Never for pleasure. And he'd never returned to the place where his family lived; although, that was long gone, the remnants of their village a distant memory in a valley grown over by grass and heather. He could never return there. It would be the end of him if he did. Too many memories. Too much darkness. Too much evil. Too much pain.

"I'll get you the tickets. First class," Lazarus heard himself say. "Stay in Edinburgh and Glasgow, then go up to the Highlands. Do a tour all over... on me. Book the time off, Clive, and give me the dates. I'll set it up."

Silence. For long seconds there was silence before Clive whispered, "What? Are you sure? I was only joking, Lazarus. I've never asked you for anything, and I wasn't really asking; you know that, don't you?"

Lazarus did know that. Clive Parnell, FBI Special Agent, had never asked him for a damn cent. Not in all the years he'd known him. Not one. And he'd struggled over the years. Lazarus knew that too, and he'd offered more than once to help him out, but Clive had cursed at him and refused. Said his payment was what he did by taking out the fuckers he couldn't. That was all the payment he needed, not his money.

He'd watched his friend get grey hair and wrinkles; he'd seen him rub his shoulder where he'd been shot, it now aching when it was cold or damp. He saw him limp in the winter because of the arthritis he was getting in his left knee, but he refused to tell him about it or moan. Yeah, he knew though. The man never asked him for anything... except to deal with the special files he sent him.

And those were Lazarus' salvation. It was a pleasure to deal with those. They helped him more than they helped Clive. If he didn't do those, his beast would be unleashed and he'd wreak bloody havoc and lose control. So yeah, he owed the man, and it was time he paid up.

"I do know that, Clive. You didn't ask but I'm doing this. You deserve a fucking holiday, so just shut up and take it... but not until you've given me the information I need on Tanith. Okay?"

"I don't know what to say except hell yes. I'll get on this straight away, and I'm typing up my vacation letter now. I'll be in touch as soon as I have anything for you."

"Thanks. Just email me when you have something and let me know the dates. I'll get your trip organized for you."

"Deal."

He hung up and sat back, hoping Clive would be able to get him something on Tanith he could work with. Then he'd have to put a team together to deal with whatever she was up to. That she was up to something wasn't in question. She was always up to something. It was just a matter of what and how bad.

When his phone rang, he was surprised to see Acelin's number appear. The Witch rarely changed protocol of contact outside the dark web. "What?"

"I think you should get out here. Ariana is going out again, and I think she's planning on doing something she shouldn't."

"Like what?"

"I can listen in on her with the spell I have up. And don't get all upset about that, but I need to know she's not up to anything she shouldn't be. Just as well because she's been acting weird since she was dropped off."

Lazarus' blood started to boil at the thought of the Witch listening in on Ariana, but he didn't have time to deal with that at the moment. "I am upset, but what the fuck does acting weird mean?"

"She talks aloud a lot. I mean, we all do that sometimes, but she does it a lot, and she's been doing it since she got back. I won't mention the kiss you two had, but she's been mentioning a guy who, apparently, she says got away with something before and now she says it's time for him to pay because she says she's feeling fighting fit and ready to take him on. His name is..."

"Evan Smythson," Lazarus interrupted. "Fuck! I'm right, aren't I?"

"Yeah, how the hell did you know that?" Acelin asked. "Shit, she's just got into a cab and taken off. I have no idea where she's gone, Lazarus. I can follow, but my car is around the corner and, at this time of night, it's going to be hard to keep up with her."

"Follow and don't lose her. Tell me where she gets out and I'll get there as fast as I can, but I think I know where she's going. I've already got this guy's details. I think she's going to his place."

"Okay, I'm heading to my car now. She's changed clothes. She's dressed all in black and looks ready for battle."

"I bet she does." Lazarus shook his head, picturing Ariana the first night they'd met.

She'd been ready for battle that night too, and it had been Evan Smythson she'd been after then. She'd cut his friend that evening, but if his pal hadn't been there, surprising her, he was sure she would've done Smythson some serious damage. Was that what she was planning now? Would she be surprised again? Would Smythson get the upper hand again and hurt her?

Or would Ariana exact the revenge she was obviously seeking on the scumbag?

Either way, he was going to intercept her. He couldn't allow her to put herself in danger like that. Smythson was twice her size and could easily overpower her, and the last time she'd went up against him, she'd ended up battered, bruised, and running for her life.

Dark Hunter

CHAPTER THIRTY-TWO

ARIANA HAD MADE the decision on the ride home. Tonight was the night Evan Smythson paid for his crimes against the women he'd abused.

He'd gotten away the last time, but no longer.

Whatever magic Lazarus had used to heal her had worked wonders. She felt stronger than she ever had. There was no reason to wait. She'd checked out the ass's social media to find out where he was; he was on there all the time posting pictures so it was easy to follow him. He made it so simple, it was laughable. Decision made, she'd perked up and tried not to think of the kiss between her and Lazarus.

Why had she done that? Why was she drawn to him? He wasn't her type whatsoever. Then again, no man was. No man ever had been. Not since... well, she didn't want to think of that. She never thought of that.

But kissing Lazarus? That had felt good. Better than good; it had felt amazing. But bad too, because it made her feel things she didn't want to. Never wanted to. She couldn't go there. Ever.

When Ralf dropped her off, he'd asked if she were all right. She'd avoided the question, asking instead if he'd let her know if they found Keena's killer. That sobered him right up, and he did say he would. She hoped he did. He deserved to know what happened, and he should be able to face whoever ended his daughter's life. No court could dole out justice for something like that. Only a father could. A father like Ralf.

She talked to herself as she got ready, finding Evan easily within minutes. He was in a bar just down the street from his apartment, drinking and having a good laugh with a couple of friends. They had several young women in their company too. Targets in her eyes. They just didn't know it yet.

"Not tonight," she swore, shoving daggers into the side of her knee-high boots. "Not when I'm coming for you, Evan Smythson."

Deciding on getting a cab to a nearby store, she'd then cut through to the adjoining street and down to the bar where she'd sit in a dark corner and wait. She knew it would only be a matter of time before Smythson would make his move. She'd done her homework on him long ago and knew he didn't wait for the end of the night. He was too impatient for that. His modus operandi was slipping a date-rape drug into a drink then taking the girl either to his apartment or out into a dark alley.

Either way, she'd be waiting and he would not get away with it this time. This time, he'd end up with no fucking dick to do any further damage to anyone. Energy buzzing through her, she almost gave up on the cab, but it arrived just before she decided to run instead. Getting in and relaxing into the seat, she couldn't wait to end Smythson's reign of terror.

Arriving at the bar, she heard him as soon as she entered; his laughter loud and brash as she took up a position in a dark corner near the door. Ordering a soda, she kept her eyes on the group of four men and five women, one of which he had his arm around, tugging into his side and whispering into her ear. The young woman shook her head and he laughed again, ordering another round of drinks while the girl, and two others, got up to head to the bathrooms.

Ariana strained her neck, watching, and saw him reach into his pocket. Yeah, here it is. And she was right. As soon as he could, when nobody was watching, he popped something into the drink where the girl was sitting. Fuck. Even though she knew he did it, knew it was coming, it still shocked her to see how easy it was for him to do with people all around, and others still sitting at the damn table.

"Won't be long now," she whispered, knowing the drug was fast acting. He'd act before it incapacitated her fully and her friends could react.

She was right. It was only a short time afterward that he rose, holding his hand out to the woman and pointing to the dancefloor. She giggled and got up, but they danced for a minute or two only before he headed to a hallway, which led to the bathrooms. Ariana suspected there was a door that also took them outside to the alley.

She got up and followed, just in time to see him pull the girl out a door propped open at the back. The young woman was now staggering and not putting up much of a fight at all. She was more than likely not even aware of where she was, or who she was with, the drug now careening through her system. She was at Smythson's mercy. Ariana's anger boiled through her at the sight, her feet flying along the corridor until she skidded to a stop at the darkened door. She bent down to pull her daggers out, stuck her head out, checked the coast was clear, and slid out into the blackness.

"That's it baby. You know you want to; open up and take my cock inside. Suck it nice and good."

Smythson stood off to the side, beside a huge garbage container, with the girl on her knees in front of him, his cock out and forcing it into her mouth. His hand tangled in her hair as he pushed her head onto him. She looked confused, with her hands on his thighs as if she wasn't sure where she was or how she ended up here, far less who the guy was or whose dick she was sucking.

"Come on, you can do better than that." Smythson tugged her hard, and one of her hands lifted to slap on his leg. "No!

Now you don't do that. You suck my cock or things will get ugly, bitch."

Ariana saw his hand lift, ready to connect with the girl's cheek, and she'd seen enough. She felt sick to her stomach, hatred boiled to the surface, and she stepped out to confront him. "Let her go, you sick fuck."

"What? Who the fuck is there?"

He released the girl and she fell to her hands and knees, crying. Ariana didn't waste any time. She was aware each second was precious. "Get inside now. Go!"

She scrambled like a crab toward the door only yards away, but she was so slow that Ariana had to hurry her up before Smythson reacted.

"Now! You have to move faster than that!"

Finally, her fight or flight system kicked in and she scrabbled toward the door much quicker as Smythson stepped out. "What the... you! You mad bitch. What are you doing here?"

Ariana cracked her neck, stalking toward him. "I'm here to finish the job, asshole."

"She's in a bar not far from Monarch, I've got the address," Acelin whispered quickly. "No idea how I didn't lose that cab, but I didn't. Anyway, she's sitting in the corner of a bar and she looks like she's watching a group in there. What do you want me to do?"

"Nothing. I'll take it from here. I'm up the street from you. I'll be there in a couple of minutes." Lazarus knew the place and was certain when he got there that one of the people involved would be Evan Smythson.

When he arrived, he could sense her immediately. She was angry but also excited. She was less than six feet from him, sitting on the other side of the wall from where he was standing on the street. Should he go in and chance being seen, or wait to see what happened?

As luck would have it, a large group of college kids arrived and he joined them as they entered. His eyes found her as soon as he crossed the damn threshold, but she didn't even look their way; she was so intent on her target. He was right. It was Evan Smythson she was staring at from her vantage point in the darkened corner. It was a good spot too. Nobody could actually see her unless they went right up to her table, and only then if they had good eyesight.

He doubted Smythson knew she was there, and she didn't know he was there watching her either. Lazarus moved to the opposite side of the bar and sat down to watch how things played out. He was interested to see what she was planning. She couldn't exactly launch herself at the guy in front of everyone, so she was safe for the moment.

Lazarus' eyes swung between Ariana and the thug, Evan Smythson. Her focus on him was so intent he almost missed it when it grew in intensity. Almost. But her heart rate alerted him to something wrong and his eyes swung just in time to see the fucker release something into the glass of the girl who had been sitting next to him. Damn him to hell. He'd drugged the drink, and Ariana had been expecting it.

He saw it in the way her body sank back, her shoulders dropped, and her head did a little dip as if she'd nodded to herself. She knew the guy was going to do it, but now what? What was she waiting for now?

What happened next had the blood in his veins turning to ice. The girl returned to sip from her drink and shortly afterward Smythson took her to the dancefloor, then rerouted her toward a dark hall... with Ariana on their tail. Lazarus took off out the front door and headed toward the alley out the back, knowing he'd find all three there, and he was right. The scene he found sickening, disgusting, and terrifying, in equal measures.

Smythson abused the girl, and Ariana saved her, with the young woman scurrying on her hands and knees back toward the bar.

"I'm here to finish the job, asshole." Ariana faced off with Smythson. Her voice hard as steel.

Lazarus saw the two daggers she held at her side as the hulking thug emerged to face her. "You're nuts."

"I'm not disputing that. I've been called worse. But you've done this for the last time, and I'm here to put an end to it."

Lazarus was about to call out, to stop her, but he didn't get the chance. Ariana flew toward her foe without another word, her feet flying across the distance and surprising both him and Smythson, who held out his fists to ward her off.

She was beautifully defiant in the face of the giant before her. Her movements gracefully lethal as she went in low, and not where Smythson expected her to attack. The moonlight glinted off her daggers' as the first one struck. Her victim shrieked in agony, his arm coming down to land a crushing blow to her shoulder. Ariana fell to her knees, but she didn't utter a sound, her magnificent strength showing as she struck another blow up into his groin with her left hand.

Blood arced all around in a glorious burst of crimson. Smythson's bellow of pain echoing down the alley. Lazarus stood mesmerized, watching Ariana doling out justice. Her leg whirling around to knock the hulking figure onto his back and his wails of pain growing louder by the second. Ariana leapt to the side, her dagger raised high before she swept it down to hack some more at the man now howling on the ground.

She was covered in his blood, but she didn't seem to notice, or care, as she sat back, staring at her handiwork. "There! You won't be able to do much with that anymore!"

She was breathing heavily as she stood and kicked Smythson. She was glorious in her victory; she'd never looked so beautiful to him than in that moment. He wanted to rush to her side and take her in his arms, crush her to him, kiss her senseless, and... and then it all went to hell.

"Evan. Evan!"

A man appeared from the darkness. One who had been at the table. He saw Ariana, then his friend. And the next second, Lazarus saw the barrel of a gun pointed at her head.

"You're fucking dead!"

Ariana turned, her face pale and hands out to her side. "I'll come quietly."

"No, you won't." He looked down at his friend, who was bleeding out so fast Lazarus gave him a few more minutes, maybe seconds. Or maybe he was dead already.

Shit. Ariana must've severed his femoral artery.

"You're not getting out of here, you fucking maniac."

Lazarus saw the determination in his eyes, in the way he held his body, in the tension of his finger on the trigger. He was going to shoot her dead.

No. No fucking way was he losing her. Not here. Not in a filthy alley, and not because of Evan fucking Smythson.

"*Stop. Do. Not. Pull. That. Trigger!*" Lazarus commanded, rushing down the alley and stopping right in front of the gun. "You will forget you saw me or the woman. You found your friend here but saw nobody else. Understood?"

The man's eyes grew glassy under his compulsion and his head nodded. Once. Twice. And Lazarus knew he'd never remember how close he'd come to murdering a woman. How close he came to taking Ariana's life.

Lazarus turned to Ariana, who was standing behind him. He was filled with a flurry of emotions. Fury and worry were top of the list. He couldn't allow this. Couldn't allow her to put herself in this kind of danger. He would not allow it. He had no choice. He had to stop her from doing this. Had to keep her safe. He had to.

Take her. Keep her safe. His beast howled.

With seconds ticking by and a dead body at their feet, Lazarus did the only thing he could. He stepped forward, knocked Ariana out, threw her over his shoulder, and sped down the back alley. He could get her to safety. He could keep her safe. He would keep her safe.

Safe from herself. For eternity if he had to.

I hope you enjoyed Dark Hunter, and I'm sure you'll love Dark Hunger, book two in the series.

A DANGEROUS MEANS TO AN END...

I'm not sure Ariana and I can survive the flames she ignored when she stormed into my life...bringing a world of newfound danger with her.

With a treacherous enemy surfacing and attacks coming fast and furious, I have to keep her safe. Protect her, not only from those hunting her but from her own demons...

...and from me.

There's a hunger growing inside me. I want her. Need her. Crave her. And my beast won't stop until I have her. Mind. Body. And blood.

Continue to see what lurks in the shadows of DARK HUNGER, book two in the latest dark paranormal hit series by Ava K Michaels that readers are comparing to I T LUCAS and SHERRILYN KENYON.

Read Dark Hunger and continue the darkly addicting Warrior of Darkness series today.

DarkHunter

Note from Ava

Thank you for reading Dark Hunter, I sincerely hope you enjoyed Lazarus and Ariana. I have to admit they are two of my favorite characters that I've written and I hope you continue their journey in book two...Dark Hunger where Ariana pushes Lazarus to the brink of...well I'm not going to tell you. You'll have to read the story to find out!

If you loved Dark Hunter, why not check out A Vampire's Thirst: Victor? You can read an excerpt on the following pages. It's a thrilling and suspenseful read, packed full with steamy paranormal romance which I'm sure you'll enjoy.

Remember to sign up for my newsletter to keep up to date with my news, and pop over to my Facebook page for a wee chat.

Until then, continue reading, and remember, always...Live, Love, Read.

Ava

Dark Hunter

EXCERPT OF A VAMPIRE'S THIRST: VICTOR

Victor allowed the blood to flow over his tongue, savoring the taste as it filled his mouth and ran down his throat. *Exquisite*!

His first taste of human blood in such a long time, and he wondered why he'd denied himself as he sank his fangs deeper into her soft skin, drinking deeply, while his hard length pounded inside her. Her moans of pleasure as she writhed beneath him spurred him on, taking him higher, her blood filling him with lust and longing for more . . . so much more.

Her dark skin felt soft beneath his touch, her back bowed as another orgasm wracked her body as his bite took her over again and again. The blood he drank was addictive, glorious, and he wanted to drain her . . . Forcing his fangs from her skin, immediately feeling the pull to drink from her again, he retracted his teeth and pushed her away roughly.

Without a word he disentangled their bodies, dressed quickly and left the private room, disgust coursing through him briefly before the damn thirst for her fucking blood reared its head again. He wasted no time in leaving the club, not even waiting on his bodyguard, rushing out and into his limo and ordering his driver to take him home as quickly as possible. Sitting back, he tried to sort through what the hell had happened . . . he'd drank human blood for the first time in over two centuries and he had no fucking clue why.

When he arrived home, without acknowledging the doorman, he hurried to the elevator quickly inputting the security code. His only wish to gain access to his home. He slammed the door, almost tearing it from the hinges, his long legs stormed over to the window where he stopped to stare out the floor to ceiling window overlooking Central Park, his reflection glaring back at him accusingly. His ice blue eyes shielding the turmoil within from anyone that had the misfortune to look his way, only he knew the hell he was experiencing, the absolute and all-encompassing torture that his mind and body was forcing him to endure. And he had no idea what the blue blazes was going on.

What the hell is happening to me? he thought for the hundredth time.

He was one of the most powerful Vampires in existence. One who held knowledge that spanned centuries, ran businesses all over the damn world with ease, and yet here he was acting like a newly turned Vampling with no control over his bloodlust or his sexual demands.

Leaning his forehead on the cool glass, inhaling deeply to still his madly beating heart, Victor fought to control his growing anger. He *had* to control it. If he lost it then his penthouse apartment would be in ruin in no time at all, but worse . . . his secret would be out. People would learn there was something very wrong with Victor Strong and that was something he couldn't allow to happen. Not now, hell, not at any fucking time, but especially not now.

He had a meeting tomorrow that was going to be worth hundreds of billions of dollars for one of his companies and he'd be a fool to mess that up. One thing he was not, was a fool. The only saving grace was that it was being done online. Thank fuck for technology. He'd already met with the people involved and everything had been ironed out . . . almost. This was the final deal breaker and he refused to allow whatever was going on inside him to muck up the months of hard work he'd put in getting everything in place of his ultimate goal to gain some lucrative acquisitions. They'd add enough to his portfolio to make him the richest man alive . . . or dead depending on your perception of Vampires. As he still had a heart, still breathed air, he never thought of himself as one of the *undead*, but that didn't stop others from believing that were so.

"Are you going to tell me what the fuck is going on?" Flint's hard voice broke the silence, but he didn't jump, merely turned around slowly and walked to the bar.

"Want one?" he asked, pouring himself a shot of expensive whisky.

"Sure." Flint joined him, leaning his ass on a stool. His dark-as-night eyes never leaving Victor's as he took the offered glass. "So, boss, what's going on with you? You never take up the offer of girls at the club, yet tonight . . . you went through three of them. What's up with that? And, that's not all, is it?"

Flint made a show of lifting his head and sniffing. Victor stiffened, his lips curling back in a snarl of warning. "Don't say it."

"What? That I smell blood? Human blood. On the man that's not fed on human blood for so long that I can't even remember how far back it was." Flint took a sip of his drink, before placing the glass down heavily. "What's up, Victor?"

"It's not illegal, is it?" Victor snapped viciously. "I have done nothing wrong."

Flint frowned, rising from the stool and looking at him with a look of confusion on his hard face. "What the hell, boss? What's gotten into you?"

Victor shook his head, trying to clear it of the thoughts cascading through his brain. Mainly the ones of sinking his fangs into soft flesh and the taste of sweet blood as it dripped onto his tongue and trailed down his throat so damn nicely. He could still smell the heady aroma of one of the girls he'd drank from earlier, her unique blend that reminded him of a good merlot he'd tasted on his last trip to Paris. Fuck! He yearned to race back and sink himself inside her once more at the same time as his fangs tore into her pale skin to . . . no. He refused to allow himself to descend that route once again.

He was strong not just in name but in everything. His steely control over his entire life wasn't limited to his Vampire cravings, but in his everyday business dealings and the way he ran his world-wide corporations with an iron fist. It was how he became one of, if not *the* richest man in the goddamn world. He would win this war against whatever it was that was eating away inside him. He was Victor Fucking Strong and nothing, absolutely *nothing* would make him weak, or bring him to his knees. Not a chance in hell would he allow that to happen. His hands bunched into fists at his sides, his nails digging into his palms, drawing blood with the ferocity and strength of his will to battle the demons raging inside him.

"Victor?" Flint's hand landed on his shoulder, surprising him out of his thoughts, causing him to jerk away angrily.

"What?"

"You're worrying me. You were out of it then and you were definitely not yourself earlier. You need to talk to me. What's happening?"

"I'm fine." Victor pushed past the man that wasn't just his bodyguard and his right-hand-man, but someone who'd been at his side for more years than he could count. Flint was his best friend and they'd saved each other's lives so many times over the centuries it was as if he'd slapped the man as he strode away from him to the window. "I need some air."

Opening the sliding door, he stepped out onto the large patio. He didn't see the glorious New York skyline, his eyes closed as he took deep steadying breaths. Flint was next to him, he felt him, his friend nearby and worried. "I'll be fine, Flint."

"Will you?" he asked skeptically.

Victor turned to him, seeing the worry etched on his face brought a vision of when they'd first met...so many centuries ago when Flint was a new Vampling and been abandoned by his maker. Victor had found him in a backstreet in New Orleans, draining a young woman. He'd barely managed to save her in time, but he did and then took the young man under his wing and taught him how to control his urges. They'd been together ever since, and they were as close as brothers. To see him looking at him like this and talking to him with such a tone, well, it hurt.

"I'm sure." Victor tipped his head.

"I'm not," Flint replied, his steely gaze never wavering as he kept watch on him. "You remind me of what I was like when you found me and that wasn't pretty."

"That's funny," Victor's lips tugged up. "I was just remembering that night in Orleans."

"I'd rather forget it," Flint grunted. "Not something I'm proud of and I'd hate to feel like that again, that loss of control. Fuck, that's definitely not on my 'to do' list ever."

Victor agreed but that's exactly what was happening to him. He could feel it growing inside him like a damn cancer, only worse. That could be cut out, carved away by a scalpel and thrown in the garbage...unlike whatever was eating away inside him.

"Vic? What is it? You look as if you're ready to rip something apart again. Are you sure you're okay?" Flint stepped toward him, his eyes searching his face and his friend looking even more concerned.

"Yes . . ." And then something strange and magical assaulted his senses. A whisper of a scent wafting inside his nostrils . . . honey and wildflowers. It was tantalizing, mesmerizing and absolutely *his*. There was no doubt in his mind that he had to find the owner. His eyes snapped open as he rushed to the balcony, looking down to the street below which was almost empty of people at this late hour. He inhaled sharply again, using his centuries old Vampire abilities to try and locate the scent, his head whipping around toward the park . . . *there*.

His legs moved quickly, speeding toward the fire escape, with Flint yelling, "What the hell are you doing? Victor, wait!"

"I can't! I need to find her!"

ALSO BY AVA K MICHAELS

This is always changing, and only a small selection of my work, so please check out my website for the most up-to-date information.

Warrior of Darkness
Dark Hunter
Dark Hunger
Dark Huntress

A Vampire's Thirst
Victor
Flint
Quinn
A Deadly Masquerade

Highland Wolf Clan
The Reluctant Alpha
The Alpha Decides
New Beginnings
Despair and Destiny
A Highlander's Return
Dilemmas
Threat's and Surprises

The Witch, The Wolf, and The Vampire
The Beginning
Double Desire
Witch Hunt

Feud of Fire
Next Generation: A Son's Fate
Next Generation: A Sister's Plea

Supernatural Enforcement Bureau
The Dragon and The Vampire
The Imprisoned Dragon and The Witch
Bureau Under Siege

A Wolf's Hunger
A Ravenous Pack
Rafe
Kade
Zohar
Sheba
Shade

Sabrina's Vampire
Sabrina's Vampire, Book 1
Assassin, Book 2
Hunted, Book 3